Usually to be found within range of a plate of hot buttered toast, a huge mug of black coffee, and with a bar of emergency chocolate tucked in her jacket pocket, Jenny Kane loves to spend her days writing in her local café.

Jenny combines her past experiences as an archaeologist, university tutor, cheese seller, newsagent, hat maker, Robin Hood obsessive and data clerk, with the sights and sounds of everyday life, to weave tales of relaxingly relatable romance.

Jenny's 'Another Cup of . . .' series has been a consistent bestseller, while *A Cornish Escape* hit the Amazon Kindle top 10 and stayed there for many months.

Jenny also writes historical mysteries under the name of Jennifer Ash.

Find out more at www.jennykane.co.uk

Praise for Jenny Kane

'I'm a big fan of Jenny Kane' Katie Fforde

'A summer read as scrumptious as its Cornish backdrop. Brilliant!' Nicola May

'I loved this frothy cappuccino of a book!' Christina Jones

'A real bit of escapism. Great and truly lovable characters to root for and beautiful descriptions of Cornwall' ***** Reader review

'I couldn't put this book down! I warmed to the characters immediately and was desperate to see how things worked out for them' ***** Reader review

'Brilliant read, heartwarming and funny' ***** Reader review

'I loved this story from start to finish. The perfect read for a weekend afternoon, with a cuppa and your feet up' ***** Reader review

'One of   ew

Also by Jenny Kane

Another Cup of Coffee
Another Glass of Champagne
Jenny Kane's Christmas Collection
Romancing Robin Hood
Abi's Neighbour

Ebook Only
Christmas at the Castle
Christmas in the Cotswolds
Another Cup of Christmas

Children's Fiction
There's a Cow in the Flat
Ben's Biscuit Tin Adventure

Writing as Jennifer Ash
The Outlaw's Ransom
The Winter Outlaw
Edward's Outlaw
The Meeting Place

A Cornish Escape

JENNY KANE

ACCENT

First published in 2015, previously titled *Abi's House,*
by Accent Press

First published in this edition in 2020 by Headline Accent
an imprint of HEADLINE PUBLISHING GROUP

1

Cataloguing in Publication Data is available from the British Library

ISBN 978 1 7861 5768 3

Typeset in 10.5/13pt Bembo Std by Jouve (UK), Milton Keynes

Printed and bound in Great Britain by Clays Ltd, Elcograf S.p.A.

MIX
Paper from
responsible sources
FSC® C104740

Headline's policy is to use papers that are natural, renewable and recyclable
products and made from wood grown in well-managed forests and other
controlled sources. The logging and manufacturing processes are expected
to conform to the environmental regulations of the country of origin.

HEADLINE PUBLISHING GROUP
An Hachette UK Company
Carmelite House
50 Victoria Embankment
London
EC4Y 0DZ

www.headline.co.uk
www.hachette.co.uk

For my beloved and much-missed grandparents x

A special dedication and thank you must go to the Dennyside Bowling Association. This UK-wide bowling club-based charity was founded by Leonard Denny in 1935. In 2014 they rasied over £40,000 for various good causes. Recently they bid in the CLIC Sargent 'Get in Character' Auction. Dennyside's winning bid enititled them to choose a name for one of the characters in *A Cornish Escape*. So, please let me introduce you to Jacob Denny – a perfect name for a Cornish potter, and a generous tribute to Dennyside's founder.

Jenny x

Chapter One

It was the muffins that had been the last straw. As Abi sat nursing a glass of wine, she thought back to the events of an hour earlier with an exasperated sigh.

Hurrying towards the church hall, Abi parked Luke's unnecessarily large and ostentatious Porsche 4x4, and headed inside with a stack of Tupperware tubs in her arms. With her handbag slung over her shoulder and her key fob hanging from her teeth, Abi precariously balanced her load as she elbowed the hall door open.

Although she was twenty minutes early, Abi had still managed to be the last to arrive, earning her a silent 'tut' from some of the executive wives who were adding the finishing touches to the tables that surrounded three sides of the hall, and sympathetic grimaces from everyone else.

Acting as though she hadn't noticed the air of disapproval, Abi made a beeline for the cake stall and plastered her best 'this is for charity so be happy' expression on her face. Polly Chester-Davies, an exquisitely dressed woman whom Abi always thought of as 'Perfect Polly', was adding doilies to plates, making the stall look as though it was stuck in a timewarp.

'Ah, *there* you are, Mrs Carter, I'd given you up.'

Biting back the desire to tell Polly she'd been working, and was in fact early anyway, Abi began to unpack her wares, 'Here you go, two dozen chocolate muffins without frosting, and two dozen with frosting, as requested.'

Polly said nothing, but her imperious stare moved rather pointedly from Abi's face to the chocolate muffins already in position on the table, and back again.

Her disdainful expression made Abi mumble, 'Are you expecting to sell lots of chocolate muffins today then?'

'No, Mrs Carter, I am not. Which is precisely why you were instructed to make chococcino muffins.'

It had been that 'instructed' which did it. In that moment Abi felt an overwhelming hit of resentment for every one of the orders she had gracefully accepted from this Stepford harridan of the community.

For almost three years Abi had been doing what this woman asked of her, and never once had she said thank you, or commented on how nice Abi's cooking was. *Probably*, Abi thought as she compared her own muffins with those provided by Perfect Polly herself, *because mine don't look like they could pull your fillings out*. Nor had any reference ever been made to the fact that she would have to catch up on her own work in the evenings, after helping out with whichever good cause she'd been emotionally blackmailed into supporting this time. Not that Abi was against supporting a good cause, but this was different. These women didn't raise funds for whichever charity was flavour of the month out of the goodness of their hearts. They did it because it was what they should be seen to be doing. It went hand in bespoke glove with being the wife of a successful man in the city, living in faux-village suburbia, and having a suitably fashionable nanny for the children.

Abi spoke slowly through gritted teeth. 'The message on my answerphone sounded scrambled. I heard it as far as "choc", so I did what I always do. I dropped everything I was supposed to be doing and made you these.' Abi nodded towards the muffins but, rather than putting them onto plates, she snapped the lids back on the tubs. 'Some of us do work for a living, you know!'

Speechless for a fraction of a second, Polly closed her ruby lips, and put her best 'so sorry for you' face on. 'Yes, well, of course, things are very different for you now you don't have darling Luke to support you.'

'Luke didn't support me! I supported me. Unlike some, Mrs Chester-Davies, I did not marry for money!' Then, collecting up forty-eight muffins she'd never get round to eating in a million years, Abi strode from the hall with her shoulders back and her head held high, trying not to meet a single one of the astonished stares that followed her exit.

As she threw the tubs of cakes onto the passenger seat of the car, Abi's hands began to shake. It had been a long time since she'd stood up for herself. She could just imagine what was being said about her in the hall as she drove away at an unadvisable speed.

'Well, I say, how ungrateful; and after we took her under our wing for Luke's sake!'

'We should make allowances, she's grieving after all.'

'I would have thought she'd like being kept as busy as possible.'

'I don't see why she works anyway. Luke was loaded!'

The various conversations Abi's mind conjured swirled around in her brain, causing her to park Luke's car with a carelessness he'd have hated, and head towards the kitchen and a bottle of wine at high speed.

She left the Tupperware tubs neglected on the passenger seat.

Now, sipping a rare glass of wine before seven o'clock at night, Abi had a sudden desire to drink the whole bottle. She was also dying to tell someone about what had happened. She was sure if she had a friend to share the ridiculousness of her exchange with Perfect Polly with, it would all fall into perspective, become funny even. But Abi didn't have friends anymore. Luke had seen to that. She just had people that she knew, and that was not the same thing at all.

Her eyes surveyed her kitchen. Abi couldn't remember the last time she'd actually studied it properly. There was no doubt it was beautiful. It had everything a connoisseur of cookery could wish for, and with its scrubbed oak units, shuttered windows, state-of-the-art Aga, and antique double sink, it was an interior designer's dream.

Abi looked down at the sofa upon which she sat. It was in total contrast to the rest of her home. Tatty, and in some places the pale blue fabric was so worn that it was virtually threadbare. This was where Abi had spent most of her time since Luke had died, either reading or sketching out new picture ideas for the children's books that awaited her attention.

Luke had hated it, but the sofa was her one rebellion. Its continued presence in their lives, and its journey from her flat, to his flat, to the corner of their kitchen, was the only thing she'd ever successfully managed to insist upon.

Abi used to think Luke tolerated it because it held happy memories of their time snuggled up on it together when they'd first begun dating. In recent years she'd come to see it was Luke's idea of indulging her. Letting his wife have one tiny piece of her own identity to hold onto in compensation for taking over the rest of her body and soul. A fact that had been hammered home to her a few months before his unexpected heart attack, when Luke had told her to buy some throws to hide her sofa from view, as it was an unnecessary embarrassment that lowered the tone of the house.

The reason Abi was living in this Surrey village, which was really a small commuter town with ideas above its station, was Luke. Well, now Luke was gone, along with his constant need to be seen to have the best of everything, and his inability to understand that the best and the most expensive weren't always the same thing.

Taking another draught of Pinot, Abi sighed. She had done her best to be the wife Luke desired, to match his required lifestyle. She'd spoken to the right people, worn the right clothes, driven the right car, and said the right things. At first it had pleased her to please Luke; but soon it had become just a role she played. Now that it was all over, Abi realised how long she'd

4

been acting the flawless wife, rather than genuinely being the flawless wife.

The quiet one from the office, Abi had been flattered by Luke's attentions, and bowled over by his good looks. Twelve years her senior, he'd been kind and courteous; not pressing the pace of their relationship, nor teasing about her lack of confidence like his fellows had. It hadn't bothered Luke, or at least she hadn't thought it had, that she was merely a temp, a part-time assistant PA to help subsidise her earnings as an artist. She had been his one rebellion against the conventions of his life.

Squeezing her eyes closed, Abi pictured Luke as he'd been in the beginning. Just over six feet tall, with sandy-coloured, well-cut hair, his broad shoulders and muscles were honed by an hour at the gym each morning before work. He'd had a lopsided grin which she'd found endearing, and an easy-going nature that none of his City colleagues had shared.

Luke had swept her off her feet – and she'd been happy to let him. More than happy. Abi hadn't been able to believe her luck. It had felt too good to be true. Which of course, hindsight now smirked at her, it had been.

Two months after they'd been married in a lavish ceremony in the Bahamas, Luke had been promoted, and in that instant the increased responsibility, combined with a salary increase that no one could truly justify, the Luke Abi had fallen in love with began to disappear.

First he had insisted they move out of his London flat, and into Luke's idea of where successful couples lived: a huge detached home in a row of identical detached homes in executiveville. Six months later, when Luke calmly informed her that it was time she stopped mixing with her arty friends because they weren't in keeping with her new lifestyle, Abi began to suspect he'd married her because she fitted the mould of what an executive's wife was meant to look like. And she did – she was a petite, fit brunette with a high IQ and excellent cooking skills, and although she didn't care about clothes, there was no doubt she had a good eye for what suited her, and always looked far less unruffled than she felt.

It worried Abi that Luke had only been dead for six months and she didn't really miss him at all. No. That wasn't true. She did miss the Luke that used to live with her when the front door was closed on the rest of the world. Only then did she get to see the occasional glimpse of the kind, funny man she had fallen in love with.

She did not miss the Luke who appeared in public. It hadn't been enough for him to have the best of everything; he had to be seen to have the best. He had become a walking statement of his success, and always had to show the world his latest cars, gadgets, and designer suits. For reasons Abi couldn't fathom, clever though Luke had been, he'd never worked out that this would turn more people away than it attracted; he was constantly trying that little bit too hard to be liked. The result was that he was seen as rather overbearing. His public standards Abi found impossible to live up to.

Well, now she didn't have to.

It had been Luke's idea, a few months after their marriage, that Abi give up going into the office and work from home. She had been delighted, keen to return to her art, but after two weeks, when the search for work hadn't been the immediate success Luke had assumed it would be, Abi had discovered he'd asked the village ladies to enrol her in all their events, and take her under their wing. In other words, Luke wanted to turn her into a lady of the village.

These twinset and pearls-wearing women were all older than Abi, and most of them had reached the stage of executive wife-ness where they could cook a five-course meal for six unexpected visiting reps at the drop of a hat (or at least employ someone to do this for them), while simultaneously running the WI, and chatting to the mayor on the telephone about why purple and silver Christmas decorations would be so wrong in the village square this year.

When Abi had seen an advertisement for a children's illustrator she had applied straight away, and had been thrilled when she'd got the job. It had taken all the stubbornness she had to ignore Luke's protests that she didn't have to work, and should just look after him and their home.

Glugging back her wine, Abi put her glass down, and with a desperate need to escape rising fast in her chest, she walked around her home from room to room. Each one was exactly as it should be. Tidy, clean, and basically soulless.

Pulling her mobile phone from her pocket, Abi leaned against her huge wardrobe doors and opened up her contacts page. There were only five. Her brother Oliver, her brother-in-law Simon, Luke's mother, Perfect Polly, and her employers, Genie Press. Abi's old phone had had her friends listed on it. But that, along with her friends, was long gone.

Angry at how easily Luke had manoeuvred her into cutting ties with her past, and even more disgusted with herself for letting him, Abi threw the phone on to the double bed, her heart pounding with fearful exhilaration as she realised that, at long last, she was ready to retake charge of her life.

Chapter Two

Fighting down the habitual rush of guilt that hit her whenever she thought about how much easier life was without Luke, Abi checked her watch. Thanks to walking out of the charity fund-raiser three hours earlier than she'd expected to, she had time to get back to work . . . or she could plan her escape . . .

Now the idea had entered her mind, it seemed so blindingly obvious that another wave of anger at her own feebleness threatened to wash over her. It wasn't as if she could blame grief, although she could probably blame guilt over her lack of grief for her recent going-through-the-motions behaviour. Certainly shock must have had a role to play. One minute Luke was there, calling over his shoulder as he left for the gym at 6 a.m. on that Friday morning six months ago. Then, two hours later, she'd taken a call from a suitably sober-sounding nurse from the Royal Surrey County Hospital.

Luke had got caught in heavy traffic on the way to the gym and, determined to complete his morning exercise session, he'd rushed through his fitness routine. Unbeknown to Abi, he'd signed himself up for intense training sessions with view to doing an Iron Man challenge. It was a dangerously foolish thing to do at the age of forty-four, even if you were fit and in good health.

That morning, fresh from doing an extreme workout in less time than he should have allowed for it, Luke had dashed to his car so he wouldn't be late for work.

It had been a sprint too far.

No one had had any idea that Luke had arrhythmia. He'd had what the consultant explained was a ventricular fibrillation, rapid, erratic electrical impulses causing the heart's ventricles to quiver uselessly instead of pumping blood. It was likely to have happened sometime during Luke's life, he said, but had probably been triggered that day by the morning's exercise routine combined with the additional stress of rushing to his car. A car Luke had never got into again.

The consultant had gone on to say that the condition was distressingly common. In her numb state, Abi's overwhelming thought at the time had been that Luke would not have liked dying of anything common.

The depth of the sigh that escaped from Abi's lips caught her by surprise, and physically and mentally she knew it was high time that she pulled herself together.

It was time to leave. Time go somewhere new, where she could embrace her inner muddle. Fighting back the good little persona that she'd unwittingly developed over the course of her marriage, she yanked her shoulders back and did her best to haul the Abi who used to efficiently temp her way around some of the most competitive companies in London back to the fore.

'I'll sell the house.' The determined stare Abi gave her reflection in the bedroom mirror was reassuringly bracing. 'I can be an illustrator anywhere as long as there's internet access. But where to go? Somewhere far, far away from here.'

Abi's head immediately filled with an image of a small slate-roofed end-of-terrace in a short row of houses in Cornwall, one that she'd fallen in love with as an eight-year-old. It had been a tiny house that her late parents had always joked should be hers, simply because it was called 'Abbey's House' . . .

'That's as good a place to start as any!' Emboldened by her snap decision to hunt down the village she, her brother, and their parents had regularly visited on holiday, Abi closed her eyes.

Where exactly in Cornwall had it been? Near Land's End, but where? She could almost feel the sea breeze playing on her skin as her memory nudged her. Abi was almost sure her mind wasn't playing tricks on her, and that the cottage had been within viewing, if not walking, distance of the sea. She could virtually hear the cry of the seagulls. Not like the gulls that made a nuisance of themselves in the parks of Surrey, continuously squawking as if blaming all around them for the fact they'd somehow found themselves so far inland, but the proper call of a seagull, living where a seagull should live.

Scooping her phone back off the bed, Abi rang Oliver's number, and headed toward the study, flicking on her laptop with a feeling of purpose she hadn't experienced for years. The call was picked up as she was halfway through typing 'slate roof cottages Cornwall' into Google.

'Hi, Ollie, you OK up there?'

Ollie laughed, 'Afternoon, sis. Why do you always make Yorkshire sound as if it's Outer Mongolia or something?'

Cursing herself, as she always did, for not phoning her brother more often, for Ollie always had the ability to make her smile, Abi laughed. 'I only do it because it annoys you. Look, Ollie, I know it's a long shot, but do you remember the Cornish holidays we used to have when we were little?'

'Blimey, they were twenty-odd years ago.'

'I know, but I sort of need to know exactly where we stayed.'

'Sort of need to know?'

Picking up on the query in her brother's voice, Abi explained her sudden desire to escape. 'I mean, the happy memories I can take with me, and the rest – well, the rest I want to leave behind.'

'I don't blame you! I've been telling you for ages to come north. You'd be very welcome here, you know.'

Abi smiled down the line, 'Thanks, Ollie, but you have your hands full with Tina and the kids anyway. The last thing you need is a confused widow cluttering up the place, giving out a "not sure where to settle" vibe.'

'You're not that bad, are you? I got the impression you were coping brilliantly. Or have you been conning your old brother?'

Flicking her gaze down the line of Cornish houses on her computer screen, Abi groaned as she answered, 'Well, that's the thing. I am coping. I do miss Luke being around, and the private Luke was a hell of a lot nicer than the public one but . . . it's like I was tired all the time trying to keep up with him. I was always trying to justify him to people I liked, or was hidden in his shadow when we were with the people he liked.'

'Which was most of the time?'

'Well, yes.' Abi hovered her cursor over an image of some slate-roofed houses that had a familiar feel about them. 'It was the muffins that were the last straw really.'

'The muffins? That one you'll have to explain.'

Abi relayed the entire chocolate-versus-chococcino debacle before adding, 'So, can you remember where we went? Right at the bottom of the county, near Penzance and Land's End, wasn't it?'

She could hear Ollie moving around whichever room he was in, 'Hang on a minute, Abi, I'm in the junk room; the photo albums are here somewhere.' There was the sound of books falling, before he said, 'Yes, here we go. They were behind the ones of my lot.' There was a noise of the plastic pages of a photo album being flicked before Ollie said, 'I was about ten, wasn't I, which means you were eight-ish. Sound right?'

'Yes. The last one was when I was eight, but we went for at least five years on the trot before that. Have you found something?'

'Think so. Tina has stuck dates on the front of all the albums.'

'Seriously? Boy, that's organised.'

'Well, you know Tina.'

An image of her sister-in-law came into Abi's head. Tina, with her no-nonsense haircut and sensibly blunt outlook on life: always mega-organised, always just a little bit frightening. One thing was for certain, Tina would be able to cope with Perfect Polly and her cohorts no problem at all.

'Here, I think I've found them. Yes!' Ollie chuckled, 'I'd forgotten you had pigtails. How cute you were. Not unlike my Kitty.'

'So I did.'

Abi felt a shot of sadness at the memory of her carefree self, so much like her youngest niece, before quickly gathering herself up with an even stronger determination to get that carefree feeling back. 'So, where were we?'

'You were right, we were right down the bottom. Here's one of us in the botanical garden in Penzance, and another by St Michael's Mount. Oh, and here we are in an empty field.'

'An empty field?'

'Yeah. Don't you remember, back in the old days there was nothing at Land's End except, well, land?'

'Of course! Any shots of the houses?'

'A few. Shall I post some of them down?'

'Would you? That would be wonderful. Thanks, Ollie.'

'It's very good of you to see me so near to closing time.'

'Not at all, Mrs Carter.' The estate agent, whose name badge declared he was Nigel Davison, settled into his chair with the gleam in his eye that all agents get when faced with the prospect of selling a particularly valuable property. 'As you will appreciate we will have to make a valuation, and if you are keen on speed, a survey might be a good idea.' He opened his diary, 'When would be good for you?'

'Tomorrow?'

Mr Davison looked flustered, 'As fast as that? I'm not sure we have anyone free tomorrow as we don't survey at weekends, but I could sort something for Monday.'

Taking a leaf out of Luke's book, and modelling her haughty response on Perfect Polly, Abi rose from her chair. 'Thank you, Mr Davison, but as this is a matter of some urgency I think I'd better try someone else.'

The panic only lingered on Nigel's face for a split second before he gestured benevolently to the recently vacated chair, 'In that case, if speed really is of the essence, then I'm sure we can accommodate you. Perhaps . . .' He glanced at his watch, 'I could view the property this evening, so that I can give the surveyor the information he needs, and we can start putting some particulars together for the sale?'

'And the surveyor will arrive . . .'

'The best I can do is nine o'clock on Monday morning.'

'Thank you, Mr Davison. I shall go and prepare for your arrival.'

'About seven? And please, call me Nigel.'

Abi was aware that her pulse had been racing with an overdose of adrenalin ever since she'd stalked out of the church hall, and eventually it was going to run out. Before that happened she needed to make one more call.

'Good evening, Simon, I hope I haven't called at a bad time.'

Her brother-in-law answered with his usual suave confidence, 'Abigail, how nice to hear from you. All well I trust?'

Not wasting her breath reminding Simon that her name was not and never had been Abigail, but simply Abi, she prepared herself for the landslide of disapproval that she was sure was about to come her way. 'I've decided to sell the house, Simon. I can't live here anymore. It's so big, and now I'm on my own . . .'

Deciding not to tell him that she was planning on fleeing the area completely, Abi left a tiny pause before adding, 'I know it is terribly short notice, but I wondered if you'd come over in an hour. The estate agent is on his way, and I'm rather out of touch with what sort of price he should offer me.' Adding a little flattery to her request, she added, 'I know how well you keep up with these things.'

'But, Abigail! That's your home. Luke's home. You can't just . . .'

'Simon, it isn't exactly a home anymore, is it. I'm lonely here and . . .'

The moment the word 'lonely' had come out of her mouth Abi regretted it. She'd always known that her brother-in-law had a crush on her, but she'd politely ignored it. Since Luke's death he had been a little more forward each time they met.

13

'You never have to be lonely, you know you only have to say and I'd be there.'

'I know. Thank you. Luke would be very grateful to you for looking after me.'

There was a pause, then Simon said, 'I'll be there in half an hour. If the agent turns up first, show him the garden until I get there.'

Still bristling from Simon's high-handed manner, and the fact that she'd brought it upon herself by asking him to help her in the first place, Abi cursed the lingering feelings of loyalty she had towards Luke's family.

Simon had arrived at the same time as Nigel, their BMWs parked twin-like on the wide gravel drive. As the besuited men had got out of their cars and shaken hands, Abi had been reminded of two stags at bay rather than two professionals about to negotiate the value of her home.

Habit had seen Abi letting Simon simply take over. He'd been the one who'd led Nigel from room to room, and he'd been the one who laughed at the first valuation, and agreed upon a much higher price. It was only when the men had returned to the garden, where Abi had been sat at the patio table feeling oddly detached from what was going on, that she became involved.

'Are you still available on Monday morning for the surveyor, Mrs Carter?'

'I am. Nine as agreed?'

The estate agent opened his leather-bound diary and pencilled down some numbers. 'I have taken Mr Carter's number; can I have your mobile number, please, to pass on to the surveyor so he can call if there is a delay?'

'Of course.' Abi dictated her number. 'In fact, it should be my number you call rather than Simon's. This is my house, after all.'

Simon's eyes narrowed slightly, and Nigel looked confused, but good manners prevented him from saying anything. 'I am sure you'll find our quotes acceptable. I will get them processed and emailed to you on Monday as well.'

As Nigel stood to leave, Abi shook his hand, before Simon escorted him back to his car.

Swallowing her annoyance, which was more at her own behaviour for not having the confidence to deal with the agent's valuation on her own, than at Simon, who was just being, well, Simon, Abi was about to politely thank him when a suspicion crossed her mind. 'Mr Davison didn't think we were married, did he, Simon?'

'He did, actually, but don't worry, I put him right.'

Her natural inclination to be polite, rather than doing what she really wanted, made Abi offer Simon a cup of tea instead of asking him to leave.

'I'd rather have something stronger.'

'But, Simon, you're driving.'

'Not for ages yet. I've decided to take you for dinner. We need to talk.'

Chapter Three

Beth peered nervously out of the window. She wasn't at all sure she was doing the right thing. Yet she knew in her heart that she'd been prevaricating long enough, and when the bright red Mini with the slogan of the local estate agents emblazoned across the side arrived, Beth experienced a rush of relief that a decision was going to be forced from her.

Closing her eyes to gather herself before letting the agent inside, Beth could feel the familiar aroma of her grandad's cobbler's shop hit the back of her throat. It had been three years since economic conditions had hammered the final nail into the shop's coffin, and although she'd tried to keep the cobbler's going with the help of her grandfather's young assistant, it had folded.

The shop had been on the market for two years, but no one had shown the slightest interest; although, to be fair, Beth had done nothing about promoting the sale. She wasn't sure how she'd cope if someone else owned the shop. Even the idea of selling the building that had been her family's business for so long made her feel sad.

'Come on, Beth, time to be a grown-up.' She went to answer the doorbell which was about to ring. 'There's no point hanging onto it. The shop is a white elephant, and you don't need it.'

The only member of her family left, Beth had no boyfriend, and at the age of thirty-two was fast giving up on the prospect of having children. She knew that by not putting the shop on the market, she was somehow keeping her life safe – but safe wasn't exactly getting her anywhere. She'd got stuck in a rut; it was time to shake life up, even if it was just a little bit.

Beth had lived in the flat for seven years, five of which had been spent helping, and then caring for, her beloved grandfather, every hour when she wasn't working at the local school, where she taught the nursery children. Since her grandad's death two years ago, she'd lived there on her own.

'Morning, Beth.' The estate agent grinned widely as the front door was opened. 'So, have you made that decision? Are you going to lower the price of the shop for a quicker sale, or vacate the flat and sell the whole thing, then?'

'To the point as ever, Maggie!' Beth smiled back. Having known her visitor since they were at primary school together, she was very used to Maggie's abrupt but friendly style. 'No, I'm not going to vacate the flat, but I do need some advice about selling the shop. I can't ignore the fact it's empty any longer.'

'Allowing me to put a "For Sale" sign up would be a good place to start.'

'OK, OK.' Beth lead the way into the shop, and stood quietly amongst the leftover cobbler's paraphernalia, trying hard not to take a lungful of the leather scent which still hung heavily in the air.

'Sorry, Beth, I didn't mean to sound like I was bullying you. I just think if you cleared this lot up and gave it a lick of paint it would be a wonderful space. You'd get no end of interest, and forgive me for mentioning it again, but you would get even more interest, and a substantially bigger sum of money, if the entire property was sold, not just the shop.'

Beth ran a finger across the top of the machine her grandfather had used to polish up the shoes he repaired. She knew Maggie was right, just as Maggie knew she wasn't telling Beth anything she didn't already know.

Maggie pulled over a dusty chair and sat down, 'Beth, listen, sweetie. Don't tell my boss I said this, because he is gagging for me to persuade you to sell up the whole property, it is after all a prime site. Sea view from the flat upstairs, tourist trade and all that, but if you're heart isn't in selling then why not reopen the place yourself?'

'I'm no cobbler, Maggie.' Beth stared at the cobwebs in the corner of the room, and the tatty blinds that needed more than a shot of antibacterial cleaner.

'As something other than a cobbler's, then?' Maggie dug out her notebook, 'Here you go. This is what we think the shop is worth on its own now. You'll see the figure is a little higher than it was two years ago, but it is dependent on you cleaning and whitewashing the place. The figure underneath is the sum you'd get it if you sold up the whole property, flat, shop, yard garden, the lot.' She ripped the piece of paper from the book and passed it to Beth, 'Think about it, but don't wait too long, because the longer you leave this place unused, the more work it'll need, and the harder it'll be to sell.'

Beth snapped back to reality. 'Sorry, Maggie.'

'Forgive me asking, but if you didn't really want me to come, why did you ask me? I'm right, aren't I? Come on, sweetie, I've known you since we were five years old, tell me the truth. You asked me here today because you thought you ought to, not because you wanted me to come. Right?'

Sighing, Beth held her hands up as if to gesture the entire contents of the place in one go. 'I did, and I didn't. I thought I ought to. I mean, what can I do with this place? I know I can't get planning permission to turn it into a house rather than a shop and flat because I looked into it after Grandad retired, and I don't want to give up teaching to run a shop, so what other choice is there but to sell?'

'That's obvious, sweetie! Rent it to someone else, of course.' Maggie shrugged in defeat. 'You know where I am when you've made your decision. But look, it's costing you money to keep this place on our books, even if you aren't advertising it as such. Call me as soon you've made your mind up, one way or the other.'

'I didn't mean to waste your time. Thanks for being so understanding.'

Watching Maggie's Mini disappear from view a few minutes later, Beth heart began thudding hard and fast in her chest as she realised that the estate agent's visit had led to her making at least one firm decision about her future. Even if it wasn't the one she'd expected to make.

She wasn't going to sell up. Not the flat or the shop. A frisson of edgy excitement tripped down her spine. It was time to clean up the space. The bigger decision about what to do with it could come later.

In case she became tempted to change her mind, Beth picked up the phone.

'You did?' Max looked far more surprised than Beth had expected him to.

'I did. But I'll need your support. I mean, I'm bound to panic about this soon; a fact that will probably lead to me doing yet another about-turn decision-wise. Will you help stop me ducking out and ringing Maggie back up again?'

Stabbing a forkful of chips, Max smiled. 'No problem. Let's think. If you can't bring yourself to sell the space then let's get scheming. There must be loads of things you could do with it. You gonna stop teaching to do this then?'

'I'd rather not. Especially as I have absolutely no idea what this is.'

'You do like to make life complicated, don't you? Aren't you supposed to make plans, research your market, and put forward a viable business idea before you clean up the premises to house it?'

Wiping a piece of bread around her plate, Beth grinned. 'You sounded like my grandad then!'

'I will take that as a compliment.' Max laid down his cutlery and peered thoughtfully into his pint of cola. 'So let me get this straight, you have one hundred per cent decided not to sell the shop. Is it officially off the market?'

'It is.'

'Was Maggie OK with that?'

'She thinks I'm crackers not to sell up completely, take the money, and run, but considering how I've messed her about between selling and not selling, she's been great.'

'The advantages of growing up in this village together, you can take a few more liberties with each other's patience!'

'I guess so.' Beth's cheeks darkened a little, 'I do feel bad about it, though, I can't imagine her boss was thrilled.'

'Don't be daft. They've had almost two years of monthly payments from you to keep the shop on their sale list, for doing sod all. It's your future that needs addressing, not theirs. Talking of which . . .' Max took a huge gulp of fizzy drink, which Beth knew would make a lesser-sized mortal burp like a trooper, but probably wouldn't even touch the sides of Max's bear-like frame, before he added, 'we have exactly ten minutes before I have to get back to the bathroom I'm in the middle of decorating, so we'd better either think very quickly, or meet later for a proper planning session.'

Beth looked at her watch. 'Max, it's nearly five o'clock!'

'I know, but the old dear is stuck without a toilet. This is a mercy mission!'

'But you're a painter, not a plumber!'

'True, but when I was decorating, she told me about her toilet not working properly, and I told her I'd fix it. Save her spending her pension money on a plumber. It's a simple job, but I need to get a few parts, so I thought I'd grab some grub at the same time.'

'Your kind heart is never going to get in the way of your stomach, is it?'

Max rubbed his overall-covered stomach. 'Are you implying I'm fat?'

'Nope, I'm saying you really like your grub.' Chuckling, Beth stood to leave, 'I would love that proper planning session though, if you're up for it. How about tomorrow night? I have a heap of marking to do tonight, not to mention all the admin stuff they throw at us at the end of each school year to plough through.'

'Perfect. Tomorrow evening, about seven? We could go for a walk before the tourist season kicks off in earnest and we can't move for grockles and emmets cluttering up the coastline, and have a good ole talk.'

'Shouldn't that just be emmets if they're in Cornwall? Grockles is the name for tourists in Devon, isn't it? Or is that Somerset? I can't remember now! Anyway,' Beth laughed, 'anyone would think you didn't like the tourists, Maxwell!'

'And they'd be right! Pain in the arse. Can't ever park the works van for bucket and spade carriers!'

Poking her best friend in the ribs playfully, Beth followed Max towards the door. 'Don't knock it; we may need the tourists to buy stuff from whatever shop I run. If I open one.'

'If you open one?' As his booted feet crunched across the gravel car park to his van Max pushed his ginger hair out of his eyes. 'You don't have any idea about uses for that space at all, do you?'

'Not a clue. But I do know it needs cleaning out before I do anything as rash as making another life choice.'

'And a coat of paint might be a plan as well.' Max climbed into his van ready to go back to his toilet-less old lady.

'I'll slap a covering of whitewash over the whole thing and go from there.'

Max rolled his eyes. 'Not while I live and breathe, Miss Philips!'

Chapter Four

Abi knew there was no hope of avoiding her brother-in-law for ever, and the longer she put off seeing him again, the worse the situation would get.

Until the previous evening, Abi hadn't really understood what it was like to seethe. Not even Perfect Polly had managed to elicit that emotion from her. But seething was the only possible word which could sum up how Abi had felt as she'd mutely watched Simon leave her home the night before, a smug self-righteous expression on his smoothly shaven face.

Smooth. That was an apt description of Simon, with his designer suits, sharply cut blond hair, and steel blue eyes.

Unshakeable. As Abi sat up in bed, her arms wrapped around her duvet-clad knees, she thought that was another description that could be applied to her brother-in-law. It wasn't that he was never wrong. It was simply that the idea that he could be wrong, or even be 'in the wrong,' never ever crossed his mind. Yet despite her better judgement, Abi couldn't help but respect Simon. She just wished she could shake the unease she felt whenever he was around.

Despite the July sun's efforts to beat its welcoming early morning rays through her closed curtains, Abi pulled the duvet tighter around herself and flicked her straying hair behind her ears as she tried to make sense of the night before.

She'd stayed sat at her little patio table long after Simon had left, only rising after the light dimmed to the point that the cold night air had cut through her long sleeves and dotted her arms with goose-pimples. Numbed into a state of speechlessness.

Perhaps if Simon hadn't tried to touch her hand while he was speaking at her (it had definitely been at her and not to her), then it wouldn't have been so bad. Abi exhaled in a frustrated noisy rush. Luke could have won the occasional award for being a control freak, but compared to his brother he'd been an amateur.

Simon had even managed not to look affronted for more than a split second when, having played his trump card, he'd placed his hand over hers, and she'd snatched it away at top speed, placing both palms out of reach on her lap.

Abi still couldn't believe he'd suggested it. Not only that he'd suggested it, but the fact he'd obviously thought it through carefully, and decided it was the best solution all round.

Their inevitable marriage, he'd declared, was not just agreeable to himself, but would be good for the Carter family as a whole. Oh, and for Abi of course, he'd added. There was no doubt she was a minor part in his calculations, rather than the main factor.

Simon had informed Abi that he'd decided it would be sensible for her to move into his house to start with. His mock Georgian home was, he'd said, far too big for him alone, and that he owned it because it would look wrong from a business perspective if he didn't have a place outside the city as well as his Knightsbridge flat. He'd considered his options, and giving her the use of the third bedroom to begin with, which he was sure Abi would like because it was light and airy and she could both work and sleep there, would be the best option for both of them. 'Although', he'd added as an afterthought which made Abi wonder if he was talking to her or to himself, 'I'd rather not redecorate, so I hope you like the dove grey furnishings. You'd only have to live there for a while anyway, as if my current business strategy pans out then I have my eye on a property in Oxford I'm convinced you'd love.'

Stunned, struggling to process what Simon was actually saying,

23

all Abi had managed to ask at that point was why and when this idea had come to him, seeing as she'd only just decided to sell up.

'After you called me about helping with the estate agent this afternoon of course. I popped in on the parents before I came here and mooted the idea to them. They saw it as the ideal solution, although they did suggest I wait a few more months. However, with you toying with the idea of moving, the time to broach the subject seemed right to me. Strike while the iron's hot and all that stuff.'

'What? What do you mean? Your parents?' Abi frowned. 'And what makes you think my moving plans are just thoughts?' I'm not toying with the idea of moving, Simon. I am moving. And I will be living on my own.'

Now, after a broken night's sleep, filled with an odd combination of dreams about being held captive by a wicked prince and his mother, which reminded Abi of a suffocating version of *Shrek 2*, and bouts of anger at Luke for having been so stupid as to take on a challenge he was far too old to do and go and die on her, Abi found Simon's suggestions even more difficult to comprehend.

She hated being talked about at the best of times, but now a picture of her in-laws all sat around Simon's dining table, port in hand, discussing what should be done about Abi made her insides shrivel. The scene refused to stop replaying over and over again through her head.

The remainder of Simon's one-sided conversation with her last night had become more and more preposterous after he'd dropped his bombshell. All the protests Abi knew she should be making aloud had become stuck in her throat in the face of her sheer indignation at the Carter family's presumptuous cheek.

He'd explained to his parents, he said, that it would be unwise to let Luke's house go out of the family – and, as Abi was still capable of having children, albeit a little late in the day, he was sure he could persuade her that she did want a child, despite Luke's claims to the contrary, and that it made sense that the child should remain a Carter.

His plan therefore, which had his parents' full approval, was to move Abi in with him and, once a respectful period of time had elapsed after Luke's death, propose to her. After all, he was far nearer to her age than his brother had been, and there was every chance that if they didn't hang around too long, that they could have the heir that Luke had always dreamed of . . .

He'd seemed amazed when Abi hadn't replied with an instant, 'Yes, that's a good idea' to his practical suggestion – a suggestion which had been delivered as if it were already a decision made.

Abi had sat there, her mouth opening and closing like a rabbit mesmerised in headlights, expecting Simon to tell her he was joking, but he didn't.

After two minutes of total silence, he had finally got the message that he'd shocked her, 'Well I guess it's a lot to take in, and we'll need to sell this place first, won't we?'

'We?' Abi had taken a slug of wine from her glass as Simon stared at her as if she was a business asset ripe for acquiring.

'Yes, of course.' Simon had looked at his watch then, and risen from his seat. 'You invited me to help. Well, it's getting late. I should be going. Call me tomorrow and we'll sort out when I should be here to check the surveyor doesn't cheat you. After all, you wouldn't know whether they are doing the job or not, would you?'

In the safety of her bedroom, Abi rested her head in her hands. Every single expletive she could think of was running through her mind, each one queuing up impatiently for their chance to hurl themselves at Simon. She was amazed he hadn't patted her on the head and told her she shouldn't worry her pretty little mind about all these man-decisions.

Abi was at a loss as to which of his statements had hurt her more. The assumption she needed someone with her because she couldn't cope on her own? The fact he and his family had not only married her off to her dead husband's brother, but hadn't even considered her feelings on this? Or the dig about Luke's lack of an heir. A son presumably.

OK, there was no contest, it was the 'you are still capable of having children, albeit a little late in the day . . .' that had stolen the last vestiges of any possible coherent responses from her head, and made her sit and listen to his assumptions like a statue, without letting fly the crippling ball of hurt that had knotted in her stomach.

It was so unfair. Abi would have loved children, but Luke hadn't wanted them. Ever. Although he wanted the trappings of wealthy suburban life, the traditional 2.4 children didn't fit into his plans. So that was that. Subject closed. She'd had no idea the Carters blamed the lack of grandchildren on her.

Throwing back the duvet, Abi forced herself to the shower. As she let the water work its magic against her tense muscles, the shock began to pass, and Abi allowed her anger to take its place. She owed neither Simon nor his parents anything. Especially not his parents! They'd made no bones about the fact that Luke had married beneath his class, and had always made sure Abi never forgot the fact. Not that they were top-drawer themselves – but they certainly thought they were, and there was no fighting convictions like that.

As she shampooed her hair in a furiously vigorous motion, Abi closed her eyes, and the image of Simon was transplanted with one of a tall cylindrical building, covered in wooden slats and topped with a conical roof.

'Of course!'

Washing the shampoo out as fast as possible, Abi jumped from the shower and, wrapping a large bath sheet around her dripping body, dried her hands and dashed to her studio room. Flicking on the laptop, she towelled herself dry as she impatiently waited for the machine to connect to the internet.

One minute later, Abi found herself looking at one of the enduring images of her early childhood: The Roundhouse and Capstan Gallery in Sennen Cove, Cornwall. She smiled as she remembered the miniature wooden parrot she'd bought from its craft shop when she was six. She'd called it Nelson, and her dad had placed it on a string and hung it over her bed.

Keen to tell Ollie that she'd remembered the name of the village, Abi switched to her email to write him a message, only to find one from him waiting for her.

Ollie had found the pictures he'd been looking for, and here they were, scanned and uploaded for her to see so she didn't have to wait for the postman to deliver them. Abi, Ollie, and their parents outside the Roundhouse when Ollie was about five and she three. Abi and Ollie on the beach, building sandcastles. And, last of all, a photograph of Abi, grinning all over her young face, pointing at a house sign that said 'Abbey's House', with a traditional Cornish terraced row behind her.

'That's it! That's my house – or one like it anyway!' With a new resolve, Abi replied to Ollie with over-enthusiastic thanks, and dashed off to get dressed.

Talking to herself as she moved about the house, Abi began to compile a list of what she should do next. 'First I need to call that snake Simon and tell him to forget all his assumptions, then I'll call a different estate agency and get another quote.'

Grateful that she enjoyed freelance status at work, so could take leave in between projects whenever she liked, Abi added under her breath as she pulled on her jeans, 'I'll email work and tell them that when I've finished my current project I'll be taking a month's break. And then I'm going to go house-hunting. In Cornwall.'

Abi happily pressed print on her computer so that she had copies of her brother's photographs to carry on her travels, in the hope someone would recognise the row of cottages in the photograph. She rang two rival estate agents, secured an appointment for a quote from both of them, then emailed work, promising them that the remaining pictures for *Davy and the Rebel Robots* would be with them by Monday morning, and then after that she was taking a relocation break.

Ironically pleased that she hadn't yet managed to bring herself to break Luke's 'no mess in the house' rule, Abi had little to do but wipe round the bathroom and make her bed before the estate agents arrived.

Scooping up her laptop and taking it to the kitchen, Abi stood for a moment, drawing breath as she snapped on the coffee machine. It was going to take at least one double espresso, if not two, before she called Simon. Her natural instinct was to ignore the situation, pretend he hadn't said all that, and just disappear. After all, now Luke had gone, there was nothing to connect them. There wasn't even any legal wrangling to sort out, as Luke had left Abi everything in his will, a fact which had left her very well off. It was something that she acknowledged made her very secure, but also very determined to make her own way. Apart from using the proceeds from the sale of the house to buy a new home, Abi had decided to only spend Luke's money if she had to. After all, she'd always paid her own way, and although her wages couldn't support her living in Surrey, they could in Cornwall if she had no mortgage to pay.

The sale of her current home alone should keep her in a style to which Luke had wished she'd become accustomed.

Giving the espresso time to take effect, Abi googled 'The Roundhouse, Cornwall: hotels nearby' and, pulling a notebook and pen towards her, began to jot down the names of all the nearest bed and breakfasts, hotels, guesthouses, and pubs offering rooms as close to Sennen as she could find. Then, with her list of hope laid out in front of her, and her perspiring palms giving away how anxious she was, Abi called Simon.

Chapter Five

'Abigail! Thank you for calling. I was just thinking about you.'

Not responding to his ominously enthusiastic greeting, Abi could hear the blood thudding in her ears as she launched into the speech she'd been rehearsing. 'Simon, I would appreciate it if you would listen to me without interruption.'

Without allowing him time to respond either positively or negatively, Abi spoke at top speed so she could get out everything she needed to say before the inevitable interruption. 'I have no idea why you believed that you could replace Luke, or that I was even looking for a new husband. The fact you and your parents have even discussed this situation without consulting me is both insulting and hurtful.'

Abi's hands were shaking but she kept going, relieved that Simon hadn't tried to butt in yet. 'I asked you to assist with the sale of the house because Luke always respected your opinion, and I hoped that I could rely on your help as I will not be on hand to supervise the sale myself. Obviously, that can't now happen. It is only out of loyalty to Luke that I'm phoning you now. I'm sure you are blissfully unaware how downright insulting you have been. I suspect that if I left without saying goodbye you'd probably assume I'd thrown myself under a bus or something. So, I'm phoning to say goodbye now. Goodbye, Simon.'

Abi hung up. Damn. That last bit wasn't how she'd rehearsed it. Her emotions had taken control of her tongue from the point where she'd said she'd supervise the sale herself. Abi had meant to sound professional and cool, not overemotional and cross. Her hands shook as she tried to block out her imagined images of Simon's stunned face as he digested what he'd been told. Her imagination, which was so essential for her work, was a real hindrance to the rest of her life sometimes.

Picking up her list of possible temporary accommodation, Abi traced a finger down it, drawing comfort from the words. She wasn't sure why she knew going to Cornwall was the right thing to do, and she was realistic enough to know that she might get there to find that all her memories were so rose-tinted compared to reality that she couldn't possibly live there. But she had to travel down there and see. She had to know for sure.

The arrival of an email from her employers, saying taking a break was no problem as long as she could commit to providing illustrations for one of the next three books due to be finished by November, which Abi knew was their polite way of saying she could take a four-week sabbatical, but no longer, was the final positive push she needed.

Replying with an agreement that she would indeed be able to honour that commitment, Abi was about to email the first hotel on her list, when the phone rang. It was Simon.

Abi stared at the flashing screen of her mobile, a knot twisting in her stomach. Tempted to ignore the call, but knowing he'd keep trying, or worse still, he'd turn up in person, she answered.

'Hello, Simon.'

'I am amazed, Abigail. I had no idea you could be so dishonest.'

Of all the opening sentences that Abi had been expecting, that had not been one of them.

'What do you mean?'

'You know full well what I mean!' Simon's voice didn't rise in volume, but it had become gilt edged with a bubble of annoyance that Abi recognised as being like Luke's tone had been if any of his plans had been thwarted, business or otherwise. 'You lied to me.'

Abi thought furiously, trying to think back over every conversation she'd ever had with Simon. 'I did no such thing.'

30

'You didn't tell me you were going away.'

'I told you I was selling up. Beyond that it is none of your business where I go or what I do. I lost my husband, Simon! I have to look after myself now, and I'm damn well going to do just that. I can't do that here surrounded by memories. Now, was there anything else you'd like to accuse me of, or can I get back to work?'

Walking through to the studio, Abi flicked open her paint box as she held the phone to her ear, laying out everything she needed to produce the last cartoon-like image required for her latest project as she listened.

'You know how much I care for you, and yet you led me on for your own ends. How dare you!'

Fighting the impulse to hang up on him, Abi took a long, audible exhalation of air; responding as sharply as she was being spoken to, 'I asked you to help me with the valuation of my home. That was all. Nothing else. Not at any time. Ever. I have politely ignored your unsubtle crush on me for years, because, frankly, it was embarrassing, and because I was married to your brother! Take a reality check, Simon! Oh, and for your information, my name, as you well know, is Abi, not Abigail.'

This time Abi did hang up. After all, what else was there to say? Ignoring the mobile as it immediately rang again, showing Simon's number on the screen, Abi pulled her large workbook towards her. She was about to draw the initial line of the sketch when the doorbell rang.

The first of the day's estate agents had arrived.

As Simon had called five more times, Abi knew it would only be a matter of hours before he turned up on the doorstep wanting to know why she was ignoring him. Keen to avoid any sort of showdown, and wanting time to think about the three different quotations she now had from the estate agents, Abi put the finishing touches to the picture before her, gathered up her mobile, the list of hotels, and got into her car.

Parking in the first available space near the river, Abi walked for a gloriously peaceful half an hour, before sitting down on a bench and ringing her first hotel. It only took three phone calls for Abi to realise that finding accommodation she could have for an unspecified number of days was going to be an awful lot harder than she'd assumed. The fact that the school holidays were due to start any day now hadn't crossed her mind, nor had the fact that she was heading to one of the most tourist-dependent places in the United Kingdom at the height of the season.

'Idiot!' She grimaced at a passing duck. 'So, do I postpone or do I carry on regardless?'

The duck quacked as if on cue, and taking this as encouragement, Abi phoned the last number on the list, which belonged to the Cairn Hotel in the nearby town of St Just, rather than in Sennen itself.

Five minutes later Abi was thanking the mallard drake profusely as it peered up at her, an incredibly inquisitive look on its billed face. 'You were quite right, Mr Duck. Thank you. I'm in!'

The kindly sounding lady on the other end of the phone, who introduced herself as Barbara, had been extremely helpful. Her rich Cornish accent had infused Abi with hope, as Barbara confirmed that she could certainly accommodate Abi for at least the next two weeks, possibly longer, although Abi would have to move rooms after seven days, if that was OK, due to previous bookings.

Having assured Barbara that she was more than happy to have a double room for the first week, and then a compact single after that, a little of the anxiety Abi felt over the magnitude of the decision she was making slipping away.

Looking at the piece of paper she'd written the three house valuations on, Abi knew that, although she hadn't liked Nigel Davison very much, as his quote was the best she'd have to go with him. She wished Simon hadn't got on so well with him. Although, she had to admit to herself, if Simon hadn't been there, the valuation may well have been lower.

Calling Davison, Abi told him that she was happy to accept his offer providing the surveyor's report was good.

'Thank you, Mrs Carter. That is good news. I'll liaise with Mr Carter about the survey times, shall I?'

'No, Mr Davison, you will liaise with me directly, and on this number, please. I'm going away for a while, so I shall leave a set of keys with you so you can show prospective buyers around the house. Is it OK to just post them through the estate agency door?'

Sounding a little confused, but good business instincts giving him the common sense not to say so, Davison confirmed they would be happy to act as agents and advisers. 'But I'm afraid it will add to the fee, Mrs Carter.'

'I rather assumed it would. Goodbye, Mr Davison.' Abi hung up, wishing she'd been able to sound as brusque and to the point when she'd been dealing with Simon. Then, with a friendly nod to the duck, Abi set off towards home, to finish off her painting and pack. There was nothing standing in her way now. The sooner she got to Cornwall the better.

Abi was only partly surprised to see Simon's BMW in the drive when she got back to the house. Fighting the childish impulse to run away and hide until he'd given up and gone home, Abi pulled up next to the flash black car.

Bracing herself for a landslide of accusations, telling her how selfish she was being in upping and leaving her family behind, Abi was completely wrong-footed as Simon climbed out of his car, his hands out before him in a 'forgive me' gesture.

'Before you say anything, I should apologise.'

Abi said nothing, but her expression didn't hold back on the fact she was flabbergasted.

'I've had a long think, and you were right. We had no right to discuss you as though you were one of Luke's assets for disposal. And I can see that was how it must have appeared. All I can do is assure you that was never our intention. Rather clumsily, we were trying to do our best by you now that Luke isn't here to take care of you. All I can ask is that you forgive us.'

Abi's hurt at being treated like a disposable object lost out to her hatred of any sort of confrontation, and her keenness to have

33

no spectres beyond the ghost of Luke himself left behind her. 'It's OK. You're forgiven,' she said curtly, 'but only as long as you understand that I am not yours for the taking, I am not on the hunt for a new husband, and I do not and never have needed looking after. When I met Luke I was a successful woman in my own right, supporting myself, and I can be that person again. I'm after a fresh start, and for that to work I have to be somewhere else.'

'Will you at least tell me where you're going?'

'Cornwall.'

'Cornwall?'

Chapter Six

'Will you look at all that lot?' Max peered into the large cardboard box that Beth was carrying along the street towards her home. 'You've got to be the most popular teacher in town!'

Smiling at the welcome sight of Max, Beth shoved the box into his waiting arms, and hooked the large envelope she was still carrying under one arm, while rescuing her handbag before it slipped off her shoulder, 'With only three teachers in the school there isn't really a lot of competition. And I can assure you, Max, my colleagues are similarly stocked up with enough smelly candles, soap, flowers, and boxes of chocolates to stock a village shop.'

'A shop like your shop, maybe?'

Ignoring Max's oblique query to a use for her retail space, Beth fished her key from her skirt pocket and unlocked the door to the hallway. Without glancing at the white door to their left, which led into the shop space, she headed up the stairs to her flat, Max right behind her.

'I get a few more gifts than the other two staff because I teach the really little ones. It's always quite emotional for them, and for their parents watching them take the daunting step from nursery to "big school" life. Because I'm the teacher that steers them on that first educational journey, I get loads of thank-you presents.'

Following Beth into the flat, Max laid the box on the kitchen table, which was full of conflicting scents from various perfumed products. 'So it's nothing to do with you being a brilliant teacher then?'

'Not a thing.' Beth lifted up two mugs to ask if he wanted tea or coffee.

'Coffee please.' Picking up the large envelope Max asked, 'Can I peep?'

'Of course.'

As Beth busied herself making hot drinks, and threw the take-away menus at him as he sat down. 'I'm feeling lazy, what shall we have?'

Max didn't bother to look, 'I imagine we'll have a large pep-peroni with extra cheese and a side order of garlic bread, with wine for you and lager for me, like we always do.'

'One day I'll astound you and say I want something different.'

'No you won't! Now go and order the food, woman, while I examine what the next generation of Van Goghs have produced.'

Beth stuck her tongue out at him and went into the living room to make the call. By the time she'd returned Max had spread as many of the large drawings and paintings out across the table as he could fit.

'These are good. I mean, considering they're by four- and five-year-olds.'

A lump came to Beth's throat and tears prickled in her eyes as she looked at the array of painted flowers, happy smiley faces, and various portraits of herself teaching. She always found saying goodbye to the children who'd come to her as little more than toddlers, and (mostly) left as rounded young children ready for the challenges of primary school, rather emotional.

'They are, aren't they. Look at the effort that's gone into most of them. They've all done one. Even Brandon.'

'Brandon? That would be the lad you've mentioned before; the one who has the attention span of a gnat and an attitude like a teenager from a soap opera?'

'That's the one. Every class has a Brandon – and more often than you'd imagine, that's what they're called – but I did my best

36

with him . . . and look, his picture is excellent. Perhaps I taught him something after all!'

Hugging his friend to his side, Max said, 'Of course you did! Come on, cheer up. They'll all do wonderfully next year, and you'll be able to watch them develop and grow while you're teaching a brand new batch of fledglings.'

'Thanks, Max.' Beth cradled her coffee. 'Do you ever wish you'd finished your teacher training so that you got presents like this?'

'So that I too could get an annual supply of bath fragrances?'

'Yep! Although the male staff at the last school I worked in tended to get chocolate, handkerchiefs, and ties rather than sickly bath stuff.'

'Makes a change from socks, I suppose!' Max began to line up the bars of soap and boxes of chocolates on the table while Beth put the bunch of carnations in a jug of water where it would survive happily until she had time to arrange them into a vase.

'You haven't answered my question.'

'No, I haven't.' He added a bottle of lavender bubble bath to the regiment of Beth's gifts. 'So when's the pizza coming, then?'

Accepting his unspoken request to change the subject, Beth picked up one of her pictures, 'It'll be about forty-five minutes.'

One at a time, Beth studied the pieces of artwork she'd been given, before piling them into a neat stack. A few of them had obviously been created by rushed sweeps of the brush or pencil, but most of them had clearly taken her young charges some time, and had had a great deal of concentration spent on them. 'It seems such a shame to stick them back in the envelope and let it gather dust, but there's no way I can hang fifteen pictures up, I simply don't have the room.'

Max stared at Beth over the top of his coffee at her, as if she was missing something obvious.

'What?'

He gestured his gaze toward the paintings.

37

Rolling her eyes, Beth said, 'Oh, just tell me, or I'll withhold your garlic bread.'

'I will put your lack of grasping the obvious down to the fact that it is the end of a busy term and you are emotionally impaired after saying tearful goodbyes to your little ones, and tell you.'

'Max!'

'You have a shop downstairs which is currently doing nothing but providing a useful home for a whole host of spiders. You could display them there, make it into a gallery.'

Putting her mug down slowly, Beth frowned. He was right of course. It was an obvious use for the space, even if only short-term, but a gallery?

'Are you being serious, Max, or was that you being flippant? I mean, galleries are ten a penny in Cornwall. Does Sennen need another one?'

'I just meant that you could use the space to show the children's work. They'd love it, wouldn't they, if they saw that their teacher was so proud of their work she wanted to show the world. I wasn't really thinking beyond that to be honest, but a gallery is a possibility, isn't it?'

Beth stroked the top picture, the thick poster paint rough beneath her fingers. 'I don't really know anything about art.'

'Do you know what you like?'

'Well, yes, but that isn't enough is it. Not in a county where artists and galleries are everywhere.'

Max glanced at his watch. 'Come on, grab your cuppa. Let's go downstairs. There is no way you can make a proper decision if you can't feel the space around you.'

Beth took a few covert deep breaths as she placed the key in the lock to the shop's internal door. She knew she had to get past the feeling she always had whenever she contemplated redesigning her grandad's shop; that she was desecrating his memory in some way.

They both stood still in the silence. Despite the dust and mud-dle, neither of which would have been allowed when Grandad had been in charge, it still felt as airy and comfortable as it always had. As the building formed the end of a row of shops, the space had made full use of the corner plot, with two huge picture windows at right angles to each other.

Her grandad had had two step-like display shelves in each window, but they'd been propped up at the back of the room next to the machine he'd used to buff up the shoes he'd mended. His workbench, which ran along the right-hand wall, was still littered with scraps of leather, pots of congealed glue, laces, tubs of polish, rags, and a vast array of pots containing things that might be useful one day.

On the wall above the bench was a set of wooden shelves that was formed of dozens of rectangular cubbyholes. Many of them held the boxes of different sized heels or soles that had been his most essential tools.

There was also a key-cutting machine, an engraver for trophies and pewter mugs, and a large selection of cardboard boxes of shoes that had never been collected, plus stocks of laces, key blanks, and all manner of bits and pieces whose function Beth could only hazard a guess at.

Breaking the hush that had descended, Max picked up the nearest box and placed it on the workbench, dislodging a cloud of dust which immediately shot up his nose and made him sneeze. Understanding that this was a big deal for Beth, even though her beloved grandfather had been gone for two years, Max spoke gently, but forcibly. 'Beth, your grandad was a good man. He wouldn't want you to waste this space. He'd want you to use it to enhance your life. I'm sure he would.'

Nodding, but saying nothing as Beth surveyed the room, trying her hardest to picture it as something other than a cobbler's shop, but knowing in her heart that she'd never be able to do that while all her grandad's stuff was still in situ.

Sensing his friend needed him to make decisions for her for a while, Max pulled his diary out of his substantial overall pocket. 'I have two days next week when I can paint this place. If I nip over when I can, do you think you can have it empty by then?'

The date mentioned snapped Beth out of her nostalgia. 'Next week? But Max, I'll never have cleared these by then.' She pointed to the machine and the wall shelves, 'and anyway, don't you have work planned for then? I thought you had two conservatories and a kitchen lined up to paint next week?'

'I do, but not for Saturday and Sunday.'

'I can't ask you to work all week and then paint this place during your time off!'

'Oh don't be so darn ridiculous, woman! If I was an accountant and offered to paint this place at the weekend you wouldn't question it, would you?'

'Well, no, but . . .'

'But nothing. First we'll have to empty this place. I suggest you get that lot advertised in the local paper and on eBay asap,' Max pointed to the machinery, 'otherwise, shall we make a start while we wait for the pizza?'

Not waiting to take no for an answer Max pulled a bin bag out of another of his copious pockets. 'Right, what of this lot is rubbish?'

For half an hour, with one ear listening out for the doorbell and the arrival of their takeaway, the two friends went through the first box, quickly filling the bin bag, while also creating a pile of leather off-cuts which Beth had quickly earmarked for future textile and art lessons at school. As they worked they threw ideas back and forth.

'After the showing of the children's work, which could just be stuck to the windows really, what then?'

'I think their pictures deserve a little more than a bit of sticky tape at each corner, Beth, but I get your point.' Max examined the wall shelves, 'They'd make great shelves for old-fashioned sweet jars. How about a sweet shop?'

'Not sure I fancy that, and anyway, I'd never compete with the one in Penzance; the fudge in that place is to die for.'

'Clothes, shoes, hardware, posh deli, café, bookshop?'

Beth sighed. 'The bookshop idea appeals, but not the others.

40

A café or food store would require too much upkeep on a daily basis, and as I said, I don't want to give up teaching.'

'You could remain the owner, but lease the place as a hair-dresser's or beauticians or one of those new nail bar things?'

Beth laughed incredulously, 'Seriously?' She looked down at the hardwearing ankle-length denim skirt and purple shirt that was pretty much her school uniform, 'A beautician's salon? A nail bar? Owned by me?'

'Alright, alright!' Max held up his hands in surrender. 'It wasn't such a bad idea, we don't have either locally, but call me a quitter, I'm sensing you don't feel comfortable with those ideas?'

Beth was saved from delivering a short, pithy reply by the arrival of their pizza.

Chapter Seven

Nerves and an inconveniently accompanying wave of guilt hit Abi as she pulled into Taunton Deane services. With the border that divided Devon and Somerset a few miles away, Abi could feel the enormity of the step she was contemplating starting to disturb her concentration.

Making a beeline for a desperately needed cup of coffee, preferably with a side order of something unhealthy and smothered in chocolate. 'Although not a bloody muffin,' she muttered under her breath.

Abi couldn't stop thinking about what her brother-in-law had said when she'd finally given in and answered one of his calls. Had Simon been right? He'd talked to her as if she'd flipped, and had suggested rather forcefully that the trauma of Luke's untimely death must have had more of an effect on her mental health than they'd all initially thought.

Abi hadn't been able to stop herself from laughing at the time, assuring Simon that she was very sane, thank you very much, and that if she didn't like Cornwall, she'd be trying other locations, but that was her business and not his, or his parents. To both humour him and shut him up, and because ultimately it really would be useful, after much consideration, Abi had decided to tell Simon she'd accept his help with ensuring a seamless and tidy sale of the house if he was still willing.

Abi had been quite proud of herself, as Simon had given her his fervent promise that he'd keep an eye on the house sale while she was away, with no expectations or agenda. Now however, as she queued for her overpriced drink, Abi couldn't help listening to a treacherous voice at the back of her head telling her Simon might be right. Perhaps her leaving was a delayed knee-jerk reaction to Luke's unexpected death.

Luke may not have been the best husband in the world, and she didn't miss being put down in public for one minute, but at the same time she'd never once doubted that he'd loved her. It was more that he always acted as if he wished he didn't.

Every day since his death it was becoming harder to remember how she'd let herself be changed from a successful businesswoman (who had admittedly been acting her socks off to portray a strong image and hide the true shy persona beneath) to the mousy wife who'd do anything to avoid the look of disappointment in her husband's eyes when she failed yet again to live up to his expectations. *I did love him, and I do miss him, but . . .*

Abi looked out of the window, trying not to let another stab of emotion get the better of her as she watched a happy family of four, all holding hands, cross the car park. Had she been so naive to dream that she and Luke could have a family like that one day?

Despite their age difference, Luke had always given Abi the impression that he wanted children – until about a month after their honeymoon. They'd been eating in a restaurant, and a family had come in with a baby that wouldn't stop crying. Luke hadn't been just indignant, he'd been plain rude to the parents about their inability to keep the infant quiet. All the way home he'd ranted about how families shouldn't be allowed in restaurants with babies, and preferably with no one under sixteen. When Abi had stuck up for them, saying that there was no way anyone could predict when a baby would cry, and that having children in restaurants from a young age helped teach them good manners and social interaction, she had been cut short with a cold look, a look she would become all too familiar with over the next few years.

A look that was followed by Luke informing her that there was no way they were ever having a creature that behaved like that! And that had been that. All conversations about having a family were closed, and every attempt Abi made to resurrect the discussion met a brick wall of silence.

Was she really striking out for a better life on her own terms, or was she running away from the hurt Luke had brought her when he was alive, and again now he was dead? Could she even do this? Determined to remain calm, Abi found a semi-clean table and sat by the window, staring out blankly across the sea of parked travellers' vehicles.

She looked down at her drink ruefully. Luke certainly wouldn't approve of her drinking coffee from a paper cup. After his mega-promotion at work, even drinking from a mug rather than a bone china cup and saucer was only something to be done when circumstances allowed no superior alternative.

Continuing to watch the chatting couples, groups of friends, and families move about the car park, tears started to gather at the corners of Abi's eyes. By allowing Luke to take over every aspect of her life, she'd missed out on so much. She hadn't meant to be so feeble – but with Luke . . .

With a sustaining sip of caffeine, Abi knew she'd been miraculously given another chance. She wished it had come about in another way, but nonetheless, it was a chance, and she was not going to waste it.

Abi suddenly had a strong desire to do all the things Luke would never have approved of. She wanted to mess up her salon-perfect hair, maybe get a tattoo, go out of the house without make-up, make friends . . .

That had been the hardest thing. None of her friends had taken to Luke. She'd tried to justify him in the beginning; to explain his haughty exterior was all an act, that he could be nice when he was on his own – but as he didn't approve of anyone Abi knew outside of work, Luke never showed them his nice side. As a consequence none of her friends saw the Luke she had fallen in love with. Now, as she stirred extra milk into her coffee, Abi found herself wondering if that side of him, the side she did miss, had been the act, and Luke's public persona had been the real one.

Knowing that there was no point in thinking that way, Abi pulled the list of properties for sale she'd printed off the computer the night before from her small backpack. None of them looked anything like the house she'd loved as a child, but as she nibbled on her bar of chocolate a smile crossed Abi's face and extinguished any idea of crying. Whether they looked like her childhood dream house or not, all of the properties displayed on the page before her appeared a lot more inviting than the sterile executive home she currently owned.

Abi wanted a house she could wear shoes in without anyone having apoplexy about dirty footprints on the carpet. She wanted a home that felt like a home, not a place that was on the verge of expecting royalty, or an impromptu visit from *Homes and Gardens* magazine.

Daydreams of long coastal walks and lazy clifftop meanderings, maybe with a dog (one with long hair that would get all over the furnishings!) filled Abi's head as she knocked back the remains of her coffee and, clutching the house details like a lucky talisman, set off back to the car.

The sun stopped shining almost the second Abi's car crossed the Tamar, the river that separates Devon from Cornwall.

Until that moment, Abi had managed to keep hold of the optimism she'd wrapped herself in while sat in the service station, but now, as the sky began to darken, her new resolve began to waver. The journey was taking far longer than she'd imagined. The route she'd planned on the internet should have taken about five hours. But as the Cornish roads became slower and narrower, she encountered countless road-works, and hundreds of caravans had slowed the traffic flow right down. Then the motorway had disappeared entirely, the sky had become steadily bleaker, and storm clouds had congregated above her. Driving fatigue and fear at the unknown path that lay ahead fought to get the better of her.

45

Never had Abi been so pleased to see a road sign as she was to see the sign for Penzance, which she knew was the closest town to St Just. As Abi drove past a large pub, mentally marking it as somewhere to visit later in the week, the first fat raindrops landed on the car, and a crack of thunder overhead heralded her arrival to the very foot of the country.

Cold in the summer clothes which had been so fitting at the beginning of the journey, but were no longer suitable for a wet evening, Abi's stomach rumbled, reminding her that she hadn't eaten anything apart from a bar of chocolate since lunchtime, and now it was coming up to 6.30.

'Yes!' Her body sagged with relief behind the wheel of her car as she spotted a signpost. St Just was only two miles away! Turning right as directed, she followed the curve of the narrow road. After what must have been four miles, Abi realised she must have taken a wrong turning somehow. Doing a three-point turn that was more like an eight-point, she drove back the way she came. Then, repeating the exercise, she did it again – and still found she'd gone wrong.

Every road sign Abi saw seem to conflict with the next, and as she drove round in circles, panic began to set in. How could she possibly be lost at this stage of her journey? Abi glanced at her petrol gauge. She was getting close to empty; she couldn't afford to be lost for much longer.

Pulling over, Abi cursed the fact that she'd lost Wi-Fi signal and so couldn't check her directions on her phone. 'Right, be logical. You know it isn't in front of you. You can't go left or right here, so it has to be behind you. A whole town, however tiny, cannot have disappeared! Go back towards Penzance, and then at least you can find a pub for food and then hunt for some petrol.'

With her pulse thumping rather faster than she would have liked, and wishing the roads weren't so narrow, Abi kept going. At last she spotted the pub she'd seen earlier. Pulling into the car park, Abi went inside, her usual reluctance to go into a pub on her own wiped away by her desire to find both food and directions.

The beaming landlady quickly settled Abi at the only free dining table. After making sympathetic noises about the state of traffic in the holiday season, and promising that Abi would have step-by-step instructions of how to get to her hotel before she left the premises, she bustled off to fetch a cup of coffee and a tuna mayonnaise-smothered jacket potato as fast as humanly possible.

Half an hour later, her coffee gone and her meal almost consumed, Abi was re-reading the list of houses she hoped to make appointments to see when she had the feeling she was being watched.

Looking up, Abi found herself looking into the smiling face of a tall rugby player of a man with shockingly ginger hair, who was walking purposefully in her direction.

'Sorry to interrupt, but Patsy there behind the bar,' he gestured towards the barmaid who waved at Abi, confirming that the man had arrived on her instructions and wasn't someone about to make a doomed attempt at chatting her up, 'told me that you could do with a few directions.' He held out a large hand. 'I'm Max.'

'Abi. And yes please! I've been going in circles. I'm not sure if I was going wrong because I was tired and hungry, or if none of the road signs actually go where they claim to.'

'You also need a filling station?'

'Yes.' It hit Abi that she was talking to a good-looking man she didn't know, and that there was no one to tell her not to. Luke would have hated this if it had happened in his company – but then it simply wouldn't have happened in the first place. She couldn't remember the last time anyone had offered her help without some kind of personal agenda of their own. Abi found herself sighing, and then she blushed. 'I'm sorry, it's been a long drive.'

'Not at all. Where have you come from?'

'Surrey. I knew it was a long way, but somehow it seems even longer!'

Max laughed. 'Those last few hours once you've crossed the border into Cornwall go on for ever, don't they?' He nodded towards the house particulars laid out on the table before Abi. 'Looking to join us in these parts, then?'

'Well . . . yes,' Abi was embarrassed at her unthinking assumption that she'd be welcome here, 'but don't worry, I'm not planning on being one of those weekenders who snap up all the good houses, and then disappear back to London to spend their wages there!'

Laughing again, Max said, 'The idea never crossed my mind. Do you know the area?'

'Not really. I loved it as a child. My parents used to bring me and my brother to Sennen every year. I'm going to try and find a house I fell in love with back then, and then look for somewhere to live.' She pointed to the chair. 'Would you like a seat, a drink?'

'Thank you, but I ought to go. I promised a friend I'd look in on her tonight. I wondered if you'd like to follow my van, if you're ready to leave that is. Patsy said you were off to the Cairn. I go right past it on my way, so you could trail me.'

'That would be so kind of you.' Abi gathered up her notes and papers, 'I'm dying for a hot bath and an early night.'

'Come on then.' Max collected up the empty plate and cup and put them back on the bar, before calling goodbye to Patsy.

'Nice motor.' He waved approvingly towards Abi's car.

'How did you know that one was mine? The car park is packed.'

'You're from London, lass, as near as makes no difference anyway, and it shows.' He smiled broadly to show he wasn't being insulting, but merely honest. 'So, if you turn right out of here, drive for about three minutes, and turn right again, you'll find a petrol station. They open at six o'clock tomorrow morning. Right now however, we are going to turn left, OK? If you stay behind my van, then I'll get you to your hotel.'

Doing as she was told, staying as close as was safe to the 'Max Decorates' van, Abi reached the hotel car park in minutes.

'Here you go.' Max jumped out of his van's cab and strode

over so he could open Abi's car door for her. 'You'll be all right here. Nice place.'

'Thanks so much, I would have still been going around in circles without you.'

'Remember the golden rule: the road signs are for the tourists, they take you the long way for everything, and they are designed to confuse.'

'Why?'

'Not a clue.' Max laughed again, 'Oh, and I hope you don't mind me saying, but if I were you I'd check out all of the towns where there are houses you want to view first, before you book appointments to see them. Some of locations are going to be smaller than you imagine, I suspect, and not all of them have Wi-Fi. Find your childhood place first though. I don't think anything else will match up until you do.'

As if he realised he might have been giving unwanted advice, Max mumbled, 'Just a thought, like,' before he quickly drove off with a wave goodbye.

Letting the heat of her bath soak into her tired shoulders, Abi found herself thinking about the kind giant of a man who'd guided her to this temporary haven. She realised with a sense of surprise that, not only had she found talking to him easy, but that at no point had it crossed her mind that he might have been leading her into trouble, or been about to proposition her. Like Patsy, the landlady at the pub, and Barbara when she'd checked into her hotel room half an hour ago, Max was simply a very friendly person.

Abi sank further beneath the bubbles. 'Friendly people. That has to be a very good omen.'

Chapter Eight

Restless since the squawks of the local seagulls having a squabble had woken her at dawn, Beth had given up on the struggle to sleep long before six. Pulling on the set of overalls Max had left for her, and rolling up both the sleeves and the legs several times so that the outfit was merely too big rather than swamping her, she stood in the middle of the shop clutching a roll of rubbish sacks.

Cranking up the radio in time to hear the tail end of the six o'clock news, Beth apologised to her grandad for what she was about to do. Flapping open the first bin bag, she took a deep breath and began to divide the contents of the old cobbler's shop into things to throw away, things to keep, and items to sell.

An hour later, as the third sack of rubbish was tied closed, Beth stretched out her back and walked over to the old shoe bar where her grandad had done the majority of his work. Trying to blank out the vision of him standing there, polishing up freshly repaired shoes and boots, Beth wondered how she'd get rid of it. Who would want it? Should she keep it? Was there any way it could be incorporated into the place? 'Maybe if I call it The Old Cobbler's Shop.' Beth spoke to the machine as she stroked it, but she remained unconvinced. The name was hardly inspiring, and could allude to pretty much anything from a café to a hardware store.

Doing her best to picture the shop space empty and freshly decorated, Beth decided to leave the hunt for specific ideas of what to sell on hold, and to face one thing at a time. First she had to decide if she would run the shop herself, or lease it out to someone else. Unsure if she wanted to relinquish control of the space, but knowing she didn't want to stop teaching either, Beth shook her head against her contrary thoughts.

Could the shop be a general store, a bookshop, or a café? Or maybe even a gallery, as Max had suggested? With its two large windows, the space would be ideal to display paintings, but there were so many galleries locally. Beth knew she needed ideas that were unique enough to make the shop profitable in an area where tourism and art and craft shops already dominated the scene, beyond the displaying of the art work her recent pupils had given to her.

It was no good. She couldn't think straight this morning. Pulling her shoulders back, subconsciously echoing a gesture her grandfather had used when he was dealing with a particularly difficult client, Beth decided it was best just to be practical and get on with what she knew had to be done. Once the place was cleared and she and Max were slapping on a fresh coat of paint, then she'd start making some choices.

Even though she'd been exhausted from driving for so many hours the day before, it had taken Abi a long time to relax enough to fall asleep. She'd lain under the duvet for hours, listening to the gulls and the rain bouncing off the slate roof above her, her mind a complex mix of ideas and insecurities about what she was doing.

Now though, with a stomach that was full of butterflies, Abi sat in the airy breakfast room, smiling at the hotel's sole waitress as she delivered her a full English breakfast. Ignoring the echoes of Luke's voice that mutely scolded her – 'Too much fat, Abi; how could you? Don't you know by now that it'll just stick to your hips?' – Abi poured herself a mug of tea strong enough to have sustained a removal man for several hours.

As she buttered a slab of thickly cut toast, Abi could see the sun breaking through the clouds, getting ready to shine its way across Cornwall. Chewing her way through some delicious bacon, she could feel her childhood calling to her. She began to eat faster. Would she be able to find Abbey's House today?

Recalling the advice Max had given her in the pub the evening before, Abi begin to build an itinerary for her day as she ate. Despite her keenness to find the house she'd loved in her youth, she was also aware there was a high chance that seeing it again so many years later could be a major disappointment. So, as much as she wanted to dive straight in and track it down, she was determined to be practical and sensible. First of all she'd fill up her car with petrol, and then she'd go to the nearest place with a cashpoint.

Draining the contents of her mug, feeling as though she'd eaten enough food to sustain her for the whole day rather than just until lunchtime, Abi stood up with a spark of excitement running through her. It was time to go exploring. Today she'd cross off her list all those villages with no broadband coverage. As the kindly ginger-haired decorator had reminded her, without that function Abi simply couldn't work.

Apart from that dose of common sense, Abi mused as she gathered up her car keys, and her bag ready-packed with maps and the addresses of all the local estate agents, she would let her heart do the decision-making.

Although she was grubby and tired, at last Beth knew she was making progress. She could hardly move for overstuffed black bin liners around her feet. Working hard and fast, she had not allowed her mind to stray from the task in hand. With every drawer emptied and the bench clear, over half of the clearout was complete. Beth's stomach growled noisily, reminding her it was a long time since she'd paused for the round of toast which had doubled as both a late breakfast and an early lunch.

Rolling off her massive overalls, throwing them on top of the bags of rubbish she hoped Max would take to the tip for her later,

Beth headed up to her flat for a shower before going to join her best friend in the pub for a much-needed plate of chips.

Sat on the low wall that ran along the seafront of Sennen Cove, Abi stared out in wonder at the beauty of the scene. Despite being gone six o'clock in the evening, the white sandy beach was still full of families making the most of the end of their day at the seaside. Mums wrapped their children in towels, sandcastles dotted the beach, pits had been dug with happy abandon, and collections of shells and pebbles sat ready to decorate sand forts, or to be taken home as souvenirs.

It was the nearby Roundhouse that held her attention however. Closed now due to the lateness of the hour, to Abi the gallery looked the same as it had when she was eight years old. A wood and granite building, it had once been a capstan for hauling boats out of the water, but was now an art and crafts centre, and, apart from Abbey's House, it formed the mainstay of Abi's childhood holiday memories of the Cove.

As she stared at the building Abi reflected on her day. She must have visited more little towns and villages in one day than she had in her whole life. She'd liked most of them; but couldn't picture herself actually living in any of them. Nothing had made Abi feel as if she was coming home. She'd struggled to damp down the knowing voice of Luke that spoke softly in her mind: 'Don't be silly, baby – just go home.' But as Abi looked across the cove, with its turquoise sea that could have been in the Caribbean as easily as Cornwall, she knew that this place, right here, right now, felt right.

Maybe she shouldn't have spent the day being sensible, and simply followed her heart and hunted down the house she remembered falling in love with as a child after all, rather than scanning the whole toe of Cornwall. The problem was, although Sennen wasn't large, it was a maze of nooks and crannies, with as many houses tucked away as there were on show; she simply had no idea where to start. Abi wished she hadn't packed her photo of the house in her luggage, or she could have shown it to Max, and he might have been able to tell her were the house was last night.

Thoughts of Max had drifted through Abi's mind on and off all day. He'd been right. She wasn't going to find anything to match her dream until she'd tracked down the house from the past. It would have been nice to share the experience of hunting for Abbey's House with him.

Abi thoughts brought her up short. She didn't know Max from Adam! Was she so desperate for friendship that she'd gladly spend a day with a man she'd met once in a pub simply because he'd been kind to her?

Not wanting to admit defeat or give in to the feeling of loneliness that was threatening to engulf her, and listening to the rumble of her stomach, Abi decided to go in search of dinner, and make a new plan on the way. Climbing to her feet, taking a lungful of the salty sea air as she did so, Abi told herself sternly that she was returning to the pub she'd visited last night simply because she knew roughly how to find it and because the food was good. She was not going there because she might bump into Max. Abi couldn't deny however that she was disappointed not to see his van in the car park. It would have been nice to have someone to talk to.

Having been greeted by Patsy, who was keen to make sure she'd had the help she'd needed the night before, Abi had settled down to eat.

Making notes about the pros and cons of the places she'd visited so far, the warming effect of her steak and chips made Abi feel more positive by the second. She was so engrossed in what she was doing, that she didn't notice the footsteps approaching her table.

'Hello again,' Max beamed down at her, 'how goes the new life hunt?'

'Oh, hello.' Glad that he'd caught her between mouthfuls of food, Abi smiled. 'Mixed fortunes, I think would be the honest answer to that.'

'Let me guess, you like everything, but you can't seem to narrow your search down because this county is both spread out and on top of itself all at the same time?'

Rather than being cagey, as she would have been with Luke in case he put her ideas down, Abi nodded, amazed Max had managed to understand and sum up the problem so quickly. 'That's pretty much it. Everywhere was lovely, but not quite . . . although I'm as sure as I can be that it is Sennen I'd like to ultimately settle in. It felt the most right out of everywhere I've been today, and well, you know . . . and then there's this house I'm sort of looking for . . .'

Abi found herself blushing, and she stopped talking. This was a stranger, and she was saying too much. He'd probably only come over to be polite, for goodness' sake. She hadn't missed that he'd been taking the occasional covert glance towards the pub door, and was obviously waiting for someone.

'I'm so sorry, I'm gabbling.' Abi knocked her notes together on the table, the abrupt need to escape stronger than her need to finish her dinner. 'Thanks for your help yesterday, but I should leave you in peace.'

'Not at all!' Max looked at her plate, 'I interrupted you, not the other way around. And anyway, you haven't finished. Besides,' he gave her an even bigger smile that did strangely pleasant things to Abi's insides, 'I'd be lying if I said I wasn't curious to know which house in particular it is you're looking for. I might know where . . .'

Her companion broke off as a woman came up to his side. She was short next to Max, but tall compared to Abi. The newcomer's dark brown hair hung loosely across her shoulders, and looked as if she had recently washed it and not worried about hanging around at home to make sure it was properly dry before she came out. Luke would have had a fit if Abi had done that.

This must be the girlfriend or the wife then. Abi was taken aback by her disappointment that the decorator was attached, and then gave herself a mental shake. Just because a man had been nice to her didn't mean a thing. Plus, Max was so far from her type it was laughable to even think about him in those terms. I do not find him attractive; he's just the first nice man to show any sort of interest in me for a very long time without having an agenda of his own.

'Abi, may I introduce my best friend in all the world, Miss Beth Philips, schoolteacher of this parish, property owner, and like yourself, a lass about to embark on a brand new adventure!'

Chapter Nine

Beth gave Abi a welcoming handshake. 'Well, that was quite an introduction! I'm pleased to meet you, Abi. So what adventure are you having then, if you don't mind me asking?'

Again taken by surprise by how genuine this new stranger sounded, Abi found herself offering Beth and Max seats, which, to her greater surprise still, they took.

'I'm either relocating or escaping from the clutches of the wicked metropolis,' Abi gave a little laugh to show she was joking about the last part, even though she knew in her heart she wasn't, 'How about you?'

'Oh, I'm in a dither about a shop,' said Beth, 'but I have to say your adventure sounds far more life-changing – and loads more exciting!'

Abi smiled. 'I'm not sure about that. It's definitely exciting, but it's also a bit scary. New area with no one I know and everything, but it feels the right thing to do now that . . .'

Aware that since her arrival in Cornwall she seemed to be suffering from a severe case of verbal diarrhoea, Abi abruptly stopped talking. She had to know someone a great deal better before telling them about Luke. Anyway, this woman seemed nice. Abi didn't want to put her off being a potential friend by admitting how weak and feeble she had been when she'd been married and kill off any respect Beth might have her before they'd had a chance to get to know each other.

Rubbing his hands together as if more than satisfied that they were all sitting together, Max called over to Patsy for a refill of Abi's drink, and two pints of the local beer for himself and Beth, along with a couple of plates of the house special fish and chips.

'So then, where have you been so far?'

Abi sighed, her determination to be upbeat waning in the face of such friendliness. It was so much easier pretending everything was OK when you were afraid to show weakness. 'Where haven't I been? Penzance, St Ives, Lamorna, Marazion . . . All lovely, but it was Sennen I fell in love with. But as it's so small, the chances of me finding a suitable home are slim. Silly to set my heart on something I probably can't have. I was wondering if I should go back to Surrey and make the best of what I've got.'

'Not silly at all.' Max was shaking his head in earnest, 'and I notice you said go back, and not go home. That sort of implies that your heart isn't in Surrey anymore.'

Beth was nodding in agreement. 'If you're relocating then it has to feel right, you can't live your life in the wrong place. I assume you work for yourself and can live anywhere, that's how it usually is for incomers.'

'I'm an illustrator for a children's book publisher, so although I don't work for myself, I can work anywhere, providing there's enough light, space, and broadband coverage!'

Max and Beth laughed. 'Then there are definitely some places that you have to cross off your list – including some roads in Sennen, but not all of them.'

Beth unrolled a hairband from her wrist, swept her brown hair from her eyes and pulled it up into a stubby ponytail, 'So, this dream house then, tell us all! Is it in Sennen village or the Sennen Cove area?'

Abi stabbed at her last forkful of food, her need to share at odds with years of reticence. Here though, she reminded herself, she needn't be the introvert she'd become since her marriage. Here she was allowed to be sociable. 'I'm not entirely sure. I fell in love with the house as a child when I was on holiday with my parents. It is definitely around Sennen, and I remember it being near the sea, but I realise that hardly narrows things down.'

Beth thanked Patsy as fresh drinks were delivered to the table, before asking Abi, 'So what's special about this house?'

With a slight feeling of self-consciousness, Abi began to explain about how her parents had joked that 'Abbey's House' should belong to her, and was relieved when neither Max nor Beth laughed at her or told her she was being fanciful.

'I just need to find it. I know the chances of it being for sale are nil, and that it will probably be nothing at all like I remember, but I don't feel I can start looking for a new home before I've squashed the slim possibility of owning it myself.'

Max tilted his head in her direction, 'And that's what you want, deep down? To own the house you remember?'

Abi gave a mini-inclination of her head as if she was embarrassed. Hearing her dream coming from someone else's lips sounded preposterous. 'Let's just say I need to lay the ghost to rest before I start being sensible. I'm pretty sure that Sennen is where I'm going to start my new life, though.' Feeling that she'd been the centre of attention for long enough, Abi asked, 'How about you, Beth? What's your new adventure?'

'How about I tell you tomorrow? Fancy a local tour of Sennen?'

'Oh, that would be wonderful! Are you sure you have time?'

Max put down the pint he'd been sipping, 'Beth's a school-teacher, lass, which makes her a lady of leisure until September!'

Beth was nervous. It had been ages since she'd spent any sort of quality time with a female friend outside the confines of a class-room. She'd surprised herself by offering to give Abi a guided tour of the bits of Sennen and the surrounding area that she thought she might have missed. The woman was a stranger, for goodness' sake! But Max had obviously liked her, and although Max was friendly with absolutely everyone, he rarely engaged women in more conversation than necessary. The distrust Max's ex-wife Lucinda had engendered in him had been all-consuming, and Beth found herself more than a little curious about Abi and her search for a house that might not even exist beyond her childhood imagination.

As she sat on a bench at the bottom of picturesque Cove Hill, where she'd arranged to meet Abi, Beth watched the narrow street before her begin to fill with the early morning tourists, as they left their accommodation in search of a traditional breakfast. The cafés were already doing a brisk trade.

Searching the steady flow of traffic hunting optimistically for a car parking space, Beth kept her eyes peeled for the dark blue Alfa Romeo Max had told her Abi drove. A few minutes later, she spotted it, and was impressed as it was parked comfortably in a roadside spot Beth knew she'd have had trouble reversing something half the size into.

'I'm impressed!' Beth waved at the woman walking towards her, her smile giving her away to be as apprehensive about their day as Beth was. 'I could never have got even my little car in there. Reversing and I have never been good friends, which is why I tend to walk everywhere I can!'

Abi felt a tiny flutter of pride, 'London parking practice. I had no idea it would pay off so well down here!'

Beth laughed. 'Well, if you can't make ends meet with your pictures you could run a course for the locals to learn city parking techniques!'

Smiling at the unexpected dig Beth was making at her own shortcomings, Abi turned to look along the row of cottages that ran along Cove Hill. 'They're so beautiful.'

'They are indeed. Incredible views as well.'

The bright blue of the clear sky and the pretty vista in each direction she turned filled Abi with a rush of optimism as Beth said, 'First things first then, a cuppa in one of the local cafés, or a walking tour of the main village and then a coffee?'

'I don't mind. Whatever you'd like? You should choose as you've given up your day for me.'

Beth laughed again. 'All I've given up is hours of tidying

and cleaning. Plus, it's the perfect excuse to put off a major decision for another twenty-four hours. You're doing me a favour, believe me!'

'That will be a decision about the new life you're about to embark on, that Max mentioned in the pub?'

'That'll be it.' Beth stood up, 'Shall we make the best of both worlds and grab a takeout coffee to drink while we walk the length of Sennen's main street? Then I'll take you on a tour of the tucked-away roads and a few of the nearby villages.'

'Sounds great.' Glad to have someone else willing to take the reins, especially as it was in such a friendly way, Abi relished the morning sun on her face as they strolled towards the cluster of cafés that huddled around the edge of the beach.

The sunshine that had been absent on her arrival was back in earnest, and with it had come the first major wave of summer holidaymakers. The café they'd walked to soon changed their mind about getting a drink straight away, 'I can't believe how busy it is. I swear there was hardly a soul here ten minutes ago, and yesterday, although it was busy on the beach, it was nothing compared to this!'

'Welcome to Cornwall during the first week of the school holidays! By this time next week, the place will have transformed from the sleepy place you saw yesterday to a swarm of people all looking for suntans, sticks of rock, and homemade fudge.'

'And out of season? What's it like then?'

'We're rarely totally without tourists, but it can be very quiet.'

Trying to imagine living as a local observing the tourists, rather than being a tourist herself, Abi asked, 'Which do you prefer?'

Ducking back out of the nearest packed café, having decided to get a drink in the village instead, Beth and Abi edged their way back between the customers waiting to be served their appetisingly smelling full English breakfasts. 'I like it both ways. I adore seeing the happy faces of the visitors. It makes me proud of the place. Amazing isn't it, that geography can bring so many people so much pleasure. And I also feel privileged on those occasions when I have the whole Cove to myself. Early on winter mornings, when the frost settles on the sand and you're the only person in sight, is quite a special feeling. Sometimes it feels as though even the sea is holding its breath.'

There was no doubt Beth loved the place, and as they began to stroll along the road towards the village, the views on all sides, across the sea or over the higgledy-piggledy cottages, reinforced Abi's sense that this was where she was supposed to be. 'I love it too. I love that the place feels alive, even when it's quiet and you can't see another soul.'

'You have seen it empty then?'

'It was pretty quiet last night, but . . .' Abi was a little uncomfortable, 'this is going to sound weird but, I remember it empty, as a child.'

'Not weird at all. Children's memories are complex things, and it is amazing what stays in the back of the mind, especially when connected to an emotional response to something.'

Abi looked at Beth with curiosity. 'That sounded like a professional opinion!'

'I teach primary school children, but before that I studied the capacity of memory in the under-tens as part of my university dissertation.'

'Wow. That's impressive!'

'And totally useless in everyday life! It was interesting at the time though.' Beth smiled as she stopped walking, and gestured to the building they'd reached. 'Max would never forgive me if I didn't point out this first landmark. This is, as you can see from the sign, the Old Success Inn, where Max will, if you aren't careful, drag you on a Thursday night to take part in the pub quiz.'

'You're not a pub quiz fan then?'

'I really enjoy them to be honest, but as a teacher everyone always expects me to know the answers to everything, and then takes great delight in gently teasing me when I don't. It's all good-natured, but I'm not always in the mood for it.'

'I can understand that.' Abi faintly remembered the quizzes she'd used to go to with friends when she'd been an art student. 'I used to rather like pub quizzes. Been years since I went to one though.'

If Beth noticed Abi's sudden air of wistful regret she didn't comment on it. 'Max will be chuffed. He is always looking for new general knowledge talent!'

Dying to ask Beth if she and Max were more than best friends, but not quite sure how to phrase it, Abi peered into The Old Boathouse souvenir shop as they passed by. Despite it being fairly early in the morning, the shop was already doing a roaring trade in postcards and buckets and spades. Although Abi had walked past the same buildings last night, she hadn't taken in much beyond the sea view and the continued presence of the Round-house, which she could see now in the distance as they walked along. Looking about herself, determined not to miss a single thing, Abi asked, 'Is the school where you work near here?'

'Other side of Sennen. Walkable if you don't mind hills.'

'I bet everyone knows you round here.'

'Oh yes, I've taught most of the young ones in the local villages. They're a good bunch on the whole. I'm very lucky to have such a great job. I really don't want to give it up?'

'Give it up?' Abi was cautious as she spoke, not wanting to interfere where she may not be wanted, 'is that the big decision then, giving up teaching or not?'

'Sort of.'

As they passed two picturesque white thatched cottages, and kept going towards the heart of the village, Beth said, 'I tell you what, let's grab that coffee after all, and I'll tell you my story if you tell me yours. Deal?'

'Deal!'

Chapter Ten

Settling into a window seat of the Toffee Nut Café, Abi and Beth gratefully acknowledged the speedy arrival of two mugs of strong coffee and the sustaining slices of saffron cake that Beth insisted they have. 'It's a local speciality, and slightly better for you than a Cornish cream tea – which I love, but it isn't exactly kind on the waistline.'

'Well, Luke would definitely approve of it, then, although having said that,' Abi picked up her slice of what looked like bright yellow fruit cake, 'it still looks far too delicious for him to have approved of.'

'Is Luke your husband?' Beth took a bite from her own cake, trying not to make it obvious that she'd noticed the cloud that had passed over her previously cheerful companion's face.

'He was. I'm a widow.'

'Oh my goodness, I'm so sorry! You're so young. I had no idea!'

'There's no reason why you should have known.' Abi began to play with her wedding ring, circling it around her finger as she stared into her mug. 'He had a heart attack. Luke was older than me, and he had a very stressful job, but it was still unexpected.'

'It must have been an awful shock!'

'Yes.' Abi cradled her mug of coffee and stared out across the street, admiring the granite cottages that seemed to reflect the warmth of the sunshine across the narrow road.

Not wanting to intrude, but at the same time consumed with

curiosity and no small amount of concern for her new friend, Beth said, 'We don't have to talk about it if you don't want to, but if you do want to offload, I'm a good listener. Just ask Max! I've been his emotional sounding-board for years, and he's mine in return.'

'He must be a wonderful boyfriend then.' Abi sighed. 'Looking back, I don't think Luke ever had the patience to actually listen to me, and he certainly wouldn't have shared anything he regarded as remotely emotional himself. That would have constituted weakness in his eyes.'

Beth would have laughed, but the expression of sadness on Abi's face stopped her. 'Really? That's a shame. Luke was missing out there.'

'I always thought so. Generation gap, perhaps. Although I don't suppose twelve years is a big enough age difference for that really.'

Quiet descended over the table for a moment before Beth added, 'And, umm . . . Max isn't my boyfriend, he's my best friend.'

Snapping out of the guilt-laden melancholy that had descended on her, Abi didn't disguise her relief as much as she might normally have done. 'You're kidding! You look and act just like a couple.'

'Do we?' Beth shrugged. 'We've been friends forever. We grew up together, and then we both decided to train as teachers. It seemed natural for us to study together, and so we applied for the same university.'

'But Max didn't get in?'

'Oh, he got in alright.'

'But he's a painter and decorator? I don't know him, but he seems like the sort of guy who would have made a great teacher.'

'He would have, and I suspect he would be a headmaster by now if life hadn't got in the way.'

The way Beth said 'life' made Abi suspect that she really meant a woman. 'Life?' Abi asked before sipping her coffee, before realising she was being nosy, 'Sorry, it's none of my business.'

Beth smiled. 'I'm sure Max wouldn't mind. Let's just say he met his wife at university and she had other plans for him, and so the teacher training ended.'

'She wanted him to be a decorator?' Abi was confused.

'No, she wanted him to be a lawyer or accountant or something high-powered. He did try, but he hated it, and she couldn't understand why. In the end she ran off with someone else. That's why he's here. He came back to the area three years ago, and has been working at his decorating business ever since in his attempts to build a new life, and pay the old witch off.'

'You weren't a fan of hers then?'

'Lucinda tore Max apart. I'm not sure I'll ever be able to forgive her for how badly she treated him.'

Beth's expression had become as dark as Abi's had been, and even though she was dying to know more about Max, Abi also wanted to lift the mood. Changing the subject, she said, 'We were going to tell each other what our new adventures were. Shall I go first, or will you?'

The arrival of lunchtime menus on their tables made both girls simultaneously check their watches.

'Good heavens!' Abi couldn't believe it. 'It's twelve already. We've been chatting for two hours!'

It had been years since she'd had a proper conversation like that. A broad grin crossed Abi's face as she allowed herself to accept that she was already making new friends here. It was more than she'd dared to hope for.

Over their empty coffee cups, Abi had heard all about Beth's grandfather and the consequential lack of relationship opportunities beyond the occasional brief physical liaison since she'd moved in with him seven years ago. Beth had explained about how she'd not been able to face emptying the old cobbler's shop he'd left to her, but now she knew she couldn't put off making a decision about the property's future any more, she was torn between running it herself, or leasing the premises to someone else.

In return Abi had told Beth about how suffocated the business wives Luke had so approved of made her feel, and how their dis-approval of her working and not just being the perfect wife had worn her down. Then, when Luke had died, the wives' inability to accept that Abi could look after herself, along with the attitude of Luke's family, had started to drive her mad.

'And that's why you came to Cornwall? To escape the Carter family and the wives of the county set?'

'That, and because I've always wanted to live here, ever since I was little.'

'Since you fell in love with Abbey's House?'

'Yes.' Not wanting to add that she also wanted to move far enough away from her old life as possible so she could escape, not only the ghost of being Luke's wife, but also to make some friends that had never met him, and hadn't known what she was like when she was with him. 'I guess it sounds a bit strange. Of all the places I could have decided to live, and I could literally go anywhere, that I have come here. But it just felt so much like the right thing to do.'

'Do you really have no idea where the house is?'

'To be honest, if my brother hadn't found an old photograph of it for me I'd have thought I'd been imagining Abbey's House. I haven't seen it since I was eight years old.'

'What happened after you were eight?'

'My father was promoted and we could afford to take holidays abroad. I was very lucky, I saw a great deal of the world, but nowhere's stayed in my heart like Cornwall has.'

Beth drained the dregs of her cold coffee. 'I don't suppose you have the photograph on you?'

'Stupidly I've left it in the hotel. I meant to bring it, but, well, to be honest I was a bit nervous about meeting you today. It might have looked a bit pushy if I'd brought it with me.'

Beth grinned. 'To tell you the truth, I was nervous as well. It's been a long time since I had a female friend.'

'Really?'

'I've always preferred male company. Women can be so darn catty. I don't have the time or the patience for it.'

Abi laughed. 'I can't argue with that!'

'So, it's called Abbey's House?' Beth looked thoughtful. 'I can't say it's a name I recognise off the top of my head, but I might when I see it.'

'Maybe if it hadn't been called Abbey's House I wouldn't have had a connection with it. A silly childhood ideal, perhaps. I always wondered if there was an old abbey or monastery around here that it was named after.

'More likely to be a family name. Maybe the Abbeys were a tin mining family or something? It could be worth having a dig into the local archives at the library.'

'That's a great idea, thanks, Beth.' Abi's confidence rose a notch as she watched a group of holidaymakers passed the window, 'I remember the house being at the end of a short row of houses. Terraced, stone built, and painted a creamy white colour. Although you can't see it in the photograph I've got, I'm fairly sure that when I was sat on my father's shoulders I could see the sea, but when I was stood on the pavement I couldn't see it, although I could hear it and smell the salty air.'

'Which probably means that it has sea views from upstairs, but not from the ground floor. That would place Abbey's House somewhere up the side of the slope that forms the village, not at the bottom, nor the top. So I guess that narrows the hunt a little,' Beth smiled.

'I really should have brought the photo.'

'Never mind. Why don't I come back to the hotel with you later and take a peep? You never know, I might recognise it on sight.'

'Are you sure? That would be great. Thanks, Beth.'

'So if you find it, are you hoping to see a For Sale sign in the garden?'

Abi blushed. 'If I'm honest, I'd love it, but that might be a miracle too far! And if it was on the market, I can't imagine that it would have the studio space I need to work from. Somehow I need to see it before I start to seriously hunt for a place to settle down in.' Abi looked about her. 'Do you think we should move? There are people waiting for tables.'

'Good plan. I tell you what,' Beth stood up, 'do you fancy coming to see my place? You could help me choose what to do with it?'

'I hadn't realised you were so close by!' Abi trailed a hand over the outside of the white-painted granite wall. It was a picturesque building, standing neatly at the street corner, its huge windows giving views in two different directions. 'I can see why you don't want to sell up and leave. This is stunning. Right in the middle of the village, and yet somehow still peaceful. You're so lucky!'

Beth was touched by Abi's enthusiasm for her home. 'So you can understand why I can't bring myself to let go of it, quite apart from all the memories of living here with my grandad. I love the place.'

Following Beth into the shop, Abi stood in the centre of the room. Beth might well not know what she wanted to do with the place, but Abi knew what she'd do with the place instantly. It was the most perfect location for a studio she'd ever seen.

With her hands buried deep in her pockets, Beth turned to Abi. 'Tell me, if this was your place, what would you do with it?'

Chapter Eleven

Holding a copy of Abi's photograph, which the hotel receptionist had kindly reproduced for them on the office photocopier, Beth curled up on the end of her armchair with a coffee in her spare hand and her phone tucked under her chin.

'So, Maxwell, I guess I can forgive you for dropping me in it when we were in the pub, and making me feel like I had no choice but to invite Abi out for the day.'

'I did no such thing.' Max chuckled, 'Anyway, I'm an excellent judge of character; I knew you two would get on. I take it you had a good day?'

'We did. She's lovely, and the poor girl has had a pretty crap time lately. She didn't say it in so many words, but I suspect Abi is running away more than relocating.'

Stretching his long legs out in front of him in the cab of his van, Max frowned. 'How do you mean? No one's hurt her, have they?'

Beth smiled at the concerned tone of his voice. Max would always be the first in the queue to rescue a kitten from a tree or help an old lady cross the road. The idea of one human being hurting another was something he couldn't bear.

'Her husband died just after Christmas. I'm not sure he gave her the easiest time marriage-wise. She didn't say that much and I didn't feel I could ask anything too personal after only knowing her a day.'

'Abi is a widow? Blimey! She can't be much more than twenty-five!'

'She's thirty-two; that I did find out. Our birthdays are really close together actually. I also think I might know where Abbey's House is. She's given me an old photograph her brother found in a family album, but I'd rather check with you to make sure I'm right before I get her hopes up.'

'Any chance of it being for sale, do you think?'

'Not a hope, but until Abi has seen it, then I don't think she'll be able to move on past the childhood memory that sent her down here in the first place.'

'A lot could have happened to the house in twenty-odd years. It might not be anything like she remembers at all.'

'That's true.' Beth placed her mug on the coffee table. 'Do you fancy nipping over here after work and taking a gander at the photo then?'

Max hooked the driver's seatbelt over his shoulder, 'If you're home I could come now. I've just this minute finished for the day. That OK?'

'I'll pop the kettle back on.'

As Max drove towards the old cobbler's shop, his fingers crossed for a parking spot, he found himself struggling not to get angry. There was no logical reason why he should feel annoyed with Abi's husband, especially as he was dead. A death that had obviously occurred prematurely if he had been married to someone as young as Abi. Yet the possibility that she might have been sad even before the death of her husband made Max's hands grip the steering wheel far tighter than usual.

Slowing to avoid hitting a couple of seagulls that had decided to take up residence in the middle of the road, Max found himself feeling curious about Abi in a way he hadn't been about a woman for a long time.

He blamed Lucinda. He'd had his trusting fingers well and truly burnt by his ex-wife, who'd run off with someone high-powered who could afford to buy his way into her avaricious heart over and over again. But there was something about Abi.

71

She seemed so fragile, and not just because she was short and petite. There was an air of vulnerability about her that she was evidently trying to hide within an invisible suit of armour.

If her husband had died recently, perhaps that would explain the way she held herself. Upright, shoulders back, as if trying to cast away every single sign of weakness, and repel any sympathy that might open the floodgates on whatever she was holding inside.

'Oh for goodness' sake, Max!' He rolled his eyes as he pulled the van into an unusually handy parking spot right outside Beth's place. 'You're letting your imagination run away with you. It's obviously been too long since you met a woman your own age.'

Still, as he let himself into Beth's place with his spare key, Max couldn't stop himself imagining giving Abi a hug. He could almost feel her tucked up under his arm, the top of her head just reaching his chest. He shook his head sharply, trying to dislodge the idea as he climbed the stairs towards Beth and a very welcome cup of tea.

'Yes, that's the one.' Max held the slightly out of focus picture of the old photograph up to the light. 'I'm sure you're right. Looks like the end of Miners Row.' He traced a finger over the two small figures in the photograph. 'I take it that's Abi and her brother?'

'Oliver. Abi hasn't changed much, has she?'

'No.' Max didn't say anything else. Even as an eight-year-old Abi had the look of someone it would be easy to snap if she was cuddled too hard.

'Max? Are you with me?' Beth waved a hand in front of his face, 'I asked you a question.'

'Oh sorry, I was just thinking.' Max put the photograph down on the table. 'What did you ask me?'

Beth sat back and crossed her arm, a playful smirk playing at the corner of her lips, 'Do I detect a flicker of manly interest in the newcomer to the parish?'

'Hardly.' Max pulled his mobile out of his pocket, making a

play of reading his emails so that Beth couldn't see the blush that threatened to spread over his face, highlighting his freckles, and giving him away. 'Now, what did you really ask me?'

'Do you have Abi's mobile number? I forget to get it from her, and I want to tell her about the house as soon as possible.'

'No, I don't. Why would I have it?'

'Maxwell? Are protesting too much?' Beth teased him gently, but when he shrugged by way of reply, she realised with a shock that he really did fancy her new friend. Beth wasn't sure if she was pleased or put out. She had never been attracted to Max herself, but there was no doubt that she'd got used to not having to share him. She'd been the one who'd nursed his broken heart back to health, and she didn't like the thought that he'd fall for someone who wasn't local and might take him away. 'You do like her, don't you?'

'Against my better judgement.'

Beth swallowed down her own selfish feelings, 'What do you mean? Abi is lovely, and it's been an age since you dated. Time to get back on the horse, maybe?'

'Says the woman who has been single for years!'

Beth grimaced. 'Boyfriends and caring for an elderly relative don't mix. And don't you try and change the subject, Max. I like Abi. She's nice, and I'm sure she could do with some kindness. Why don't you ask her out? She likes pub quizzes.'

'How did you find that out?'

'We passed the Old Success, and I told her you liked doing the quiz there.'

'Oh,' Max shrugged again, 'well, it makes no difference. I may well ask her to come along to the quiz as a friend, but not as a date. I mean, look at her and look at me. If I hugged her she'd snap, and I can't imagine I'm exactly her type. And, to be honest, I'm not that keen to risk a relationship with another executive-type woman.'

'Abi is hardly that.'

'I bet her husband was though, wasn't he? I bet he was a real high-flyer.'

'Luke. His name was Luke,' Beth realised she'd been right to be afraid that Abi's previous life would put Max off, although she understood why, 'and, well, yes, I think he was something big in the City.'

'I rest my case.' Max decisively put down his mug, closing the subject, 'Now, what are you going to do with the photo, pop it back to her at the hotel?'

'I'm sorry, but Mrs Carter isn't here.' The receptionist greeted Beth with the disappointing news. 'I believe she's gone into Penzance to meet a few estate agents. Can I give her a message for you?'

'That would be very kind, thank you, I'll just write a note.'

Beth scribbled the address of the place she and Max believed to be Abbey's House, together with directions, her mobile number, and an invitation for another day out soon, if Abi fancied it. She placed it in the envelope with the photograph, handed it over, then headed home again.

Abi clutched Beth's message in her hand. She'd read it three times now, and as she sat on the edge of her bed, ready to text a thank you to Beth, she found herself having to steady her breathing.

Max and Beth had tracked down the house. Abbey's House. Suddenly her plan to drive as far north as Hayle to visit more estate agents, having decided it was time to pull herself together and look for real home, and not some fantasy house she'd seen as a little girl, was put on hold. Tomorrow she was going to take a look at the outside of the house that had lived in her subconscious since she was a young child being carried on her father's shoulders.

Abi squeezed her eyes closed, trying to shut out the shadow of Luke's voice, telling her to prepare to feel let down. She knew in her heart of hearts that this time his spectre was probably correct. But if her dream was about to end, she wanted it to be good for at least one more night.

74

Chapter Twelve

Abi knew she was in the right place as soon as she turned her car into a row of tiny stone terraced cottages.

Her heart thumped in her chest as she parked at the far end of the street. Taking a long exhalation of sea air, Abi rose slowly from the driver's seat. She could feel the mixture of anxiety and excitement, which had been somersaulting in her stomach since the hotel receptionist had given her Beth's letter the evening before, threatening to spiral out of control.

For a split second Abi had considered asking Beth if she'd join her on this pilgrimage into her past, but she'd quickly changed her mind. If she was going to be as disappointed as she suspected she would be, then Abi knew it was better to be by herself.

Even though Abbey's House was at the other end of the row, Abi wanted to approach on foot, just as she had as a child. It was pure fluke that she'd missed this street of houses on her first day hunting around Sennen.

Miners Row, although tucked out of sight from the main village, was only a ten-minute walk up the hill. She hadn't been far from it when she'd given up looking before. Beth's earlier guess had been correct. It was high enough up the slope to be able hear the waves and inhale the salty aroma of the sea, but not high enough to give sea views from the ground floor. Yet, because it was secluded from the bustle of the village's main streets, the air had a peaceful edge to it.

Abi forced herself to walk slowly, wanting to put off the moment when she knew she'd finally have to give up on her dream and move on until the last minute. She wanted to take in every inch of the line of six homes; all connected, each pair at a slightly steeper gradient than the next, so that every other roof was a metre higher than the next. Glad she was on her own, Abi felt oddly emotional as she moved along, images of her much-missed parents and her younger brother walking with her, but stuck in another time, quite literally another century.

The feel of the place was precisely as Abi remembered. She could almost hear her mother telling Ollie off for walking along the low stone wall that ran the length of the little square front gardens.

Each wooden front door was painted in the bright red gloss she remembered and, unsurprisingly as it was only half past eight in the morning, a few of the windows were still covered – not by curtains, but with the wooden shutters that had fascinated Abi's younger mind. Not fake ones like Luke had fitted to their house, but originals.

Abi's mother had told her the windows would probably have seats cut into the stonework from the inside. From that day on Abi had longed to live in a house with a window seat when she was a grown-up. And when her mother had added that such seats were the absolute perfect places to sit and lose yourself in the pages of a book, she was sold on the idea for ever.

It was very quiet. Not even the usual background noise of cawing seagulls disturbed the stillness of the air. Everyone that had to go to work for the day had obviously already left, and no one else appeared to be up yet. Abi stopped outside the third house, trying hard not to peer ahead to her ultimate goal, and increasingly conscious that if anyone was watching her from within the houses she might look like a lost tourist or worse, an incompetent burglar casing the joint.

The little square garden immediately before her was neat and tidy, and the presence of a pile of upturned buckets and spades drying out by the front door suggested that this was a family home.

Or perhaps, Abi happily speculated, it belonged to grandparents who had their grandchildren to stay on holiday.

The slate on the connected roofs glistened grey and blue as the sun made the flecks of granite in the brickwork flicker and shine. She wondered what the buildings looked like from the back. Abi had always assumed that they'd have the traditional long narrow gardens running out behind them. She could picture raised flower beds and vegetable plots, with discreet patios and wooden summerhouses in which to draw, read, and relax in the glow of the balmy seaside summer, or huddle with a hot chocolate and a cosy blanket in the depths of winter.

What Abi didn't see was a single For Sale sign. She was a little disappointed but not at all surprised. No one would ever want to give up living here if they didn't have to.

Trying not to make her staring obvious, Abi's pulse drummed faster in her neck as she walked toward the last two houses in the row.

Her feet stopped moving and her chest constricted with sadness. Unbidden tears gathered, resting at the corner of her eyes. The neglect of the last two houses in the row was painfully striking compared to the state of the other four obviously loved and cared for homes.

Abi forgot her resolve not to stare. Her legs wouldn't move as she took in the crumbling brickwork around the front door, the overrun garden with its tiny lawn just crying out for the attention of a mower. The upstairs curtains were drawn and tatty. As she studied the rotting window mullions she wondered when they'd last been opened.

Now Abi looked more closely, she saw that the house wasn't one cottage, but two that had been knocked into one bigger property. It broke her heart to see that the house that had stayed in her mind almost her whole life wasn't being loved. But it was the condition of the wooden house sign, Abbey's House, faded and half hanging off its supporting post, that took the tears that had been brimming and pushed them in a waterfall down her cheeks.

Abi almost stumbled over her own feet in her haste to move. Knowing there was no way she could drive safely, she abandoned her car and walked into the village. She had to think.

She sharply told herself that her distress was her own fault for chasing the happiness of her childhood. It had been bound to lead to disappointment. How could it not, after so many years away? Abi angrily wiped the tears from her face as she imagined hearing Luke's taunts. She wandered blindly towards the heart of the village, not really sure where she was going, but knowing she needed to walk; to be somewhere else.

Max tucked the bag of sandwiches he'd bought for his lunch into one of his big pockets, waved goodbye to the shopkeeper, and set off towards his van and a day of tiling a shower room. His key was in the lock when he spotted Abi. He frowned as he saw her marginally avoid bumping into a man walking in the opposite direction. It was as if she hadn't even seen him.

Quickly locking the van up again, Max hastened across the road after her. 'Abi!' Convinced something was wrong, he chased after her, amazed at how fast she could walk for someone with such short legs. 'Abi, wait!'

Catching up with her, Max placed a hand on Abi's shoulder. One look at her tear-stained face and puffy eyes told him that she hadn't even been aware of him calling her. She looked spaced out. Gently taking her hand, Max swivelled Abi round and steered her into the nearest café.

Sitting her down in the corner of the tearoom Max exchanged a familiar greeting with the waitress behind the counter, mouthing the urgent need for a large pot of coffee and two cups as quickly as possible.

Speaking quietly, as if coaxing her to respond, Max said, 'Have you eaten today, Abi?'

There was something about the ordinariness of the question that brought Abi back to reality. She peered around her, taking in the quaint table clothed surroundings properly for the first time. 'Max?'

'Morning, lass. You look very pale, are you OK?'

'I couldn't face breakfast, I was too nervous.'

'Nervous?' Max suddenly became aware that he was still grasping her tiny palm. Feeling self-conscious, he laid her hand carefully on the table top and let go.

Trying and failing not to sigh, Abi said, 'I went to the house. Just to see.'

'Ah.' Max said nothing else for a while, letting Abi gather herself, as she blew her nose and wiped her eyes.

Thanking the waitress as she brought a large coffee pot and two cups to the table, Max said, 'Can I have a large stack of hot buttered toast as well, please?'

When they were on their own again he said, 'The house wasn't as you remember it?'

Abi went to pour the coffee, but her hands were shaking so much that Max took the pot off her. 'Let me. Do you have milk and sugar?'

'Just milk. Thank you.' Abi felt horribly embarrassed. 'I shouldn't have come here.'

'You needed food and drink. And no way was I leaving you in the street like that.'

Abi shook her head sadly, 'No, I meant I shouldn't have come to Cornwall. How stupid to chase a childhood dream at my age! You'd think I'd know better.'

Shaking off the impulse to pick Abi up, wrap her in his arms, and tell her that whatever it was, it was going to be alright, Max pushed a cup brimming with coffee towards her. 'You did what you needed to do, and that was to come to a place where you felt safe as a child; at a time before your world hadn't been tilted on its axis.'

Abi, her face still pale but for two high points of pink on each cheek, frowned in confusion.

'I know she shouldn't have, but Beth told me about losing your husband, and about how you hadn't fitted in with the other city wives. I hope you don't mind. She was worried about you.'

'It was kind of her, but she need not worry.'

79

'Oh course she should. You're a friend, and you're sad. Beth wants to help. We both do.' Max averted his eyes from the lost expression in Abi's eyes, glad that the waitress chose that moment to deliver the piping hot rack of toast and real Cornish butter. 'I'm going to butter this and you are going to eat every scrap, and before you tell me you're not hungry, I don't believe you.' Not pausing for Abi to argue, Max went on. 'I have to pop outside to make a phone call, and then I'm coming back. Seems to me that it's been far too long since anyone listened to you properly.'

Abi started eating without being aware that she was doing so. She felt a total fool, and Max's kindness was making her feel worse.

How could these people read her so well and so fast? Did she have 'I am running away from an unhappy life' tattooed on her forehead or something? It didn't help that Max was right. It had been a long time since she'd properly offloaded her troubles onto anyone, and, somehow, seeing Abbey's House looking so run-down and neglected had undone the securely padlocked box she kept closed up in the confines of her mind.

A box which contained every hurtful comment, every inch of guilt from the times she'd known she'd unwittingly let Luke down, every friend she had unwillingly sacrificed to make her husband happy. And then there was the sense of failure. Firstly, because she'd allowed it all to happen – because, for all Luke's faults, she had loved him. And secondly because she was crammed to the hilt with regret that once the initial shock of his demise had passed, she simply couldn't manage to make herself miss her husband. The relief of being free of his demands and rules was just too strong.

As she thought, butter trickled down her chin, and slowly the crunchy, creamy calories began to return Abi to her senses.

Enough. Enough now.

As Max came back to the table, slipping his mobile back into his pocket, she poured him a coffee of his own. 'Thank you.'

And as he sat down, his kind, friendly face a picture of smiling concern, he said, 'Never mind the thanks. Just talk to me.'

Chapter Thirteen

It was almost midnight, and despite her chunky woollen jumper, Abi shivered against the chill as she sat in the hotel garden watching the star-studded black sky.

She hadn't been able to face going back to the pub for her evening meal, nor seeing Max. He must think she was some sort of emotionally screwed-up nutcase. He'd probably have reported back to Beth by now, and although Abi didn't mind that as much as she might have in the past, she wasn't up to any show of sympathy tonight.

She had managed to eat more of her dinner than she'd thought she would, but had soon escaped the bustle of the dining room. Feeling stifled indoors, Abi had wrapped herself up warm and gone outside, settling herself onto one of the soft cushioned garden chairs on the sculpted patio.

Max hadn't said much after he'd rescued her. He'd listened. He hadn't interrupted her as she'd spoken. Abi knew she'd told him far more than she'd intended to about her marriage, about how she'd met Luke and fallen in love with him, but how stifled he'd quickly made her feel once they were married only six months after they'd met. Abi had explained about the muffin incident, and how the disapproving looks and comments of that particular gaggle of wives had been the final straw, in far more detail than she had to Beth.

She'd even told him about Simon's attempt to keep her in the family. It was as if, once Abi had begun to share with him, the floodgates had opened and she couldn't stop.

Staring up at the sky now, picking out the few constellations she knew, Abi felt a comforting glow at how angry Max had been by the time she'd stopped talking. The ire he'd directed towards the Carter family in particular had stunned Abi with its venom, so much so that she'd found herself defending them. Abi had told him it was just how they all behaved, and they saw keeping Luke's financial assets within their control as normal and sensible, rather than cruel.

That was when Max had taken a visible deep breath and placed his large palm over her hand. 'Your defence of them shows a great deal about how good a person you are, but they sound monstrous. Whatever you decide to do, or where you decide to go if Cornwall doesn't work for you, don't go back to them. They'll squash you.'

Max hadn't said much else. He'd just squeezed her hand hard once, and apologised as he stood to go. 'Work is calling me, Abi, thanks for talking to me, lass. Why don't you go back to your hotel and grab some rest. Don't make any decisions today, you've had too much of a shock.'

Then he'd left.

'So,' Abi addressed the outline of the constellation of the Plough as she sat in the closing dark, 'Should I give up and go back?' As she spoke up to the stars she remembered how Max had spotted that she called Surrey 'going back' and not 'back home.'

Abi wasn't sure at what point the house on the outskirts of Guildford had stopped being her home. Now she considered it, she thought it was probably before and not after Luke's death. It wasn't a realisation that she liked.

'But is Cornwall the right place?' Abi shifted her stargazing to the belt of Orion.

A cold shiver washed over her. Her mother would have said someone had walked over her grave. In the stark starlight she could almost see Luke, a spectre in her imagination telling her how foolish she had been to come to Cornwall in the first place.

'Perhaps you're right, Luke.' Abi pulled her knees up, resting her feet on the chair seat, so she was hunched in a tight ball on the chair, her arms wrapped over her legs. 'And yet, I've only been here a few minutes and I've already made two friends.'

Friends who interfere.

'Friends who care enough to interfere.'

You used to pride yourself on being self-sufficient and not needing anyone but me.

'I had no choice but to believe that, Luke. It's how I survived the isolation – by telling myself it was my choice.'

It was your choice.

'One you forced me to make.'

I did no such thing.

Abi closed her eyes. Yet again her imagination was taking her in pointless circles. She knew she had been weak, that she should have argued with Luke, stood her ground, and that he might even have respected her for it – although she doubted it. But what was the point of beating herself up about it now? How many times was she going to have this conversation with herself before she accepted that she'd been given, albeit in a manner she would never have chosen, a fresh chance? An opportunity to make a life wherever she wanted to be.

You have to go back. You have to go home. To our home. Your dream house is no longer a good dream. Our home has everything you need in it, a studio, comfort, space, a garden, a sunny conservatory – everything. You've had your running-away moment – now it's time to grow up and face reality.

Abi jumped as footsteps rapidly approached from out of the dark.

'Oh sorry, petal!' Barbara smiled, 'I didn't realise you were out here. Are you OK with coming inside so I can lock up, or would you like me to leave you the key so you can lock up after you when you're ready to come in?'

Abi uncurled her legs. 'Sorry, I hadn't realised the time. I'll come in now. Thanks.'

Barbara paused to look up at the sky. 'The stars are magnificent, aren't they? Looking up at them always makes me feel so tiny somehow. My husband always used to say that if you stared at the stars for long enough they'd stare back and a little of their soul would light your life forever.'

'I like that idea.'

'He was a great one for sitting and looking. My Sam was a man who always had time to actually look properly.'

Abi wasn't sure if she should ask, as slightly awkwardly she said, 'Sam?'

'Motorbike accident.'

'Oh, I'm so sorry!'

'Thanks, love. Eight years ago now, but not a day goes by when I don't miss him. It gets easier though – not nicer – just easier.' Barbara led Abi back into the cosy embrace of the hotel, 'Can I get you a drink or anything to heat the bones before bed, petal?'

'No thanks.' Abi smiled gratefully at the hotel proprietor and walked thoughtfully up the stairs.

Beth turned her car radio down as she pulled up outside the Cairn and waved to Abi, who was sitting on the wall waiting for her. Beth hadn't been sure what state she expected Abi to be in today. Max had given her a brief account of finding Abi after her disappointment with the house the previous morning, but he'd been unusually taciturn about what she'd told him.

Prior to driving to St Just to collect Abi, Beth had manoeuvred her car up the narrow backstreet of Miners Row. She'd walked that way so many times, but it wasn't until this morning that she'd really looked. As soon as Beth had seen the broken house sign and the poor state of repair that Abbey's House was in she had understood something of the grief that had flooded her new friend.

'Hi, hun!' Abi beamed as she climbed into the car, 'this is so kind of you, are you sure you have time to escape from sorting out the shop again?'

Beth couldn't help but laugh. 'No problem, I am one of life's prevaricators when I'm out of the classroom! Max can never understand how I can be all sensible and decisive at school, but be totally scatty and unable to make a decision about my own life.'

'I get that. Making decisions for other people is easy. You just follow common sense and the rules set down by your job or whatever, but personal decisions – they can be a total nightmare.'

'You've got it!' Laughing again, Beth edged the car back out onto the road and pointed it towards the Minack Theatre. 'How about you, though, are you sure you want to take time out from your house hunting?'

Abi stared straight ahead as she answered with a question of her own, 'Did Max tell you about yesterday?'

'He said he'd seen you and that you were very upset about the state you found Abbey's House in, and that he'd got some food down you before he went to work.'

'He was incredibly kind. Did I make him very late for work?'

'Not at all. He let his client know he'd be delayed, and they were fine about it.'

Abi stared into her hands as she spoke, her voice barely above an embarrassed whisper. 'I'm very grateful to him. To you both. I'm rather embarrassed to be honest. I haven't behaved well, crying and moaning to people I've only known for five minutes. And you've been so kind and . . .' Abi could feel emotion attempting to nudge back up her throat, '. . . and anyway, I've made a decision.'

'You haven't, have you? Damn, that means I'll have to!'

Thankful for Beth's light humour, Abi looked out of the window at the close high hedges that seemed to line all the narrow roads. 'I tell you what; let's just enjoy our day out. I know I've only just got here, but I already feel as if I need a break! Then after the show we'll get down to sharing some serious decisions.'

'I'm liking that plan!' Beth slowed down as they negotiated a narrow blind curve in the road, 'it follows all my principles of denial and putting things off!'

Abi hadn't been prepared for the Minack Theatre's sheer breathtaking beauty.

As Beth opened the car boot and pulled out an armful of thick tartan rugs and a wicker picnic hamper, Abi stood and stared, her mouth open in awe at the sheer wonder of the view before her. Surely there was no place on earth more suited to a performance of Macbeth.

'We don't need all those blankets, do we? It's a gorgeous day.' Abi could feel the sun's rays piercing her T-shirt, and was already wishing she'd worn shorts and not her trusty blue jeans.

'These aren't to cuddle up in. Although if you come up here when the sun isn't shining and it is freezing, you'd be glad of them. The wind can really whip off the sea here. The blankets are to sit on. The granite seats may look awe-inspiring, but they can become rather personal to sit on in a very short time if you aren't prepared!' Beth passed two plump cushions to Abi. 'We'll definitely need these as well!'

As Abi looked, she saw that everyone else was also pulling travel rugs, cushions, and picnics from their cars, and the happy rush of contentment that she hadn't experienced since her first morning in Cornwall washed over her again.

It only took a few minutes of sitting on the carved stone seats before Abi was grateful for Beth's foresight in bringing the blankets and cushions, and within twenty minutes, both women had one of the travel rugs over their knees and their jumpers back on despite the sunshine, as the breeze from the sea had had decades to develop the skill of invading the bones with an expertise that could be admired if not appreciated.

Despite its chill however, the breeze simply added to the hauntingly striking atmosphere. 'It feels as if this place has been here forever. It looks like a Roman amphitheatre, but the Romans never made it this far south, did they?'

'It really does look like it should be Roman, doesn't it? But the Minack's only been here since 1932.'

'Really? Wow, I'd have guessed eighteen-something, though I'm not sure why.'

Beth opened up a flask and began to pour out two cupfuls of

aromatic coffee. 'It does have a romantic Victorian air to it, doesn't it? In fact it was built by an amazing lady called Rowena Cade and her gardener. They carved every seat out of the granite cliff face. It must have been a real labour of love.'

'Was it always meant to be a theatre, or did that come later?'

'I'm not sure, you'd have to ask Max. He's the fount of all local knowledge, but I have a feeling that it was always meant to host performances. I do know that the first production here was *The Tempest*. I mean, can you imagine anywhere more idyllic for that than here? With the sea actually present, having a starring role!'

While Beth popped into a gloriously old-fashioned homemade sweet shop to buy a supply of rum and raisin fudge, Abi stopped to admire the statue of Sir Humphrey Davy high along the raised pavement of Market Jew Street in Penzance. She'd seen it the day before, but hadn't paused to look. The words of Barbara talking about her husband came back to Abi as she examined Davy's life-saving lamp. Life should be about looking and not just seeing.

Beth, already munching a lump of fudge as she walked out of the shop, offered the pink and white striped paper bag to Abi, 'Do you want to peer in the estate agents' windows while we are here, or shall I whisk you off to Marazion so we can sit on the beach overlooking St Michael's Mount?'

'What a silly question!'

Beth grinned. 'Good stuff. I love Marazion! We could get takeout coffee and walk along the beach if you like.'

Abi smiled back at her new friend. Suddenly, despite her disappointment with Abbey's House, Cornwall was feeling a lot more like she'd hoped it would.

Chapter Fourteen

Having taken off their shoes and socks, the girls walked along the sand, giggling like children as the lap of the sea broke over their toes.

Abi stared out across the bay towards St Michael's Mount, proud and isolated on its little island.

Noticing the line of Abi's gaze, Beth said, 'We're a bit late tide-wise to walk out there today, but we could go soon if you like?'

'I would love that.' Abi watched as a little shuttle style boat pulled up on the beach and despatched a dozen or so tourists. 'Mind you, the boat looks fun as well.'

Beth grimaced. 'Max loves it, but I get seasick.'

'But you live in Cornwall?'

Beth laughed. 'They say Nelson suffered from seasickness and he was one of the greatest naval heroes of all time.'

'Good point.' Abi dug her toes into the sand, enjoying watching the sea set them free again. She looked at her watch; it confirmed what the quiet state of the beach was already telling her. It was already seven o'clock, and many of the tourists had gone back to their hotels and rented cottages for their evening meals. 'Thank you, Beth, it has been a wonderful day. Just what I needed. Can I take you out for a meal soon to say thanks? And Max as well; I owe him big time for his kindness.'

'Not at all. Although a meal out would be great.' Beth sat on the sand and stretched her naked feet out in front of her. 'It's been so much fun. As much as I love my flat, I almost can't face going back.'

'I know what you mean.' Abi stretched her legs out in front of her as well, 'once we go back, we'll have to think about all those decisions we've avoided all day.'

'Successfully if not triumphantly avoided, if I may say so!'

'You may indeed!' Abi trailed some of the fine yellow sand through her fingertips, 'I think this is the first time since I lost Luke that he – and how to structure my life without him – hasn't been at the forefront of my mind.'

They watched as a man walked his dog along the front. The black Labrador was splashing in and out of the waves with an abandon they could only envy.

'I think I'd rather like one of those.' Abi tilted her head to one side as she watched the dog chase after a stick thrown between the shallow waves.

'A man or a dog?'

'Definitely just the dog! You?'

'I think I could go for both!' Beth giggled. 'We didn't actually have our chat about making decisions, did we?'

'Perhaps we decided not to?'

'Just one more hour of non-decision-making then?'

'You have a deal!' Abi sniffed the sea air. 'I can smell chips. Let's get some!'

Scrunching up the chip wrapper and throwing it into a nearby bin, Abi sucked the remaining traces of salt and vinegar off her fingers in a gesture of pure decadent bliss.

'Well then,' sounding far more decisive than she felt, Abi turned to Beth, 'what do you want to do with that shop of yours?'

Beth slugged back the remains of a can of cola and shrugged. 'I don't know. I do know what I don't want to do with it, but that hardly helps.'

'Of course it does.' Abi began to brush sand from her feet before putting her socks and trainers back on. 'What don't you want to do?'

'I can't see myself sitting behind a counter and selling things, which, as it's a shop, is rather a major drawback!' Beth pulled on her own shoes, and in unspoken agreement they began to walk towards the car park. 'To start with I'm going to use the space to display the pictures my last reception class of children did for me as a leaving present.'

'Oh, what a lovely thing to do! And having seen the space, I'm sure it would make a superb gallery.'

'That's what Max said, and to be honest, the idea does appeal, but there are so many galleries in Cornwall. I don't think I could make it cost-effective. And then there's the other problem.'

'The other problem?'

'I don't want to give up my job, so I'd have to employ someone to run the place for me, and if it was some sort of gallery, then I'd never bring in enough cash to afford that.'

Abi was about to suggest that they go back to Beth's and have a good stare at the place to see if they could come up with any suggestions, and to see if she was brave enough to share her idea that the shop would be an excellent studio this time, when Beth's phone burst into life.

'Hi, Max, good day tiling?'

Abi sat on a nearby bench just out of earshot and looked about her. Today had been a good day. A really good day. She had, in a miraculously short time she realised, done two of the things she had most wanted to do on leaving Surrey. She had made friends of her own, and she had found Abbey's House.

Her disappointment at the sad state of the house was still acute, but Abi no longer felt as though all her dreams had been dashed. With some mature reflection helped by a good night's sleep, off-loading to Max, a magical day of Shakespeare, fudge, and chips with Beth, Abi knew facing all the demons Luke had left her with had done her good. There had been so much grief backed up inside her, not only from the loss of her husband, but of the loss of her happiness some time before that. She'd felt so cheated by her marriage, and by the man she had loved so much at first, but who had slowly undermined every bit of confidence she'd had.

Abi was also sure now that this was the place for her, but that she also couldn't stay unless she found somewhere that made her heart happy. Knowing she had to be sensible, Abi decided to give herself two days to find out what was available to buy in the region. Then, if nothing fitted her expectations, she would get to grips with the idea of going back to Surrey and house-hunting from there. She couldn't justify staying in a hotel indefinitely until a suitable home came along, when she could sort out the sale from Surrey and house-hunt in Cornwall at the same time via the Internet.

Beth waved, telling Abi her call was over. 'Max has been having a think while he was tiling.'

'Really?'

'Yes, he always reckons he does his best thinking while he's tiling.'

'Fair enough,' Abi nodded, 'I always do my best thinking in the bath.'

Beth laughed, 'Really? You two are a right pair, aren't you!' She bent down to unlock the car, 'Anyway, he said that if you wanted to find out who lives in Abbey's House, then you should ask at the village post office. They know everything and everyone in that place!'

Climbing into the car, Abi asked, 'How is knowing who lives there going to help me?'

'Well, Max thinks that if the house is so unloved, then perhaps you could make an offer to the owner? They may be open to it? Can't hurt to try – if you do want to live there, that is?'

Abi tried hard to keep the flame of hope that had instantly leapt up in her chest from showing on her face. 'It's a huge long shot, though. I mean, I can't just walk up to the front door and say, "Excuse me, but can I buy your house", can I? And although I love it from the outside, I may hate it on the inside.'

'True, but if you don't try you may always regret it. I mean, if the house was obviously being looked after and loved it would be different, but it isn't, is it?'

'You've seen it?'

'I drove that way before I came to collect you this morning. It would need a lot of work if the owners said they'd sell.'

Abi watched the sea disappearing from view out of the car window as Beth slowed to follow a tractor that was taking up the entire width of the road.

Abi smiled. Max was such a lovely man to think of even more ways to help her, but she kept the thought to herself. Relaxing back in her seat, watching the Cornish hedges go by, Abi sighed softly. Even though a tiny fleck of hope was nudging at her thanks to Max's idea, she had to be sensible. 'I've decided to go back to Surrey and have a rethink.'

Beth almost swerved the car in surprise. 'What do you mean? You've just got here, and you've hardly house hunted at all yet.'

'I know, and it isn't exactly what I want to do, but I have to be practical. Coming here was exactly what I needed, but if I want to sell the house in Surrey I ought to be there to do that. I've left my brother-in-law in charge, and I'm not sure I can trust him to help me as much as he claims he will. So, I'll give myself two more days of searching for what is realistically available here house-wise, then I'll take a few days as holiday to think things over, before I go back until a suitable property comes along. I can't live in a hotel forever.'

'But you will stay to find out who lives in Abbey's House, won't you? I've been thinking about it. It might be unloved and run down because the owner isn't living there. Loads of people own property here but work up in London or Bristol or something. If that's the case, they might be up for an offer on a property they obviously can't maintain? Surely it can't hurt to find out, and it would be better than going back to making muffins and thinking up excuses for why you don't want to paint scenery for the local amateur dramatic society.'

Even though she knew Beth could be right, Abi was determined to keep a firm grip on common sense, and not raise her own hopes high again. Yet she couldn't quite stop contemplating that, just maybe, she could get to see inside the house, and perhaps fall out of love with it, or even persuade the owner to sell . . .

Beth's phone rang again as they approached the sign to St Just. 'Can you get that for me, hun?'

'Beth's phone, Abi here . . . Oh hi, Max, look, thanks again for yesterday. I hope I didn't mess up your day too much . . . What? Really? Are you sure? That was so kind, you didn't have to do that . . . well thanks. I'll tell Beth . . . Yes, I'd like that, thanks . . . see you, then. Bye, Max.'

'Well, don't keep me in suspense, what has he found out?'

'How did you know he'd found something out?'

'Because once Max has an idea in his head he's like a dog with a bone. I bet he couldn't wait for you to go to the post office and popped in there himself.'

'Yes! That's exactly what he did.'

'And?'

'Apparently they told him they weren't allowed to give out confidential information, but suggested he went to the library in Penzance to look up the property on the electoral roll. The house belongs to a Mr Stanley Abbey.'

Beth negotiated a particularly awkward bend in the road before saying, 'Abbey is the surname, not a reference to a building, then.'

'Yep. And it would appear the house is still very much in the Abbey family.'

Chapter Fifteen

Beth leaned back against her grandfather's empty workbench, her phone to her ear. She could hear Max rummaging around in the back of his van as she spoke. 'Abi's coming over this afternoon to help me sort the last few cardboard boxes of stuff out, and hopefully visualise a few uses for the old place.'

'Good idea, it'll be useful getting a fresh set of eyes to run over the shop.'

'She's had a quick look before, and to be honest her ideas were pretty much the same as ours, but I think she needs another problem to think about. Did you know she was planning to go back to Surrey in a few days' time?'

'What?' Max stood up suddenly, banging his head on the roof of the van, causing him to swallow back a curse and rub at his scalp as he replied, 'But she's only just arrived in Cornwall. I thought now I've found her a contact name for Abbey's House, she'd at least do a bit of research and see if there is any possibility of it going on the market in the near future.'

Beth didn't miss the hint of dismay in her friend's voice, and any doubts she'd had about him being interested in Abi beyond having her as a new friend disappeared. She was also sure that Max would do nothing about it, especially if he believed Abi was going to run back to Surrey without acting on the help he'd gone out of his way to give her. It looked as if she was going to have to act as fairy godmother if everyone was going to live happily ever after. 'I don't know, Max, I'm pretty sure

Abi is simply doing her best to be practical and avoid further disappointment. Anyway, I wondered, as we've more or less finished clearing the space here apart from the polishing machine, if you had time to come over tonight for a colour scheme think?'

'Sure. Be about seven o'clock, is that OK?'

'You are wonderful! Thanks, Max.'

Having warned Barbara that she might be checking out the day after tomorrow, Abi had left the Cairn earlier that morning with a new sense of purpose.

She'd had two early meetings with two different estate agents, and was now holding a handful of house particulars, all of which were just a little short of dream house status, but all of which had the potential to be homes she could learn to love.

Still determined to be both positive and practical, Abi knew that even if none of them had space to use as a studio yet, they at least each had enough garden in which to build one. In fact the only drawback that these properties had was that none of them were in Sennen. But as Sennen was basically only a couple of streets with the occasional house built off at an angle, Abi wasn't surprised she'd found nowhere there to buy.

Parking her car as near to Beth's flat as she could, Abi clutched the details of a three-bedroom cottage in the small village of St Buryan, further inland, and to the east of Sennen, and a two-bedroom end-of-terrace house in Gulval, just north of Penzance, to show her friend.

Calling out her arrival as she pushed open the unlocked door into the shop, Abi found Beth with her arms wrapped around a cardboard box, in the process of stacking it on a neat pile of several others by the end of the workbench.

'Wow, this place looks so different. You've worked like a Trojan!'

Wiping a stray hair from her eyes, Beth poked it under the bandana she was wearing to keep her long fringe out of the way.

'Thanks, hun, I seriously underestimated how much time getting the last few bits and bobs sorted would take.'

'It's always the little things that take the time.' Abi scanned the space, which now had a swept floor and no clutter at all. 'So, does this mean it really is decision time for you now then?'

Beth wiped her dusty palms down her dungaree-covered legs, 'It is, unless I can think up some more delaying tactics, of course!' She nodded towards the house particulars Abi was holding. 'And do they mean that you've come to some conclusions as well?'

'I have done a sweep of every estate agency and property-management company in the entire West Country. Well, that's how it feels!'

'So does that mean you have some places to view, and we won't be losing you to the Home Counties yet?'

Abi smiled at the hopeful look in Beth's eyes. She still wasn't used to the fact that someone wanted her to stay simply because she was her, and not because they required something from her. 'I have two places to see tomorrow afternoon, then, unless one of them is just right, I'll go back to Surrey until something more suitable comes up. I do intend to come back once that happens though.'

'But that could take years,' Beth tried not to sound too disappointed, 'and you haven't investigated Abbey's House yet.'

Not meeting Beth's eyes, Abi ran a hand over the smooth wooden bench. 'How can I? I can't turn up on a total stranger's doorstep and ask to snoop round their house. It would be a bit pushy, if not rude. And to be honest, I'm not that brave.'

Beth had a quick read of the house particulars that Abi had brought with her. 'They both look lovely, but they're a bit further from Sennen than I thought you wanted?'

'True, but property in this area is like gold dust.'

Knowing this to be true, Beth couldn't argue. 'Well, if you fancy a second pair of eyes when you go to see them, then just ask.'

'That would be great, thanks, Beth. I have a feeling I'm going to get lost trying to track them down!' Changing the subject, Abi put her hands on her hips and surveyed the space around her as she said, 'Any conclusions this end then?'

Abi experienced a rush of pleasure as she and Beth heard the distinctive sound of Max's work boots come into the hallway. Despite herself, Abi knew a light glow of pink was beginning to bloom across her cheeks. Hoping that her companions would put it down to the hot weather, Abi was asking Max about his day, when Beth started fiddling with her mobile phone.

Max, who had sat himself on an upturned bucket, added, 'Well, I must say you guys have worked wonders.'

Abi held up her pruned hands. 'Thanks, we've been scrubbing the walls with soda crystals. Unbelievably, you can now see that they were painted white all along!'

Beth waved her phone in her friend's direction. 'Abi has been an angel. I could never have got this far without her this afternoon. I was going to treat you both to pizza and a bottle while we talked colour schemes, but I've just received a text from the school's headmistress.'

Abi frowned. 'I didn't hear your phone? Hope everything's OK.'

'Looks like I must have knocked it onto silent by mistake. I'm always doing that! She wants to see me ASAP about the new curriculum. I'm so sorry; I'm going to have to dash. Can I stand you both pizzas tomorrow night instead?'

'Sure, no problem.' Abi felt a little awkward about being left on her own with Max now she'd privately accepted the fact that she fancied him a little bit (though only a little bit, mind). After all, she told herself firmly, you need a new boyfriend like a hole in the head. It's friends you need right now.

Beth fussed around. 'I must go and have a quick wash and then get over to her place. I'm really sorry, guys.'

As Beth virtually herded Max and Abi out of the shop, Max suspected he was being set up. Flashing Beth a look that clearly told her he didn't believe her flimsy excuse in the guise of a disappearing act, and that he was going to be having a serious word or two with her about this later, Max steered Abi onto the street.

'Looks like it's just you and me, lass, fancy a bit of company over dinner?'

Dishevelled from working hard with Beth, scrubbing the walls with a bucketful of warm water infused with soda crystals, Abi was very conscious of her creased and grubby clothing, even though she was standing next to a man wearing paint and plaster-spattered overalls. 'I'd love to, but look at me. I'm a mess! I ought to go back to the hotel to change first.'

Max winked. 'You look fine to me, lass. However, if it would make you feel better, why don't I pick you up from the Cairn in half an hour, and we'll go over to Lamorna?'

'If you're sure you don't mind.'

'Not at all, the Wink's a lovely pub. You really should try all the great local eating and drinking spots before you buy a place.'

Abi loved the Lamorna Wink instantly. They sat in the evening sunshine garden under a parasol, munching their way through the biggest plate of cheesy nachos she had ever seen. Max had already thoroughly examined the house details for the Gulval and St Buryan properties she'd brought with her to show him, and declared both nice little areas. It was only after they were beginning to see a glimpse of plate underneath the heaps of sour cream and guacamole that he asked what he'd been longing to ask since he'd walked into Beth's shop.

'You aren't really going to go and see these houses, and then drive back off to Surrey before you've knocked on the door of Abbey's House, are you?'

Playing with a nacho between her fingers, Abi sighed. 'It's like I said to Beth, I can't just go up to a stranger's front door and demand to see inside their home. It's rude for one thing, and well . . .' she played the nacho chip through a mini mound of sour cream, 'I'm not local, am I?'

'What's that got to do with anything?'

'Oh come on, Max, please don't think I'm ungrateful to you for finding out that the house is owned by Stanley Abbey, but you know as well as I do that a person who isn't local, who is obviously trying to buy a village home out from under its occupant, won't be looked on kindly. I'd be seen as just another interloper who wants to buy up village property.'

Max was about to protest that Abi was going to be living and working there, but he knew that there was an element of truth in what she was saying. He gave her an appealing half-smile. 'I don't suppose you have any Cornish blood hidden away in that pint-sized body of yours?'

Taking a fortifying sip of wine, Abi returned his smile. 'Don't think so. I just had eight childhood holidays down here.'

'If Beth was here she'd be telling me to pretend to be your brother or something; something to give you credible Cornish roots just in case!' Max laughed, 'but I've been around here far too long to miraculously discover a long-lost sister or acquire a wife overnight.'

They both went quiet at his mention of a wife, before Max added, 'But I will come with you if you like. If you decide to pay Mr Abbey a visit, that is. For moral support.'

Dismissing the idea of faking Cornish ancestry as insane, Abi accepted Max's offer of accompanying her to the Abbey House. 'You're both right, aren't you? You and Beth, I mean. I can't go back until I've at least tried to see inside Abbey's House. Thanks, Max, I'd really appreciate the moral support.'

'Tomorrow morning, then; so that you can view it before visiting the more far-flung cottages you've appointments to see?'

Abi gulped. 'You're on.'

'Good.' Max took a draught from his pint of cola. 'And, anyway, I'm more than a little curious myself. I thought I knew everyone in this area, but Mr Stanley Abbey is a new name to me.'

99

Chapter Sixteen

What on earth was she going to say? Abi's mind had gone through every possibility of how to explain why she was knocking on a complete stranger's door. In the end, as she'd half-heartedly chewed on the toast and marmalade she'd forced herself to eat for breakfast, despite her nerves having stolen her appetite – determined not to go all pathetic on Max again – she decided that honesty would definitely be her best policy.

Telling Mr Abbey, if he was even in the house when they called, that she used to come to Sennen on holiday as a young child and had fallen in love with his house because her parents had always joked it should be where she lived because of her name . . . well, it might sound a bit weird, but at least it was the truth.

Glad that Max, who was currently sat parked up behind her car in his van, was with her in case the reaction she received was less than friendly, Abi did her best to calm her racing pulse.

Calling on her long-forgotten business confidence, she decided to approach knocking on the front door as though she was nego-tiating with a difficult client, and she'd dressed for the occasion. Too late, Abi had realised she looked a bit too 'city' for the area, especially compared to Max, who was wearing his overalls, com-plete with their splashes of paint, so he could head off to work afterwards.

'Come here, lass,' Max rummaged around the passenger seat of his van and pulled out a folded-up sweater, 'you look a million dollars, but if you don't want Mr Abbey to see you as a London interloper, it might be an idea to play down the "stunning girl from the wicked metropolis" look.'

Secretly warmed by Max's words, Abi obediently, took off her jacket and swapped it for one of Max's oversized jumpers. It immediately felt far too hot in the early sunshine, but at the same time, as she rolled up the sleeves several times, Abi found herself infused by its comforting nature. Holding back from making her inhalation of its Max-type aroma from the wool obvious, Abi took a deep breath, and they both approached the house.

Opening the wooden gate and walking up the short path to the front door felt as though it was taking forever, and yet was still far too short a walk as they stood on the tatty rush doormat, which had possibly once had the word Welcome written across it.

Abi glanced up at Max. Standing side by side with him, she felt both tiny and safe at the same time. As she raised her hand to knock she hesitated. She could hear Luke shouting at her. 'What are you doing, woman? Have you taken leave of your senses? If the owner didn't want this house it would be for sale. You just get yourself home right now.'

Feeling Abi tense beside him, Max said nothing, but reached down and scooped her hand in his, engulfing it in his palm, amazed at how cold it was compared to his. She was obviously far more nervous than she was letting on. Max held her hand a little tighter and with a nod of encouragement, smiled as Abi raised her free hand, and knocked twice against the flaking red painted surface of the door.

A minute passed, and there was no sign of life. Abi was turning to leave, when Max thought he heard something.

'I think there's someone in there.'

'They'd have answered by now, surely? It's probably a cat or something.'

A couple of seconds later Abi saw that Max had been right, for now she could also hear a shuffling coming from the other side of the wooden door.

It still felt like an age between knowing they weren't imagining the sound and hearing the scrape of a key turning in the lock. Abi squeezed Max's palm harder, her imagination filling with visions of a cantankerous old man, furious at having his privacy disturbed, who was about to let fly at them. Her insides tensed as, ever so slowly, the door was edged open.

'Oh hello, how can I help you?'

Relief grabbed at Abi from the inside and rushed through her whole body. They were confronted with an old man, frail and holding a hooked walking stick, but with the biggest smile Abi had ever seen.

Disarmed by his friendliness, Abi suddenly forgot the start of the conversation she'd rehearsed and said instead, 'To be honest I'm not sure you can. You'll probably think me very silly, but . . . Oh, what a gorgeous dog!'

Mr Abbey's smile became a chuckle, as he opened the door a little wider so he could lean against the door frame, and the biggest golden retriever Abi had ever seen stood loyally by her master, looking quizzically up at the visitors. 'This is Sadie. She was supposed to be called Sandy, but when my granddaughter was really little and she was a pup, she made Sandy sound like Sadie, and the name stuck. Anyway,' Mr Abbey ruffled his dog's coat as he looked at Abi, 'I very much doubt a pretty girl like you could be silly, but why not risk it, and tell me why you've brightened a very dull day by knocking on my door.'

Bolstered by the old man's playful flattery and the continuing comfort of Max's hand, which was sending signals of potential happiness to Abi's brain that she didn't have time to confront now, but would definitely return to later, she told Mr Abbey about her family holidays. About how his house's name sort of matched her first name and how she'd always dreamt of seeing the inside of his home. She also added quickly, lest he think her too impertinent, 'But I realise that this is rather cheeky of me, and that you don't know me from Adam, Mr Abbey, so perhaps I should leave.' She began to ramble, as she turned to Max, 'What were we thinking? Mr Abbey might think we're con artists or something. I'm so sorry, sir. We'll leave you in peace.'

Abi had let go of Max's hand and was retreating down the path before she heard Mr Abbey call out, 'So is it Abbey with an "ey" or Abbie with an "ie"?'

Her face blotched with embarrassment, Abi muttered, 'With an 'i', like it's short for Abigail, although it isn't Abigail. I'm just Abi.'

'Well then, Just Abi, I think I'm old enough to make decisions about who I invite into my home, don't you? And after a lifetime of working with people, I think I'm a fairly good judge of character – although of course, if I'm wrong, well, you're never too old to learn another lesson, are you? So, why don't you and your young man come inside and tell me all about those family holidays? And do call me Stan, all this "Mr" business makes me feel as old as I really am!'

With a friendly encouraging shove from Max, Abi smiled apologetically, 'Thank you, Stan, you're very kind.'

'You've done your homework if you know my name, or did you guess from the house?'

Max answered, as Abi's nerves seemed to have stolen her tongue. 'To be honest, Stan, I looked you up on the electoral roll. I wondered if the house was empty, and it seemed the best way to find out.'

Supporting himself on his stick, moving slowly but with determination through the dimly lit hallway, where the wallpaper had obviously been good quality once but was now faded and beginning to peel at the edges, Mr Abbey said, 'Well, I'm not at all surprised you thought it was empty. The state of it from the front, and in the rooms I don't use anymore, is frightful. As you can imagine,' he waggled his stick to illustrate his point, 'as I'm not as sprightly as I used to be, decorating can be a touch of a trial.'

By comparison, the old man's living area, which had open patio doors leading into a conservatory and exactly the sort of long Victorian terraced garden Abi had imagined, was tatty but clean and obviously much-loved.

'It's beautiful. Thank you,' Abi turned to Stan, a little disturbed by just how much emotion was tightening in her chest, 'it is every bit as lovely as I imagined as a child. You are so kind for letting me see.'

'Well, you can repay me by making us all a nice cup of tea, and then letting me hold you hostage for an hour or so. Sadie and I don't get many visitors.' He pointed to the floor by his feet, and the dog obediently settled herself down, but kept her head alert, paying close attention to this interesting yet unexpected change to their obviously quiet daily routine.

Stan waved a hand back towards the narrow corridor they'd just come down, 'Kitchen is second door on the left, would you mind, Abi? It'll give you a good chance to see if my kitchen matches up to your childhood imagination as well. Don't hold the dust against me though, will you?'

Wishing that her emotions hadn't started spending so much time on her sleeve, Abi didn't dare speak in case she started to cry, but wandered towards the heart of the house as Stan and Max went to sit in the garden.

As she crossed the threshold into the kitchen, Abi could picture herself standing at the sink, washing up as she admired the view afforded by the window which looked out of the side of the house, across the countryside which she knew would lead on to the coast. Squeezing her eyes closed, Abi forced herself to stop her daydreams in their tracks. This was Stan's house, he clearly adored it; and she didn't blame him one bit. It may have been run-down, but it was so packed with character it could virtually talk to you on its own.

Breathing in the slight aroma of dust and damp, Abi admired the cream-painted cupboards, the Belfast sink with its built-in wooden draining board, and the small semi-circular oak table wedged into the corner. Lifting up the kettle, Abi tried hard not to enjoy turning the old-fashioned style tap to fill it with water.

Telling herself that whatever happened, she must absolutely not fall in love with the house even more than she already had, Abi began to hunt for a jar of tea bags or a teapot and some cups.

'Stan belongs here.'

All her determination, which had been on shaky ground to start with, dissolved into tatters the second she realised that what she'd assumed was a full-length cupboard at the far end of the kitchen turned out to be a walk in larder.

Standing inside the door, Abi inhaled the scent of long-forgotten spices, coffee grounds, and bread. Little hooks lined one side of the tiny room, holding cups and mugs and jugs, while the shelves directly in front of her were bedecked with every size of plate, bowl, basin, and pot anyone could ever need. Adding to this ramshackle collection was a plethora of baking tins, roasting pans, casseroles, steamers, colanders, sieves, and an ancient pair of weighing scales.

On the last wall, also divided into shelves, sat Stan's culinary supplies. Some looked new and entirely edible, but others appeared as though they could date from Stan's infancy, and Abi didn't even want to think about what might be inside the old flour sack that was propped against the far corner wall.

The whistle of the kettle boiling brought Abi back to herself. Gathering together three cups and saucers onto a tray, she found all her other supplies, and made up a pot of tea before risking opening an ancient-looking fridge to find some milk, relieved to find that, in there at least, nothing too far past its sell by date was lurking.

Max and Stan were chatting around a patio set in the garden as Abi carefully carried her wares through to join them. Sadie, however, had shifted her allegiance, and now had her head happily resting on Max's large lap, and was relishing being fussed under his big hands. Abi smiled at the sight, although she was surprised at herself for feeling a tiny jolt of jealousy toward the dog. She couldn't help thinking it would be rather nice to be on the receiving end of a caress from those large palms.

105

'Ah, here's your good lady.' Stan smiled his generous grin up at Abi, as Max shrugged apologetically in her direction. Abi guessed Stan must have assumed they were married, and Max hadn't had the heart to correct him. Not such a daft conclusion, Abi told herself as she laid out the cups and saucers.

'Do you take milk and sugar, Stan?'

'Yes please, now do sit down and take the weight off your feet.' As Abi did just that he asked, his brilliant beam dying a little, 'Tell me, what did you think of my kitchen?'

'It's charming! I must admit, I have rather fallen in love with your larder. My gran had one like it in her kitchen, and I used to adore being sent to find things in it when she had one of her massive baking sessions.'

'Mary, my late wife, loved it, it was her little haven. You haven't lived if you haven't tasted her ginger cake.'

Stan was quiet for a while, before carelessly adding a frightening number of sugar lumps to his tea cup. On seeing his company's exchanged glances he laughed, 'No need to worry about my teeth, chaps! Not had any real ones in years.' Stan chuckled again and then more seriously added, as he gestured to the garden, 'You can see the problem here all around you. I know I can't live here alone much longer. I have old Mrs Teppit who comes in twice a week to make sure I'm not dead, and to do some washing and cooking and stuff, but it's basic maintenance this place needs, and frankly I'm not up to it anymore.'

Max, his cup almost to his mouth, put it back in his saucer. 'I could sort the place for you, least I can do after you've let Abi have a peep at your private home.'

'You are very kind, me'andsome, but we're talking more than a new coat of paint. You've . . .' Stan splashed a little of his tea into the saucer as he put down his own cup, '. . . caught me at a time when I'm in mid-indecision. Do I sell up and move into a home, or do I pay for a carer to live here with me?'

Abi gazed across the flower beds badly in need of weeding, and the patio which, now she looked at it properly, had tufts of grass growing between nearly every stone. 'But you clearly love it here, would you really want to leave?'

'That's the problem in one, my dear. I do love it. Not only that, but I feel I ought to keep up the family home. The question is, who for? There is no actual family left in this country any more. My daughter and her children emigrated to Australia. So it's just me and Sadie now, and sometimes being here seems to rub that in a bit, if you see what I mean.'

Resisting the urge to give Stan a big hug, and talk him into finding a live-in carer so he could stay in the place he loved, even though it would put paid to her own dreams of living there, Abi was interrupted by her phone ringing.

'I'm so sorry, I should have switched it off. Will you excuse me?'

Trying to dismiss the voice that told her that it was good that there was a phone signal from Abbey's House, as there was no way she'd ever ask such a nice man to leave his home so she could buy it, Abi wondered down the garden to answer the call.

'Oh, hello, Simon.' A shiver trickled down Abi's spine. 'How are you?'

Chapter Seventeen

Abi quietly tiptoed back to the patio. The men looked so content sat together, like a grandfather and grandson chewing the fat. How does Max fit in to people's lives so quickly? His ability to be at ease with people so fast was a quality that Abi could only admire, and envy.

She returned to the table in time to see Max pass Mr Abbey a business card, 'Honestly, Stan, I mean it, if you want help doing this place up, or just getting on top of the maintenance that needs doing to keep living here, then give me a call,' Max turned his attention to the big, watery canine eyes looking up at him, 'and if this gorgeous creature fancies a longer walk than a trot in the garden, just say the word, I'd be happy to take her for a stroll along the coast anytime.'

Max looked up at Abi, about to ask her if she fancied taking Sadie out for a walk so she could have a change of scene, but one look at her told him that something had happened, although he wasn't sure from her expression if that something was good or bad. 'You have news?'

'Someone is interested in buying my house. I need to go back to Surrey right now, apparently.'

'Surrey?' Stan's already wrinkled brow creased. 'You live all that way away?'

'Yes and no,' Abi sat back down, 'I'm in the process of relocating down here.'

'I don't blame you, my girl, it must be awful for you to be so far away from such a generous man.' Stan nodded approvingly at Max.

Thinking it easier to let Stan assume she was living with Max, rather than think she was after stealing his home, Abi changed the subject. 'Did I hear you say about going for a stroll along the coast? Do you have a favourite place around here, Stan? I haven't had a traditional Cornish cream tea since I arrived. Anywhere you can recommend?'

Abi knew she should be pleased that Simon had tracked down a potential buyer for her house so fast, but even though she had been planning to go back to Surrey the following day, meeting Stan had changed everything.

Now she had a proper reason to return to her marital home, Abi didn't want to leave after all. Whether he was interested in selling up or not, she wanted to be around to make sure Stan was OK. If Max hadn't come across Stan before, that had to mean he'd been living as a virtual recluse; and for a person so obviously highly social when he was given the chance, that couldn't be good.

Before they'd knocked on the door, although she had hoped the residents of Abbey's House would be friendly, she hadn't expected to like them, and even to find herself instantly caring for them – but that is exactly what had happened.

Having thanked Stan again, and cleaned up the tea things for him, Abi and Max promised to come and visit him soon, and take him to The Queens Hotel in Penzance for a cream tea the following Saturday, an offer that was met with both glee and an invitation for Abi to explore the rest of the house next time she came by.

As they stood by their vehicles on Miners Row, Max picked Abi's hand back up. 'Come on then, lass, tell me, what exactly did your brother-in-law have to say?'

Wishing she knew if Max was holding her hand because he wanted to, or because he was a nice man and it was a comforting thing to do, Abi said, 'Apparently he's found a cash buyer for Luke's place, but to clinch the deal I have to go up myself. Simon did originally say he'd sort all the house sale stuff for me, but now he wants me up there.'

'What do the buyers want to meet you for? I mean, can't the agent do it all? It's not like anyone ever buys a house because they like or don't like the property's previous owner.'

Abi didn't mention the rest of her conversation with Simon to Max. She was confident that he would not have approved of Simon's continued persuasion techniques to get Abi to change her mind about selling the house, which very much had an edge of 'don't let Luke down' about them, and had ended up feeling not unlike emotional blackmail.

'What did you tell him you'd do?' Max reluctantly unlocked his van door, wishing for the first time in his life that he didn't have to go to work, and could stay and talk to Abi instead.

'To be honest, I bent the truth a little. I told him I couldn't come back yet as I'm in negotiations for a place of my own.'

'But?'

Abi sighed, 'But I did promise to return if the buyers are definite about the sale, so I can meet them and sign the paperwork.'

Beth was sat in the middle of her shop floor with all the pictures from her last class of pupils spread around her legs when Abi found her.

'Hey, how did it go with Mr Abbey? Was he there?'

'Oh, Beth, he is adorable. I think I loved Stan, that's Mr Abbey of course, as much as his house.'

'Really? So you won't be asking him to leave his home then?'

'No way.' Abi shook her head, 'I couldn't. He belongs there, and although I did love it, I would never forgive myself if I evicted an old man from his family home.'

'So you didn't tell him you were interested in buying it then?

I take it you would have liked to, now you've seen inside – if the situation had been different.'

'It would have been just right for me, but no, I didn't tell him. We told Stan about it being the place my family joked should belong to me all those years ago, and that I had always been curious about seeing inside. Anything else would have been cruel in the circumstances.'

Beth's eyes narrowed, but twinkled with mischief at the same time. 'We?'

'Max came with me, didn't he tell you?'

'No, he didn't mention it.'

'He was a star. I'd never have had the nerve to knock on the door otherwise. Although . . .' Abi paused, her face colouring slightly.

'Although what? Come on, don't leave me in suspense!'

'Stan sort of assumed we were a couple. I guess he spotted that we both had wedding rings on, and put two and two together and made . . .'

'Five?'

'Yeah.' Abi didn't add that the fact she had been holding hands with Max when the door was opened (purely for comfort, she told herself). 'Why does Max still wear a ring? I thought the divorce was a while back now?'

'Three years.' Beth cast her eyes across the pictures on the floor as she spoke, 'At first he left it on because he loved Lucinda despite what she did to him, and then he kept it on to repel other women. He never wanted to be hurt again, and to be frank, I don't blame him.'

Feeling that the subject had been closed, Abi crouched down and picked up the nearest children's picture of the seaside, 'These are wonderful. You're definitely going to display them in here then?'

'I am. I was just trying to work out the logistics of it all, and of course, I need to get a couple of coats of paint up on the wall whatever I decide to ultimately do with the place.'

'Do I detect a note of positivity? Has a decision beyond show-ing off your ex-pupils' artwork been made?'

'Well, that sort of depends on a few things.' Beth paused, before saying, 'I think we need a spot of coffee and a slice or two of cake. I might have a proposal for you.'

'But you might not?'

'Cake first. Then I want to hear everything about this morning.'

'On the condition that you tell me what your proposal is straight afterwards?'

'Even if I don't think it is still a proposal I can make once we've chatted?'

Brimming with curiosity, Abi followed her friend out of the shop and into the sunshine. 'Especially then!'

'I don't think I have ever spent so much time in coffee shops!

Beth looked surprised. 'Not even in London? I pictured you bent over a table in one of the main coffee house chains, mochac-cino to hand, and scribbling sketches for your latest kids' book.'

Abi snorted. 'Luke would never have allowed that. He would have seen it as common. I could have got a respectable take-out coffee to take back to my studio, or to the office, when I used to work with him. But sitting down outside of the work space dur-ing working hours was not on.'

'Even if you were working at the same time?'

'Even then.'

Beth scooped up a large spoonful of sugar to put in her coffee. 'So didn't Luke ever have business meetings outside of the office, in cafés and stuff?'

'Oh, yes, but that was different.'

Beth frowned. The more she heard about Abi's late husband the less she liked him. 'It wasn't different, Abi.'

'I know.' Stirring her own coffee, Abi felt she should explain. 'He wasn't always like that. Luke was so kind, and I fell for him big time.'

112

'So what happened, if you don't mind me asking?'

Taking a sustaining bite of homemade Victoria sponge for courage, Abi began to tell her story. All the time she spoke, she kept her eyes on the table, playing her cake fork through her sponge. It was only after she'd stopped talking that Abi dared raising her eyes to see if the expression on Beth's face.

Her friend however, was not looking at Abi as if she was feeble. She was looking as angry as Max had done when she'd told him about Luke's family. 'Say that last bit again. Your brother-in-law, Simon, expected you to start going out with him, and then marry him so the house could stay in the Carter family?'

'Uh-huh.' Abi took a long drink from her fast cooling coffee.

'And this is the same Simon who called you this morning and insisted you return to vet a suitable buyer?'

'Yes.' Abi caught the look in Beth's eye. 'You don't think there is a buyer, do you? You think he's made one up to get me back there.'

'That is precisely what I think.'

Abi thought carefully before dismissing it. 'I can't see it. I made it pretty clear to Simon before I left that I wasn't interested in remaining in the Carter family. He was quite astonished by how assertive I was to be honest; probably put him right off me as a future girlfriend.'

'Ummm.' Beth didn't sound convinced. 'So what will you do? You aren't going to go rushing back to Surrey now, are you? I know you'd planned to go before you'd met Stan, but if you go Simon will think it's because he told you to, and that would be a boost to his ego that it doesn't sound as though he needs.'

Feeling so relieved that Beth hadn't lectured her on being the doormat she was well aware she'd been for the past few years, Abi ate some of her sponge. 'No, not now I've met Stan. And,' she waved her cake fork in Beth's direction, 'definitely not before you've told me all about your proposal!'

'You haven't told me all about Stan yet!'

'You're prevaricating, woman!'

'I know, I told you, I do that a lot outside of school.'

Abi stuck out her tongue. 'Right, Miss Philips, I will give you the edited highlights. Then you'd better spill the beans or else!'

'Or else what?'

Abi giggled. 'I have absolutely no idea, but I'll think of something!'

Chapter Eighteen

Having filled Beth in about everything that had happened with Stan, Abi tapped her teaspoon against her cup as if calling the meeting to order.

'Your turn. Tell me about this proposal of yours before my curiosity makes me burst!'

'OK, but before I do I want you to understand this. You do not have to agree just to please me. This has to be a choice you make carefully, don't agree because you think you ought to. It seems to me you've done enough pleasing people at the expense of your own happiness to last a lifetime. Agreed?'

'Agreed.'

'Right then.' Beth poured the final dregs from the coffee pot into their mugs. 'I have considered pretty much every concept possible about what to do with my grandad's shop, and I've decided to take your advice.'

'My advice? I was trying not to give advice about the shop so that you made your own decision!'

'I know. I wasn't sure why you were so cagey, and just repeated what I'd already mused about cafés and bookshops and stuff when it was obvious you could see the old place all done up and sorted. I appreciate that you didn't try and push me into anything.'

Cupping her mug of coffee, which was too cold by now to drink, but still pleasant to hold, Abi smiled encouragingly. 'And so?'

'I want to do something Grandad would approve of. I know

he wouldn't have liked anything he considered, and I quote, "all modern and silly".'

'Not going to be a sushi bar then!'

'Hardly!' Beth grinned. 'I'd like it to be an artist's studio with a difference.'

Abi bit the inside of her cheeks, forcing herself not to show any reaction until Beth had finished speaking.

'I don't want to give up teaching, so I'm going to need someone to run the place for me, which is where you come in – but only if you want to. I want you to be my studio gallery manager.'

Doing her best to keep her rising excitement in check, Abi said, 'When you say a studio gallery with a difference, what did you actually have in mind?'

'Well, I thought I could have half of the space as a studio with a full-time resident. Someone who wouldn't mind if the public watched them at work. And the other half can then be booked up by artists, schools, potters, and such like on a monthly basis to display their work.'

'Like a franchise, you mean, where freelance workers could rent space for a few weeks at a time?'

'Exactly.'

'You could do the same with the studio, you know? You could rent it out on a quarterly or monthly basis. Although monthly wouldn't work for everyone, some artists need longer in one place at a time to complete a project than others.'

'Oh, no, I don't want you to just run the place, Abi, I want you to have the studio part! I mean, I can't think of anywhere around here where the artist in residence is a children's illustrator rather than an oil painter or something. You'd be perfect!'

'Are you sure? I assumed you'd take a commission from each artist? I wouldn't be able to actually sell my pictures, because they belong to the publisher as well as me.'

'True on the commission front, but I will expect a cut of the profits from those who hire the gallery side. And you could sell the books you've illustrated, couldn't you? I could take a percentage from those sales.'

'A book corner? I'd love that.' Abi beamed, but quickly forced the animation from her face. 'But, Beth, are you sure? You haven't known me five minutes, how do you know I wouldn't mess it all up?'

'Of course you won't mess it all up! Plus, if you work in a place where people can drop in and out, you'll get to meet the locals as well as the tourists. That's got to be better than being isolated by working from home all the time. And if you worked here you could stop limiting your house-hunting to places with a space suitable for converting into a studio room.'

Abi couldn't keep the pleasure from her face. As much as she loved working alone, Abi had to agree that Beth's proposal would mean she could have the opportunity to meet new people on her terms. That would make a lovely change from only encountering those who were deemed 'suitable' for her to meet. 'OK, I admit it. I'd love to!'

Getting up, Abi rushed around the table and gave her new friend a hug, 'You have no idea how grateful I am that I got lost on my first day down here! If I hadn't, I'd never have met you and Max!'

'Come on then!' Beth got up as well, 'Let's get back to our gallery. We have planning to do!'

She could see it all so clearly, and now that Beth had made the decision by herself, Abi felt able to share her ideas and enthusiasm more openly. 'I'm guessing this would be the side you had in mind for the studio.' Abi gestured to the right of the shop, with the advantages of half a picture window for natural light, but also space for the addition of artificial lighting for winter days and a walled corner for supplies, and the all-important coffee table. It also had two sets of electric plug points already in place, which would be extremely useful for setting up her laptop, recharging her phone, and keeping a kettle handy.

Beth nodded. 'Exactly, and then the larger window space can be for our visiting artists.'

'What sort of people did you have in mind for the art side of things? You mentioned painters and potters; did you want to keep everything on an entirely arts and crafts footing?'

'Everything! Literally anything and everything that could come under arts and crafts. I will have three rules. Firstly: you and I will both have to like the work. Secondly: no crochet. I can't stand the stuff. It's only one step from that to those awful little dolls with the crinoline dresses they used to put over the spare toilet rolls in the seventies!'

Abi giggled. 'And the third rule?'

'Third: they have to be local to Cornwall, or maybe Devon. There are a lot of galleries down here, and although a good number of them feature local works, far too many of them feature art from London-based artists, or those who claim to be local, but only live here at the weekends.'

Abi winced. 'So, really, I shouldn't work here then? I . . .'

'I knew you'd say that! But that is quite different. You are moving here and intend to stay, and more importantly you don't pretend to be local when you're not. That's the difference.'

'A very convenient difference?' Abi's eyes twinkled mischievously, reminding Beth of Max for a moment.

'Maybe! But it's my shop, so I make the rules, and if those rules work to my advantage then so be it!'

Abi couldn't help but laugh. 'You sounded like a teacher then.'

Beth hopped onto the bench that ran along the back of the shop. 'Do you think I should leave this bench here, or pull it out?'

'Leave it. Pictures, pots, books, and all sorts could be displayed there for sale. It's a nice space, and it's far away enough from the window for anything left there not to fade in the brightness of the sunshine during the summer months.'

'Good point. I guess we'll need blinds to pull down when it's really bright?'

'And a good-quality floor covering. Something hardwearing. This one is good, but this carpet has obviously been here a very long time.'

Jumping back onto the floor, Beth agreed. 'Since before I was born. There are wooden floorboards underneath. We could rip up the carpet and polish up the wood. We should write a DIY to-do list for the shop itself, and then another list of all the different sorts of people we'd like to invite to exhibit.'

'At a competitive price.'

Beth frowned. 'How much is a competitive price?'

'Not a clue, but I can find out.' Abi paused, 'If you want me to, that is? I mean, this is your place not mine. I don't want to take over.'

'Don't go all timid on me now, I'll welcome all the assistance I can get!' Beth ran a hand over the bench. 'This is going to need a good sanding-down and a varnish as well.' She pulled a note-book and a pen out of her bag and jotted it down, along with 'paint walls' and 'redo floor'.

'What else is there?'

'Blinds.'

'Oh yes.'

'A till, an accountant, and we need to register for tax.'

Beth looked panicked. 'Errrr . . . that part of it I am not look-ing forward to! Where do I start?'

'I'll help, I'm already freelance, so I've done all that stuff before, and I'm sure Max must have as well. The decorating firm is his own business, isn't it?'

'Of course! Between the two of you, you'll know everything official I need to do. Thanks, Abi!'

'You'll also have to work out fees for guests, and decide exactly what commission percentage you want to take from each sale. Oh, and you'll need to work out how much I'll be paying for renting space per month.'

'What? Don't be daft. You're going to be more than earning your way by sitting in here every day so I can go to work. Anyway,

I don't suppose the gallery will earn enough for me to be able to pay you a wage for running the place for ages.'

'But, Beth, this is your business! You can't let me take up half your selling space for no fee, especially as I'm already getting paid for my work by someone else.'

'I am not charging you for the space, Abi. Not while I can't afford to pay you a wage for running the place. End of argument.'

Seeing Beth in full teacher mode made Abi giggle. 'Yes, miss!'

The next hour disappeared in a flurry of list-making and planning. It was another hour after that before Beth summoned up the courage to ask Abi what she'd been dying to know, just to make certain her new business manager wasn't going to desert her anytime soon.

'Umm . . . look, I know this is a bit personal, but I need to know if you're definitely going to take the job.' Beth fiddled her pen between her fingers as they both sat on the floor of the shop, before shyly continuing, 'If you can't sell the Surrey house you will stay down here, won't you? I mean, can you afford to take on two houses, one down here and one up there?'

Abi looked embarrassed. 'Well . . . I can actually. Luke was really well off, plus I've always earned my own money.' Picking at her fingernails, Abi mumbled, 'I don't want to use Luke's money for anything if I can avoid it. The Carters always made me feel like a gold-digger and I wanted to prove them wrong . . . but now the house is mine, and it's worth a small fortune, so yes, I can afford to do what I like.'

'Wow. You don't sound very pleased about that.'

Abi shrugged. 'It has always felt wrong having money I didn't earn.'

'You are a very unusual woman, Abi Carter!' Beth joked as she straightened up, 'and you are also quite a catch. Don't tell Max though, about how much your house is worth, I mean, he is always put off by women if they have money.'

'Put off?'

'Oh come on, Abi, don't tell me you hadn't noticed he fancies you?'

Abi's face coloured from pink to beetroot, 'well I guess I wondered if maybe he did.'

Beth spoke kindly, 'You like him too, don't you?'

Shaking her head Abi said, 'I will neither confirm nor deny that statement, but I do know it's too soon for me. It's just too soon.'

Beth put her hand on her hips as Abi got to her feet, 'I understand that totally, hun. Life, on the other hand, doesn't work like that.'

Chapter Nineteen

Abi didn't exactly decide to ignore Simon's summons, but after leaving him a phone message confirming that she was happy for him to sort out the sale without her, she felt she could get on with helping Beth.

The next three days passed with lightning speed as Abi and Beth pored over crafts catalogues and designed adverts to send out to prospective studio incumbents. Abi spent ages writing out a shortlist, and then a much longer list, of all the people she thought it might be worthwhile approaching. Every now and again Beth peered over Abi's shoulder and made either positive or negative noises. Just as Abi was about to close the browser window for a particularly good potter's web site, Beth glanced in her direction. Her eyes caught the photo of the potter himself in the corner. 'Ohhh, nice! I'm not sure what his pots are like, but he'd be welcome here anytime!'

'Beth! Honestly, you need a boyfriend!'

'I do! And that there potter would fit the bill perfectly!' Smirking playfully, Beth winked at Abi. 'If his goods are as hot as his photo, we'd make a profit in a week!'

Much to Abi's gratitude, neither Beth nor Max had mentioned the fact that she was still in Cornwall, even though it was days since Simon's call. Each time she had a crisis of conscience and decided she ought to go to Surrey, Abi sternly told herself that it was more important to establish her new life than to revisit the one she'd left behind. The fact that she jumped slightly each time her mobile went off was something Abi kept quiet, as she engrossed herself in the plans for the shop. She wasn't just dreading hearing back from a disgruntled Simon: Abi was also fielding calls from the two Cornish estate agents she'd seen properties with.

The cottages had both been sweet. A little on the compact side, but now that her studio space was sorted out, there was no reason that she shouldn't buy and live in either one of them. Both nicely located, both benefitting from very rare parking spaces, both with manageable gardens and easy access to a local shop, pub, and the seaside. Yet something was stopping Abi putting in an offer on either of them. When discussing it with Beth she said it was because she wanted to hold out for something a little closer to the forthcoming gallery/studio, but in her heart Abi knew it was because she couldn't shift the idea of Abbey's House from her head. Until she found a place that was as perfect as that one, no other property was going to stand a chance.

Rinsing her hands under the kitchen tap, Beth called over her shoulder to where Abi was sat at the table crossing off a few tasks from their eternal list. 'Did I tell you that Max has arranged for us to borrow a friend's floor polisher? He reckons it'll take about four runs over the wooden boards to return them to their original glory. It's arriving today.'

'Then do we varnish them, or will the polisher be enough, do you think?'

'I'm hoping it'll be enough, but I guess a coat or two of varnish might toughen up the floor a bit more, make it easier to keep clean and stuff. It'd take lots of time to dry though. I might ask Max what he thinks first.'

'I'll add it to the list anyway, just in case.' Abi scribbled it down and then checked her phone for the date. It was already the first of August. 'Are you still set on getting this place open before you start back at school in September?'

Drying her hands on a towel, Beth leaned back against the sink. 'Do think that's pushing it a bit? I'd like to have everything up and running while I have the time to pitch in. By September I'll be back to planning lessons. Am I being unrealistic?'

Abi smiled. They'd had this conversation several times since Abi had first broached the subject of when Beth was planning to open. When she had first asked, Abi had expected Beth to say in time for Christmas, not that she was hoping to be up and running within a month.

Sounding more certain than she was, Abi calmed her friend, 'It'll be just fine. Now this place is as empty as it can be, I'll crack on with the polishing as soon as the equipment arrives. I've used one before, and although it can be tough going, it isn't difficult. We're lucky it is only a small space really.'

'You don't think it's too small do you?' An edge of alarm began to flicker in the tone of Beth's voice.

'Come and sit down.' Patting the seat next to her, Abi said, 'Look, Beth, it is a great space. If it was any bigger we wouldn't be able to heat it properly in the winter, plus, the less established artists, who are the ones we're really targeting after all, you know, those who don't have their own galleries to exhibit their work, would be too intimidated by not being able to fill their half of the shop.'

'Thanks, hun. I sometimes think I'd have been better to sell up like the estate agent said in the first place.'

'Don't be daft. You'd never have forgiven yourself, especially if someone came along and did turn the place into a nail bar or something! You'd hate seeing it under someone else's control.'

'True.' Beth pulled Abi's list towards her and ran an eye down it. 'How come every time I look at this there is always more on it than there was before?'

'Because I keep thinking of more stuff we have to do.' Abi handed the pen over to Beth who'd put her hand out for it.

'And there's something else that needs to go on this list.'

Abi frowned. 'There can't be!'

Beth wrote in capital letters at the bottom of the page, 'FIND ABI A HOME.'

'Oh, that.' Abi coloured a little. 'I'll find somewhere soon. Barbara has said I can stay on at the Cairn for a bit longer as long as I don't mind staying in a single room. The double I'm in has been booked from tomorrow by a holidaying couple.'

'I rest my case!'

'Sorry?'

'Although the fact that you are referring to the manageress by her first name is great on a friendly-with-the-locals level, it also means you've been there too long!'

'I know, but I can't –'

A banging on the door downstairs, much to Abi's relief, cut her off mid-excuse. 'That must be Max's friend with the polisher.' She jumped off her chair and was down the stairs to answer the summons before Beth had the chance to pursue the last item on the list further.

It wasn't Max's friend. It was Max.

Trying not to appear as pleased as she felt, Abi said, 'Hi, Max, you not working today?'

'Finished a tiling job this morning, and I'm not due at the next place until two o'clock, so I offered Dave to drop this off for you guys. Saves him leaving the farm.'

'A farm? Why would he need a floor polisher at a farm?'

'He rents out rooms. Last year he did a barn conversion and it worked out cheaper for him to buy his own machine and then hire it out to others.' Max carried the machine through to the shop as though it weighed nothing, and plonked it down. 'Where does Beth want to start with this?'

'I'm doing it, and I'll have it in the far corner, please, so I can work backwards.'

'You're doing it?'

Abi didn't miss the look of doubt of Max's face, 'Yes, Beth has plenty to be getting on with. We've got a shortlist of people to

125

call who we'd like to offer the first few months in the gallery to. We're hoping a reduced rent will encourage people for the low-season slots.'

Max looked impressed, but still unsure. 'Sounds great, but are you sure you can handle this? It's heavy work, and you're so tiny.'

'I have done this before, you know.'

'You have?' Max looked incredulous.

'Yes!' Abi felt oddly put out. She didn't like the fact that Max obviously thought she was too puny for manual labour. 'Now, why don't you go up and see Beth? I'm trying to persuade her to varnish the floor afterwards as well, to make it extra tough. Perhaps she'll believe that it's a good idea if she hears it from you.' Abi unwound the cable and plugged in the machine, and taking the protective goggles that were hanging on a hook above the machine's handle, snapped them into place. 'Now if you'll excuse me, I have a floor to polish.'

Turning her back on Max, Abi mentally crossed her fingers. She'd been at university when she'd helped her friend reclaim an oak floor as part of an art installation; she just hoped that she could remember how to use the machine so that she didn't look a total idiot when she switched it on.

Abi needn't have worried however, for Max had gone, leaving the space behind her feeling much bigger than it had before. Concentrating on the patch of floor immediately in front of her, which wouldn't be seen as clearly as the rest, Abi decided to use it as a test area.

Sorry Max had gone, Abi was also glad he wasn't there to witness her turning the machine on and almost being dragged behind it as it shot forward. Bracing every muscle in her arms and shoulders, Abi let the polisher glide with her assistance, rather than taking her on a random path across the floor. Stoically ignoring the continual jarring of every bone in her body, she consoled herself with dreams of the hot bath that would be waiting for her once she returned to the hotel.

*

Beth raised her voice over the thump and hum of the polisher downstairs, 'Do you think she's OK with that thing? I can't stop thinking about that episode of *Friends*, when Monica hires a polisher and it ends up in a disaster!'

'She said she'd be fine.'

Not missing the tone, Beth asked, 'What's the matter?'

'Nothing at all. Why should anything be the matter?'

'Max, you sound like a sulky child who's been told there's no toffee left on bonfire night. What's wrong?'

'Nothing!'

Beth was fairly sure the honest answer to that question would be 'Abi's the matter, but I'm not sure why,' so she left it alone. 'Are you sure you can still fit in decorating the shop, Max? Abi and I are quite capable of slapping some emulsion on.'

Max winced. 'I have no doubt that you are perfectly capable. Although I take exception to the fact that you think that paint should be "slapped" on anywhere! But if Abi says she can paint the walls, then who am I to interfere!'

'Have you two fallen out?'

'Of course not.' Max picked up the list of prices Beth had been working out for the gallery side of things. 'Are you charging enough?'

Letting the matter of Abi rest for a moment, Beth took her notepad out of Max's fingers. 'Initially yes, but I want to fill up the first three months quickly. I'll charge more for the Christmas slot, and then Abi thinks we should slowly increase prices once the tourist season starts again in the spring.'

'Abi thinks? What about what you think? This is your shop, after all.'

'Well, I agree with her. For heaven's sake, Max, what is the matter with you today?'

'I told you, I'm fine!'

Beth was about to press the point when Max's phone began to ring from the depths of his overalls pocket.

'Oh hello, Mr Abbey . . . sorry, yes, Stan . . . is everything alright?'

There was a pause while Max listened, nodding occasionally, before he said, 'I can come over now if you'd like? I have an hour before my next job. I could trot Sadie down the road and back for you as well if you wanted? . . . OK, I'll see you in a minute.'

After he'd hung up, Max headed straight to Beth's front door. 'Stan wants to talk to me about the house.'

Beth was puzzled. 'To you? But why?'

Max ruffled a hand through his hair, 'Abi didn't tell you that Stan assumed we were married then?'

'She said she thought he might have, but she wasn't sure. Why does he want to speak to just you?'

'I have no idea, but I'm about to find out.'

Chapter Twenty

Max felt unsettled, and he didn't like the reason why. He knew he'd minded that Abi hadn't wanted his help with the polisher. Logically it wasn't surprising. She was setting up a new life after years of being controlled, it was important to her self-esteem to do things herself. There was no way Abi could have known that he had deliberately arranged his day so he could be the one who dropped off the machine, rather than leave it to Dave to drop it off. Yet Max couldn't stop the feelings of rejection.

'Don't be so stupid, man.' He muttered under his breath as he swung open the garden gate. 'Just because you assumed she wouldn't have a clue how to use it, and you could impress her by teaching her how. Time you stopped making assumptions about Abi Carter.'

The front door of Abbey's House was already ajar as Max strode up to it. He sped up, 'Mr Abbey? Stan? Are you alright?'

Stan appeared from a side door, 'Not to worry, Max, I opened it up early, as it can take me a while to get to the door these days. I overestimated how fast you'd get here.'

'As long as you're OK.' Max closed the door behind him and followed the old man through into his living room. 'Are you still up for that trip into Penzance tomorrow? Abi's looking forward to her first Cornish cream tea in years.' Max patted his stomach, 'And so am I, although I don't really need one!'

The room was cold despite the sunshine outside. At the side of the house, the window was small, and the sunshine hadn't managed to do more than warm the sill and the inside of the thick curtains. Max couldn't prevent himself from wondering if Abi would have put a blind there instead.

Easing himself into his armchair, Stan pulled a rug over his knees as Sadie waddled into the room and, with a friendly sniff in Max's direction, settled herself over her master's feet.

In front of Stan on a cluttered coffee table sat a pile of very official-looking papers, many of which looked as if they'd been around for a while.

'Do sit down, Max.' Stan picked up the top piece of paper, and was about to pass it to Max when he stopped, his head cocked to one side. 'Are you alright, me'andsome? If you don't mind me saying, you don't look quite as chipper as you did last time you were here?'

'I'm fine, thanks, Stan, just concerned about you to be honest. Is everything OK?'

'Absolutely. And you are sure I'm not interrupting your working day?'

'Not at all, your call was timely. I'd just dropped off a floor polisher to a friend. She's doing up the old cobbler's shop on the corner of the main street.'

Stan smiled. 'Jack's old place?'

'Yes.' Max wasn't sure why he was surprised that Stan should have known Beth's grandfather; after all, Sennen had always been a tiny community, 'Did you know him, then?'

A chuckling Stan nodded. 'Oh yes. Jack was a regular Jack-the-Lad when we were young. Sad to think he's gone now.' Stan paused, his memory briefly visiting the past, before he added, 'Not that I saw too much for him in the last few years. I can't get far under the steam of these pins of mine, and the poor man was bedridden.'

Max shook his head, 'If only I'd known you guys were pals. Jack's granddaughter, Beth, is my best friend. I know she'd have got you together somehow.'

'Little Lizzie? I've not seen her since she was a tot.'

Max raised an eyebrow. 'Does Beth know that she knows you? I mean, when Abi and I told her about this place, she didn't seem to register it beyond the fact she'd seen it before. But in a place this small that is hardly surprising.'

'I doubt the lass knows me, me'andsome. I went away for a fair while. Lived up country with my daughter Sally for a decade. I came back here when she upped sticks and moved to Australia five years ago. Took the kiddies and everything.'

Not wanting to prod at the sorrow which was evident in Stan's voice, Max said, 'Well, I'm sure Beth would be delighted to meet you. She has big plans for her shop; I think Jack would have been proud of her.'

'I'm sure he would. He was always so full of Lizzie when she was little,' Stan sighed, as if having to leave the comfort of his memories was a real effort, 'and yes, I'd love to meet her. Thank you. Another one for cream tea tomorrow? If that's still OK with you and the missus, of course?'

'Of course it is. We're both really looking forward to it.' Max was about to add that Abi and he weren't exactly together, when Stan pushed the piece of paper that had been flapping in his hand towards Max. He looked down at the paper as Stan spoke.

'As you can see, these are the original deeds for the house.'

'Crumbs, Abi would love to see these.' Max traced the looping writing with his eyes. 'So how far back does this place date?'

'Early nineteenth century, although it's obviously been adapted since then. If you have a good hunt around the house, you can spot all the different decades of building in action.'

Max smiled. 'So was it built for the local tin miners?'

'Yes. If you read the tiny lettering, it says it was an associated building. The whole row was. And then if you read this one,' Stan passed over another document, 'it tells you when the row of houses was bought from the landlord and sold off to individuals.'

'Was that when this house and its neighbour were knocked into one?'

'No, that was a couple of years later.' Stan passed over a third paper. 'My great-grandfather did that. He owned three of the houses, these two and the one next door. He sold the third, and had these two knocked together.'

Max scanned it, noting that this paper was much more recent, less faded and produced on what must have been an ancient type-writer. 'Fascinating. Thanks, Stan, this is great! Can you bring them on Saturday? Abi would love to see these. I'd call her now to have a look,' Max paused, 'but she's in the middle of polishing a floor.'

'You said that like it was a bad thing.'

'Oh, I'm old-fashioned I guess. Abi is such a little thing. I don't like to think of her being dragged around a floor by a machine!'

Stan chuckled again, 'And there I was thinking I was the old 'un. Women do stuff, me'andsome. They do all the stuff we used to do. Can't say I like it meself, but it's how it is, and Abi seemed a very capable young lass to me.'

'She is, isn't she?' Max heaved a sigh, 'Sometimes I think I was born a couple of generations too late.'

Stan smiled as Sadie adjusted her position over his feet so that she could give Max a look of companionship that was almost human. 'I know the feeling! Anyway, the reason I dragged you from your work is to tell you my news, and I wanted to do that without Abi being here.'

After Stan had finished talking Max sat very quietly before say-ing, 'Are you sure you want to do this? I mean, neither Abi nor I would want to think this was our doing.'

'Not at all. It's been on my mind for a year or more, your visit was merely the push I needed to get me to act.'

'How about I see if Abi is free this evening? We could bring fish and chips. But only if you're sure?'

'If we can eat them out of the paper then you're on. I haven't had them like that for years!'

Max laughed. Every now and then Stan was more like a kid

than an eighty-eight-year-old pensioner, such was his enthusiasm for the little things in life. 'You have a deal. Oh, and Stan . . . please do something for me. Think hard this afternoon. I won't tell Abi what you've said, that way if you change your mind then no harm will have been done. OK?'

'OK, me'andsome. You have got yourself a deal.'

Abi reclined luxuriously in Beth's bathtub. There wasn't an inch of her that didn't ache, and she was unbelievably grubby. On the plus side, after three hours of being buffeted about the room by the polisher, the floor of the shop had been sanded and polished to within an inch of its life. Beth had been so impressed that she'd driven straight to the nearest hardware store, risked incurring Max's wrath by buying some floor varnish without his recommendation, and had already started applying the first coat.

Listening to Beth's radio through the floor as she soaked her limbs, Abi mused over Max's request that she join him for fish and chips that evening. It could be a date, but there had been something about the tone of his voice when he'd asked that made her suspect he had a different ulterior motive.

Ever since Beth had voiced her suspicions about Max finding her attractive, Abi had been mulling the idea at the back of her mind more frequently. He was so different to Luke. But was he too different? Did she actually find Max's big frame, broad shoulders, and apple face attractive, or was it just a case of anyone who was a million miles from Luke, and who was kind to her, would pique her interest at the moment?'

Anyway, it was too soon. Far too soon. She hadn't had her freedom for long, and had had it guilt free for even less time. 'Besides.' Abi spoke to the bath water as she got out and watched it slosh down the plughole at speed, 'Beth implied that Max didn't trust women with money, so that's me out then. Assuming Simon doesn't try and diddle me over the house sale.'

Not wanting to think about Simon or the house, Abi pulled

her grubby clothes back on, hoping that Max wouldn't mind the fact she was crumpled and dusty from the day's work. Even as she thought about it, Abi knew he wouldn't. That was something she definitely found attractive about Max. He took her as she was. She didn't have to pretend. Luke, on the other hand, would have gone mad to think that she'd put on the same clothes she'd been wearing after a bath as before – though Abi knew she wouldn't have if there'd been a choice. Beth had insisted she use the bath here rather than waste time going back to St Just, only to have to drive back again afterwards to see Max.

'Yum! They smell amazing.'

Max had arrived with a neatly wrapped bag of fish and chips under his arm, as Abi walked out of Beth's front door. 'Beth told me you liked them. So, floor all sorted?'

'Yep. Well, my bit of it is. Beth's just finished putting the first coat of varnish on. So as you can imagine, she is now in the bath, easing her aches and pains. I have to admit it might have been hard work, but it is already looking worth it.'

'You get on with the machine OK?'

Abi laughed. 'Once I got the hang of it. I'd forgotten how heavy they were. Where are we taking the chips? To the harbour?'

'Not this time, although I'd love to another night, if you fancy it of course, although you probably won't. I mean, you're busy and . . .'

'I'd love to, Max, thanks.' Abi gave him a smile that told him it was OK, that she knew he liked her, but she appreciated his patience. 'But where are we off to now?'

'To see Stan. He called me at lunchtime. He has something to tell you.'

'He does? Any idea what?'

'Yes, but it should come from him.'

Abi looked at Max suspiciously, and trying not sound worried, said, 'He isn't ill, is he?'

'Not beyond the usual aches and pains that go with the fact he's eighty-eight years old.'

'Crumbs, is he as old as that? I would have put him a decade younger.' She thought for a while, before saying, 'Do you have chips for Stan as well?'

'Yes, he's really looking forward to eating them out of the paper.'

'Oh good, that's the best way to have them! Apart from sitting on the beach watching the sea at the same time, of course.'

Max's eyebrows rose. 'You like doing that?'

'Love it. There is something just right about watching the sea while having a hit of well-salted, vinegar-laden chips.' Abi noticed that Max was looking at her in an odd way. 'What?'

'I don't know many city girls who like doing that sort of thing.'

'Then you need to meet more city girls!' Abi allowed herself a grin. 'This city girl also likes long cliff walks, paddling in the sea, and building sandcastles.'

'Sandcastles?'

'Yes, why should children get all the fun?'

Max's mouth turned up at the corners as his inclination to pick up Abi and give her a bear hug returned. 'I'll try and remember that.'

Abi stopped as they turned into Miners Row, and stared at Abbey's House. She'd almost been scared to come back again, just in case the extreme emotional reaction she'd had before hit her for a second time. She was glad Max hadn't told her this was where they were coming earlier in the day, or she'd have been a jumble of nerves by now.

'You alright? I'm sorry, I hadn't considered that it might be difficult for you to come back, but Stan asked and I didn't want to let him down.'

'Quite right. Stan is lovely.' Abi took a deep breath. 'I'm fine. I can't quite believe I'm going to get another look inside the house.'

'You really loved it, didn't you?'

'I wish I hadn't, but yes, I did.' Abi opened the gate, 'Don't worry, though, I have no intention of upsetting Stan by telling him I once dreamed of buying his home. This house is Stan's. It is where he belongs. I may be a city girl, but I'm not a ruthless one. If I had been, believe me, I'd have fitted in so much better!'

Chapter Twenty-one

Abi had never eaten fish and chips so fast. She was dying to examine the documents Stan had found, but she flatly refused to touch them with fingers that were salty and dotted with grease from their dinner.

Stan had chuckled at her obvious pleasure, and despite his evident enjoyment of his highly unhealthy supper, he declared that seeing Abi's glee at the prospect of learning more about the house she'd fallen in love with was as delicious as the battered haddock, which was so fresh it was almost flapping.

After washing her hands with the utmost care, to eradicate every single trace of grease and vinegar from her fingers, Abi finally sat back on the sofa, next to the fire that Max had got going in the grate – and even then she still wiped her hands down the legs of her jeans.

Max raised his eyebrows at her playfully. 'Shall I go and see if I have any white cotton gloves in the van?'

Abi stuck her tongue out at him. 'I'm just taking care, that's all. These are very old and special.'

Stan's now familiar chuckle added to the warmth of the room. 'Nice to think some things in here are older than me!'

Taking her time, Abi revelled in the thrill of discovery as she read through the deeds one at a time, deferring to Stan every now and again where she couldn't read the faint text and flowery handwriting.

Vaguely aware that Max was moving around them, quietly

tending the fire, clearing up the empty fish and chip papers, and then disappearing for a while before returning with a hot pot of tea and three mugs, Abi read on and on until, smiling widely, she passed them back to Stan.

'Thank you. You were so kind to dig those out for me.'

'Max said you'd like to see them when he popped over at lunchtime.'

'He came here at lunchtime?'

'Yes, sorry, didn't he say?' Stan's forehead crinkled a fraction.

'No. He said he'd spoken to you, and to be honest, we've been working all afternoon. There hasn't been a chance to chat.' Abi wasn't sure why she suddenly felt wary. She had assumed that the chance to look at the deeds was the reason why she'd been brought around for fish and chips. Now she wasn't so sure. Rallying quickly, lest Stan should think her ungrateful, Abi said, 'It was a lovely surprise though. I adore old documents and things.'

'You two have so much in common.' Stan seemed very pleased with himself, and Abi was beginning to wonder if he was matchmaking – which seemed unlikely as he thought they were a couple anyway, but . . .

Max came back into the living room with Sadie, whose love of sneaking chips off people's laps had seen her confined to the kitchen while they'd been eating. As he sat down next to Abi, Stan began to speak.

'Right then, Abi. It's getting late, and as I don't really function much after nine o'clock, I think it's time I came to the point.'

In need of reassurance, but not sure why, Abi reached out a hand to stroke Sadie's golden back as she looked from Max and Stan. She'd been right. They had been up to something earlier.

Putting down his mug of tea, Stan sat back in his armchair; the lone sound in the compact living room was the flicker and rustle of the fire, which even though it was summer, was essential in the thick-walled little room. 'Now then, Abi. I have a proposition for you.'

'Another one? That'll make two this week.'

'I'm sorry?' Stan looked puzzled.

'Beth, that's Max's best friend, she is reopening up her grand-father's old cobbler's shop as an art gallery and studio, and she's asked me to help her run it.'

Stan nodded. 'Jack would have approved of you; I have no doubt about that.'

'Jack?' Abi looked at Max.

'Stan knew Beth's grandad back in the day. I'll tell you about that later. Stan, I think you had a proposal for Abi?'

'Yes, yes, of course.' Stan paused then launched in. 'I have been thinking long and hard since you knocked on my door the other day. To be honest, you made me confront a choice I have to make. A choice that I've been putting off making.'

'What do you mean?' Abi looked at Max, who put his hand on her knee, the urgent look in his eyes telling her to keep quiet until Stan, who sounded as if he was talking to himself rather than to them, had finished speaking.

'I know I can't go on looking after myself properly and the house for much longer. And really, the company of other people living around me would be nice. I could get that in one of the new homes or sheltered flats they've built over in St Buryan. But I've been here so long, you see. My family has, as you saw from some of those documents, lived here for a long time. But my daughter has no intention of returning, and my grandchildren are more Australian than Cornish now, so they won't want to live here, not soon enough to stop this place falling into rack and ruin anyway.'

Stan stopped, and the pause in conversation lasted so long that Max began to think Stan had changed his mind. 'You know I was genuine in my offer to do this place up, don't you?' he said.

The old man inclined his head. 'I do. You are a very nice young man, but we both know that this place requires a lot more than a quick lick of paint, and you have paid work to get on with. Which brings me back to my point.

'Abi, Max, I want to see this house go to someone who will

care for it, and preferably to a couple who might let me visit it from time to time. A couple just like you two.'

Abi tried to speak, but no words come out.

Stan raised a hand in understanding. 'I know it'll take some thinking about, especially as the house is worth quite a bit, and you might not be able to afford it. I'll get a valuation, although I think you can safely assume I'd be happy to do the sale privately if you two are interested, that way we'll all save a fortune in sales fees.'

Guilt and horror vied for first place as Abi realised that she might be responsible for Stan feeling he couldn't live in his family's home any longer. 'But, Stan, we can't. I mean, this is your home! If I'd believed for one minute that you saw our visits as a scheme to turf you out of your home then I'd never have been cheeky and knocked on the door.'

'Not at all.' Stan leaned forward in his seat. 'Abi, your arrival on my doorstep was exactly what I needed. Until then the only person I saw in the week was Mrs Teppit, who comes along to clean up and do a bit of shopping for me now and again – and to be frank she's no spring chicken herself, and could do with retiring.'

'But Stan . . .'

'Abi, Max told me you were selling a house, which means you must be looking for a new one. Have you found one yet?'

'Well, no. Not yet.'

'And, if you don't mind me asking you both such a personal question, do you think you could afford a place this size should it go on the market?'

Abi nodded, trying not to notice Max's eyebrows rise again as he learned she could afford to buy such a sort after property without hearing what the valuation might be.

'In that case,' Stan said, 'why not take yourself off and have a proper look at the house?'

'Max?' Abi looked at him beseechingly. 'Can you come with me?'

'Quite right.' Stan clapped his hands, bringing Sadie off Max's lap onto his own feet. 'This is a decision you should make together.'

Propped against the kitchen table, Abi's lungs struggled to inflate properly. 'Max? What the hell is going on? Why does Stan still think that we're married? I thought you'd told him about his mistake?'

'I was going to, and then life got in the way, and then when he told me that he was planning on selling up at lunchtime, and that he wanted to sound you out himself, I didn't know what to say. I also wanted him to think about it some more. There was every chance he would change his mind. If I'd explained his mistake it might have prejudiced him one way or another, and I didn't want to do that.'

'But now you have to tell him. We have to tell him.'

Max cupped Abi's hands in his. 'Can you really afford this place?'

'If the sale of the Surrey house goes through then yes.' Abi was self-conscious, 'Is that OK? I mean, Beth said that you didn't like women with money. If it helps, I wish I didn't have it. I mean, it wasn't a nice way to become wealthy.'

Max squeezed her hands tighter. 'Beth was sort of right, but believe me, you do not fit into that category of woman. I'll go and sort things with Stan. Promise. You go and enjoy having a poke about the old place.'

'There's no point.'

'What?'

'Stan wants his home to go to a couple. We aren't a couple. He'll withdraw his offer when he realises we've been dishonest, even though it was unintentionally.'

Max's stomach somersaulted as he spoke softly. 'We could be a couple one day.'

'Could we?' Abi felt both hot and cold at the same time. She wasn't sure if she could take any more shocks for the minute.

Max lifted her chin up so he could look into her eyes. Abi thought he was going to speak, but he said nothing at all. She hadn't registered Max was going to kiss her until his lips met hers in a soft embrace, which sent every confused nerve in her body ricocheting through her. Melting in his welcome arms, Abi realised that although he may have been one of the tallest, broadest men she'd ever met, but he was also one of the gentlest.

As Max slowly lowered her to her feet, Abi realised she hadn't even noticed that Max had picked her off the floor. 'I've wanted to do that since I spotted you in the pub the first night you were lost.' He swept a stray brown hair from her eyes. 'Is this alright? I didn't want to rush you.'

Wrapping her arms around his waist, Abi rested her head against his firm body. 'I wanted you to as well.' She hugged him firmly, before reluctantly letting go, 'But we don't know each other. Not yet anyway, and I need time, and well . . . there's so much to learn.'

Abi smiled up at his apple face, fighting her rapidly growing craving to join the dots of his freckles with her fingertips. 'And we will learn about each other, if you want us to. But right now, we are going to come clean to Stan. I would love to own this house, but no way could I do that if I felt I'd conned him out of it.'

Hand in hand, resolved to coming clean, they went back to the living room where they'd left Stan. But he wasn't alone.

'Simon! What are you doing here?' Abi let go of Max's hand as she registered the look of thunder on her brother-in-law's face.

'A new man in tow already, Abi?' Simon gave Max a glare which would have made a lesser man wither, but Max just held the newcomer's expression for a moment before putting out his hand. 'You must be Abi's brother-in-law, pleased to meet you.'

Blanking Max completely, Simon pushed past Stan, who suddenly lost all of his colour, and if Abi hadn't guided his elbow back, so his backside hit the soft cushions of his armchair, she was sure he'd have fallen.

'Simon, I asked what you were doing here. How did you find me?'

'Find you? Find you? You're supposed to be at home sorting out the sale of Luke's house. And here you are having an affair with a tradesman! How long exactly has this been going on? Did Luke know about it? No wonder he had a heart attack!'

142

'Don't be so damn stupid! Just because you've always felt guilty about having fantasises about stealing your brother's wife! I'd never cheat on anyone'

'For God's sake, Abigail! His body is hardly cold!' Simon more or less spat out the words.

'A fact which didn't stop you trying to step into his shoes only a few days ago! And need I remind you – again – that my name is not Abigail, and never has been!'

Max could see Abi was shaking, and yet he was proud of her for sticking up for herself against this snake. Had her husband spoken to her like that? He felt a chill run down his spine, and he had to ball up his fists in the pockets of his overalls to stop himself from reacting in a way which would have been satisfying for him, but not at all constructive, and would probably have ended up with Simon having his jaw wired and him facing a GBH charge. Turning his attention to Stan instead, Max noticed how pale the old man had gone, 'Are you alright, Stan?'

'He said he was Abi's brother, not her brother-in-law. He said he'd been here as a child, and Abi had told him to come.'

'You said you were Oliver?' Every single second of resentment that had bottled up inside Abi during her marriage threatened to explode, but one look at Stan, quickly caused her to take a firm grip of her emotions. 'Stan, are you OK?'

The old man murmured, 'I'm so sorry, he said . . . that man said . . .'

'It's OK, Stan. It isn't your fault.' With a nod at Max, Abi said, 'Will you stay with Stan, please? Make sure he's alright, while I have a word with Simon.' She turned to her unwelcome visitor. 'Outside!'

Abi stalked out of the cottage and down to the road. Spinning around to face him, she had her mouth open to ask how he'd known where she was, when Simon took hold of her elbow, and dragged Abi into the back of his car, making her look and feel every bit like a kidnap victim.

Chapter Twenty-two

Abi's voice was hoarse from shouting by the time Simon pulled his BMW into the first lay-by he came to and twisted around in the driver's seat. Wrenching the mobile phone from a livid Abi's hands, Simon stared hard at his sister-in-law as she sat as far away from him as was possible, semi-cocooned with her knees under her chin on his back seat.

'Now then.' Simon was evidently trying hard to keep his temper under control. 'I am prepared to listen if you care to explain yourself.'

Abi suspected it had been a struggle for him not to add the words 'young lady' to the end of his sentence. He was certainly looking at her like a father regarding his teenage daughter after an unfortunate piece of body piercing or a tattoo.

'Let me out of this bloody car!' She rattled at the car door, pointlessly, for Simon had overridden the locks. Taking a deep breath, and as haughtily as she could manage, Abi said, 'How dare you steal my phone! I have to call my friends to tell them I'm alright. They'll be worried.'

Simon grunted, 'No point, there's never any signal in this cursed part of the world,' before dropping her mobile out of her reach in the footwell of the passenger seat.

Trying not to feel panicked by the loss of her one source of communication beyond the car, Abi kept every word she uttered as level as possible, 'Simon, will you please tell me what you are doing here, and how you found me at Stan's house?' Without giving him time to answer, she went on, 'And if you have made Stan ill, or shaken him in anyway, I will never, ever forgive you.'

'For goodness' sake, Abigail! You can't have known the old man for more than five minutes.'

'It only takes a few minutes to know if someone is a good person or not, and Stan is my friend.'

'And the giant in the overalls who was pawing at you? Is he a friend as well?'

Abi could feel the fight draining out of her. It had been a long day. She was already tired from polishing the floor. Then she'd had three major shocks to her system: Stan's offer, Max's kiss, and Simon's arrival. Abi knew she didn't have the energy for a pointless conversation which Simon wouldn't give up on until he'd won. He and his late brother were very much alike in that way.

'Max is my friend. He was giving me moral support because he is a good person, that's all.'

'Oh, really?' To Abi's relief, Simon dropped the inquisition, and restarted the engine and pulled the car back out on to the road.

'For fuck's sake, Simon! You just don't get it, do you? Some people are kind because they are good people. People with no agenda, and no profit to make. Not everyone is like you, with an ulterior motive for everything they do!' Abi's anger evaporated into a quiet resentment as her throat stung after its unaccustomed barrage of insults and confused anger. 'Look, Simon, Luke has only been gone a few months. Do you honestly think I'd be ready to start again with someone else just like that? I am trying to make a new life for myself, a fresh start away from the constant reminders of the past; exactly as I explained to you before I came south.'

'Then prove it!'

'How?'

'Come back with me and sort out these buyers. That's why I'm here. They want to meet the owner and not just her representative. But they won't keep their offer open for much longer. You have to come now.'

145

'Now? I can't. No way can I drive back to Surrey at this time of night. I'm shattered. I'd have a crash or something.'

'I'll drive. I got down here last night and stayed in Penzance. It's taken me all day to track you down.'

'What?' Abi couldn't believe it. 'That's insane. I can't come! I have people depending on me. I have . . .'

'You have Luke's home to sort out,' Somehow Simon held back the snap from his voice, and adopted a coaxing tone which was somehow even more annoying, 'that is what you have to do. He was your husband, or doesn't that mean anything to you now you have new friends?'

Simon was pressing every guilt button Abi had, and she knew he knew it. Then with a jolt, she realised that they'd driven past the road that led to St Just. 'Simon, you don't really mean now, do you?'

'Yes. We'll stop at Bristol for some dinner.'

'But we can't! All my things are at the hotel, I haven't got my car. I can't just go . . . This is kidnap!'

'Beth!' Max bounded up the stairs, 'Beth, is Abi here? Beth!'

Scrambling off her sofa, picking up on the worry in Max's voice, Beth replied cautiously, 'Isn't she with you? Did her brother find her?'

Max pushed his way into the living room, searching the space, as if needing to see Abi's lack of presence for himself rather than just taking Beth's word for it. 'She really isn't here, is she?'

'No. What's going on?' Beth could feel alarm rising in her gut. 'Max?'

Max had got his mobile out and held out his hand while he made a call, 'Hello, The Cairn? I'm sorry to bother you again, it's Mr Pendale, has Abi Carter turned up yet . . . OK, perhaps you could ask her to call me as soon as she gets back.'

'Max, please! What the hell is happening?'

Sinking down on the sofa, Max looked as if he'd had the stuffing knocked out of him, a sight that was far more worrying to

Beth than his previous worried concern. 'Beth, was it you then, who told him where to find Abi?'

'Oliver? Yes. I would have come as well, but he caught me while I was in the bath, and so I couldn't really. I thought Abi would be delighted. I know she's very fond of her brother.'

'I'm sure she is.' Max put his hand on Beth's knee, 'But that wasn't Oliver.'

'What? Who was it then?'

'Simon. Luke's brother.'

'What?' Beth frowned, 'Are you sure? What would he come down here for?'

Max shrugged. 'The only reason should be the house sale, but he was so, I don't know, proprietorial. He spoke to Abi like she was a possession, not a person. His possession.'

Beth squeezed her eyes shut, 'And I sent him straight to her! Oh, God, I'm so sorry.'

'It's not your fault. If it had been Oliver, then you're right, Abi would have been delighted.' He pressed another number into his phone and pushed it to his ear, hearing the dialling tone from Abi's mobile mocking him down the line.

Tears started at the corner of Beth's eyes. 'What have I done? If he's hurt her . . . I never dreamt I was causing trouble. I thought that I was going have a happy phone call from Abi later saying thanks for delivering her brother.' Beth began to cry, 'I even pictured you and Mr Abbey greeting him with a tour of the house.'

Putting his arm across his best friend's shoulders, Max exhaled softly. 'This isn't your fault. As far as I can tell, this is all about Luke, the house, and Simon not getting his own way.'

Abi scrambled into the front seat and snatched her mobile from the floor of the car as they pulled into the Michael Wood services just north of Bristol. Taking no notice of Simon at all as he spoke, Abi climbed out of the car, hooked her bag onto her shoulder, and sent a text to Beth: Only enough battery to send 1 text – tell

147

Max I'm OK. On way to Surrey to sort house. Be in touch asap. A x

In her silence in the back of the car, Abi had been determined to stay where she was until there was either the opportunity to escape back to Cornwall, or until they got to Surrey, and she could at least wait until Simon had left her to sleep before sneaking out and getting a train home. Mother Nature had other plans however, and Abi's full bladder was making it a matter of some urgency that she found a ladies', and fast.

Stalking past Simon, Abi dashed to the toilets. Taking her time, running her hands under the cold water, she tried to think logically. She was reasonably sure that Simon didn't mean her any physical harm. He was suffering from hurt pride after she'd turned down his advances. Perhaps he really had come to find her because he needed her to sign paperwork for the house, and that it was simply seeing her holding hands with Max that had triggered his irrational behaviour?

Strengthened a little by the reply to her text that had instantly come through from Beth after she'd sent hers telling her that she, Max and Stan were relieved she was OK, and that she could call anytime, Abi remembered how safe she'd felt when Max had held her in his arms. Determined to keep that thought foremost in her mind, knowing it would help her through whatever Simon was about to throw at her next, Abi went to read the next text that had just beeped at her, but her battery flickered, and her phone groaned it was out of juice before she could see who it was from.

Simon was waiting for her outside of the bathroom. 'I need a coffee. Come on.'

Taking her by the elbow slightly too firmly to be a friendly gesture, he steered her towards the Costa, and ordered them each a large Americano and some boringly healthy granola bars.

Ignoring the pseudo-rabbit food, still full from her fish and chips, and slightly queasy from the events of the evening, Abi sat at the nearest table, not wanting to be out of earshot of the waiting staff in case she needed help, and silently sipped at her coffee.

Simon's expression was becoming a little uneasy for the first time since his unwelcome arrival on Stan's doorstep. 'I'm sorry, Abigail. I guess I was a bit heavy-handed.' He reached out a placating hand in an attempt to be forgiven, but Abi drew it back at speed.

'I would agree with that. Stealing me away from my friends – I believe most people would call that kidnapping – not letting me go back to the hotel to collect my clothes or let the owner know that I'll be checking out for a night, to say nothing of jumping to a lot of conclusions which you have absolutely no right to jump to.' Abi held the soup bowl-sized thick china cup firmly, savouring the warmth seeping through her fingers. 'Tell me how you found me, and exactly what you want. Now. Before I throw this coffee over your suit, call the police, and scream for help – not necessarily in that order!'

'Oh don't be ridiculous, Abigail, you'd never do anything like that! And anyway, why would the police believe you? I'd tell them you were just being hysterical after the sudden death of your husband.'

'You utter snake!' Abi gripped her coffee cup tighter, looked her brother-in-law right in the eyes, and, with the thought of Max spurring her on, whispered through clenched teeth, 'I've done a lot of growing up since I was widowed, Simon. I am not the pathetic little thing that living with your brother made me, so I suggest you come clean right now about what you want. Last chance.'

'I told you. I need you to sort out a sale of the house. But yes, there is one other thing. I'd like you to consider changing your mind about the sale.'

'Excuse me?'

'I want you to at least think about staying in the house yourself, or maybe keeping it and renting it out. You'd make a fortune in rent, and you could stay nearby to make sure your tenants looked after the property.'

149

Staring into her coffee, Abi marshalled her emotions before replying, 'Do I really have to explain my position to you all over again, Simon? I want to make a clean break. I had to leave. And although I understand that you and your parents have lost someone you loved as well, you have your own homes. You do not need me to keep the house simply to be able to remember Luke.' Pushing the remains of her coffee away, Abi stood up. 'Now, was there anything else, or shall we get this charade over with.'

'Charade?'

'It's late, and as it is now much quicker to return to Surrey than to drive back to Cornwall, I might as well come with you. I can meet these buyers, collect a few more of my things, and start to pack up my stuff for my final move south.'

'You've found somewhere to buy?'

'I told you on the phone. It seems you pay as little attention to what I say as your brother did.'

The house felt large, soulless, and eerie. It had taken a lot of protesting from Abi and a further threat to call the police for Simon not to come in with her. In fact, she'd been rather surprised he'd driven her home and not held her hostage at his place. In the end, once she'd promised to call him before she contacted the estate agents the following morning, Simon had left her alone.

Abi tensed as she turned on the lights in the living room and looked around her. She half expected to see Luke sitting in his favourite leather armchair.

So, you've come back then. I knew you would. I knew you'd never be strong enough to manage out in the world on your own.

Abi closed her ears, trying not to hear the mockery from Luke's ghost. A ghost, she realised with a start, that hadn't bothered her in Cornwall for several days. Then, with a determined stretch of her shoulders, Abi took her phone charger from her handbag, plugged in her mobile, and hoping that Max wouldn't be annoyed at her calling so late at night, pressed his number.

Chapter Twenty-three

'And you really are sure she's OK?'

Stan's hand shook a little as he lifted the bone china teacup to his lips.

Beth's smile projected more reassurance than she felt inside as she sat next to him at the smartly clothed table. 'I've had a couple of messages from Abi this morning. As she's in Surrey, she's going to make the best of the situation and take care of the sale Simon has set up and then get back here as soon as she can. After all, she would have had to go back at some point to sign things, so it might as well be now.'

'And as I said, she called me last night,' Max added. 'Abi was more worried about you than herself, Stan. She feels so guilty about us misleading you about being a couple.'

Stan raised his hand, 'Don't you worry, me'andsome. I should never have assumed. Thinking about it, it was you both wearing wedding rings that did it. I thought they linked you to each other, not to other people. I'm right sorry to hear about your separate circumstances. Still,' Stan beamed down at the cream tea that had magically appeared on an old-fashioned cake stand, the type that always reminded Beth of Miss Marple, 'I'm glad you've found each other, and now I understand the situation correctly, my offer is very much staying open.' Picking up a scone, he added, 'Now then, until young Abi gets back, I suggest we get on with these. I can't tell you how grateful I am for you bringing me here.'

Staring out of the huge picture window and across over the sea towards St Michael's Mount, Stan gave a happy sigh. 'My Mary used to love it here. Always insisted on putting the jam on before the cream, mind! I swear she only did it to wind me up!'

Beth laughed. It was hard to feel worried about whether or not Abi was coming back in the face of such enthusiasm for their afternoon tea. Beth had barely slept, mulling over what the future held for her studio gallery if Abi didn't come back. Even though Abi had sworn she would return, if something happened, if Simon did something to prevent her return – Beth didn't want to think about what – who would run the gallery? They were too far down the line to change her mind about the use of the shop now.

Instead of voicing her anxiety and dampening Stan's excitement, Beth took an unhealthily satisfying wodge of thick Cornish cream and smeared it extravagantly across her scone. 'So, Stan, I think it's high time you told me why Grandad was known as Jack-the-Lad!'

Two hundred and sixty-something miles away, Abi had awoken to the silence of the suburbs. No seagulls called overhead, and she couldn't hear the sound of Barbara preparing breakfasts in the kitchen below her room for those holidaymakers desperate to secure prime beach positions for the day. Everything was unnaturally still. Had it always been like that?

Luke had liked to listen to Radio Four first thing in the mornings, but as he was usually up and out of the house before she'd risen from the depths of their duvet, the house had been quiet when Abi had begun her days. Funny how she hadn't noticed the eeriness of it until now.

Checking the bedside clock Abi saw it was far later than she'd thought. Leaping out of bed, she went straight to the one part of the house that she'd genuinely missed while she was in Cornwall – the power shower. Enjoying the thump of the water on her shoulders and through her hair, Abi planned her day. She knew that the only way to get ahead of Simon was to beat him to the estate agent's and arrange to meet the new buyers by herself. Then, having already decided that, providing they weren't suggesting less than £20,000 lower than the asking price, she'd take whatever figure they were offering, Abi then planned to ring a few removal firms, and get costings on a complete house pack up and move. She had no intention of staying there long enough to do all the packing into cardboard boxes herself.

Pausing as she scrubbed shampoo through her hair, Abi spoke to the cubicle before her. 'I think I might get in a house clearance guy as well. I don't want half of this stuff.' However she pictured it, she couldn't visualise the furniture that Luke had chosen fitting into any Cornish cottage. Funny how fast this place had stopped feeling like home. Abi smiled. 'Perhaps Simon did me a favour? If I hadn't come back maybe I wouldn't have realised that, mentally at least, I've moved on.'

Abi wasn't sure if she dare allow herself to think about Abbey's House. If Stan really had forgiven her for misleading him as Max said he had last night, then maybe she should picture her things in Abbey's House. Deciding not to tempt fate, Abi tried not to visualise her beloved sofa in Stan's kitchen. 'Whatever happens,' she told her towel as she dried her damp locks, 'wherever I end up, my old sofa is coming with me.'

'Please could you say that again? I think I must have misunderstood.'

Abi had been waiting outside the estate agency door for it to open at nine, determined to speak to Nigel Davison before she was due to see Simon at ten o'clock.

Her brother-in-law had sent her a text just after eight o'clock, summoning Abi to the coffee house that was sat opposite to the agent's to discuss 'our options.' It hadn't been lost on Abi that Simon had said our options and not her options. She had a horrible suspicion that over coffee he would make another attempt at trying to worm his way into her affections and persuading her to stay.

Now, sat on her own opposite Nigel Davison an hour before Simon had planned, Abi's brain was struggling to understand what she was being told.

'I'm sorry, Mrs Carter; naturally I assumed your husband had told you.'

'My husband?'

The estate agent's ultra-smooth exterior was beginning to look ruffled. 'Perhaps we should wait until he gets here before we continue? To be honest I wasn't clear on your husband's reasons for taking the house off the market. I assumed he'd made a private sale.'

With her entire body bristling with anger at Simon's latest act of almost-criminal interference, Abi raised her voice to make her point very clear, 'Mr Davison, I put my house on the market, not my husband. It was me that invited you to put the house on the market and not my husband, for one very good reason.'

'Which was?'

'My husband is dead, Mr Davison. That is why I put the house on the market. If you recall from our last meeting, I was keen on a quick sale.'

The estate agent blanched as he said, 'But the gentleman with you at the time, the one who showed you around? That was Mr Carter. The same Mr Carter who cancelled the sale.'

'That was my brother-in-law. Mr Simon Carter, not my late husband, Mr Luke Carter. He, Simon that is, promised me he'd look after the sale for me while I was setting up a new life in Cornwall. He summoned me back here today to discuss a sale, and meet the buyers. I was under the impression we had a meeting with you at ten o'clock this morning? I was also under the impression that he'd made it clear to you, during your initial visit to my home, that he'd assured you we were not married, in case of any misunderstanding.'

Nigel Davison did not look happy. 'What can I say? Mr Simon Carter assured me you were married, and I'm afraid there is no such appointment for you and him arranged with me this morning. I was very puzzled when he took the house off the market

154

just as we'd had such an excellent offer for the property, but he was deaf to my persuasions. He led me to believe that you had both decided to rent the house out to provide rolling funds for another property venture, although he didn't tell me what that venture might be. My diary is fully booked today, and the only reason I had time to see you, Mrs Carter, was that you were here on my arrival.' Davison ran a hand through his perfectly gelled hair. 'It seems we have both been duped. I can only say how sorry I am. Is there anything I can do?'

Another property venture? Abi could feel her insides clenching in anger but she was determined to use it to her advantage rather than to show it. She'd been a businesswoman once upon a time, and she was about to be again, albeit in a much more relaxed and fun way with Beth in Cornwall.

'There are three things you can do for me, Mr Davison. The first is to phone the buyers that were interested and ask if they still want the house. The second is to reduce my agency fee by fifty per cent, as you should have checked with me before taking the house off the market, as we agreed. Third, if my brother-in-law comes in here in relation to the sale of my house, you'll call me instantly.'

Looking decidedly uncomfortable, Nigel fiddled with a pile of paperclips on his desk, 'I'm not sure I can waive half of the fee, Mrs Carter. After all, it wasn't my fault.'

'Mr Davison, I am sure you value your company's reputation far higher than that.'

The estate agent looked hard at Abi, as if trying to decide if she was bluffing. After an uncomfortable minute, he pulled a folder out of his desk drawer. 'I can certainly phone Mr and Mrs Adams to see if they'd still be interested in buying your home.'

'Please do. Now.'

'I'm sorry, Mrs Carter I have a meeting in ten minutes, I can't possibly . . .'

'Now.'

Nigel inclined his head a fraction, and started dialling the number.

Trying not to show the shake that had started inside her, Abi got up and let him make the call in private, standing by the window of the shop and staring across at the café opposite. She wondered if Simon was in there yet. She didn't think she'd ever been so furious with anyone in her life. How dare he? And what the hell did he actually want? Her, or her humiliation? It couldn't be money, surely – he already had more than he could ever spend . . . but if he needed money for an additional investment . . . All Abi knew for certain was that she never wanted to set eyes on Simon Carter again as long as she lived.

'Mrs Carter.' Nigel was waving for her to approach, 'Mr and Mrs Adams are still interested. They'd love to buy your home, if you're willing to drop the price by ten thousand?'

'Deal.'

Nigel nodded and returned to his call.

Abi made another decision, and as Mr Davison hung up the phone, a satisfied look on his face, she said, 'I'm going back to the house now to collect up a few of my things, then I'll be returning to Cornwall. This is my number.' Abi pulled his notepad towards her and wrote down her mobile number. 'The signal isn't always great down there, so this is my hotel number and the address as well. If you can't contact me on those numbers, you can call my new employer, Beth Philips. She can be relied upon to pass on any message.

'There is one more thing you could take care of for me. I do not wish Simon to be able to have access to my home, but nor do I fancy trying to take his keys off him.'

This time Mr Davison was ahead of her. 'You wish me to arrange for a locksmith to change the locks?'

'Please.'

'That is no problem. We have a new locks policy on all houses we sell anyway. I'll have a spare key available here for you so you can get in to sort out your removal requirements. Is that acceptable?'

'Thank you, Mr Davison. Once you have that sorted, I will

156

arrange for a removal firm. Oh, and if Mr and Mrs Adams want any of the furniture – apart from anything in my studio, and the sofa and dresser in the kitchen – they are welcome to have it included in the sale of the house. Just let me know. I will call you once I'm back in Cornwall, and we can arrange things from there.' As an afterthought Abi scribbled down her email address. 'You can contact me this way as well.'

'Excellent. If necessary I can get all the signatures we need through your solicitors via email or using a courier service. Do you have a solicitor in Cornwall?'

'Not yet, but I will get one as soon as I'm back.' Abi stood to leave, hoisting her bag up onto her shoulder. 'Thank you, Mr Davison.'

The estate agent offered his hand for her to shake, 'You are very welcome, Mrs Carter. I'm very sorry for the misunderstanding. I'm sure your husband would be very proud of you.'

Abi gave him a sad smile. 'That, Mr Davison, I doubt very much.'

Not so much as glancing at the coffee shop where she was due to meet Simon in twenty minutes' time, Abi hailed a taxi. Asking the driver to wait, she went inside her former home, filled a hold-all with a few clothes, and quickly returned to the taxi.

'Where to now, miss?'

'London Waterloo, please. It's time I went home.'

Chapter Twenty-four

It was with a sense of surprise that Abi woke up to see the sign for Truro station whizzing past the window. She hadn't intended to fall asleep. The last station she remembered passing was Reading about half an hour after she'd caught her connecting train from Paddington. Perhaps, Abi mused as she watched the Cornish scenery flash past the window, it was relief at escaping Surrey without having to see Simon that brought about her exhaustion.

The man next to her was not the same man who'd been sat in the aisle seat when she'd nodded off. Abi smiled at him apologetically. 'I hope I wasn't snoring or leaning on your shoulder or anything embarrassing?'

He returned her smile. 'Not at all. You looked very peaceful.'

Abi blushed. 'Thank you.' It had been years since anyone had commented on her sleeping. No one but Luke had witnessed her slumbering state since they'd first moved in together.

She didn't often speak to people on trains, usually adopting the terribly British line of hiding her face in a book, or staring out of the window with music blaring in her headphones, but as she hadn't thought to pick up a book, and listening to music would start her thinking about what she'd left behind her, Abi broke her usual rules. 'Have you been there long?'

'Since Westbury. You?'

'All the way from London. I was lucky to get a seat really. I'm on my way to Penzance.'

'Right to the end of the line then.' Her fellow passenger's

green eyes reminded Abi of Max's, although his hair, longer and dragged into a tiny ponytail, along with his goatee beard, made him look more like a student, although she guessed he was at least in his late twenties. Abi had the nagging feeling she'd seen him somewhere before, but as she'd never been to Westbury she dismissed the idea. 'No wonder you fell asleep. Isn't that about a seven-hour journey?'

'Seven hours and forty-eight minutes if the timetable is to be believed. You?

'I'm Penzance bound as well. Job interview. Well, sort of. You?'

'I'm off on an adventure, I suppose. Something of a fresh start actually. I'm moving down here to manage a friend's new gallery.'

Her companion looked at her curiously. 'What's it called?'

Abi shrugged, 'I honestly have no idea. It's a brand new venture. The place used to be a cobbler's shop, run by my friend's grandfather. Now it's going to be fifty per cent studio, where I can draw my pictures, and fifty per cent gallery, with a different artist taking on the space every month.'

'That sounds fascinating. Do you have a business card?'

'I'm afraid I don't. That is one of the things I will have to sort once I'm settled. I guess we'll need to do flyers and get a few adverts out there as well.' Abi retrieved the bottle of water she'd bought at Paddington from her bag and took a swig, 'I gave Beth a list of artists whose work looked interesting online to phone a few days ago, but I can't imagine she's had time to do anything about it. When I left her to go and sort out the sale of my house, she was still putting sealing varnish on the shop floor.'

'So this really is a new enterprise for all concerned then.'

'Yep. I'm really excited about it. I just hope I can run the place for Beth alright while she's at work.'

'What does she do?'

'Teaches. I'll be her manager in residence during term time in return for the studio space.' Abi wondered why it was always so easier to tell things to strangers on trains than people you knew well.

The man reached into his rucksack and pulled out a bag of Maltesers, offering the packet to Abi before crunching into one himself. 'What sort of thing do you paint, if you don't mind me asking?'

'Children's picture book illustrations, so it's more drawing and colouring than painting as such; although there is a bit of that. And sometimes it's all done on the computer, it depends what's needed for each individual piece.' Aware she was rambling, Abi abruptly finished with, 'I totally love it though.'

The smile on her fellow passenger's face widened further, 'Tell me, do you believe in coincidences?'

Abi's forehead crinkled. 'I think so, why?'

'Because a Beth Philips did phone at least one of the numbers on that list you gave her. My name is Jacob Denny. Cornish potter, born and bred. You must be Abi Carter; I'm pleased to meet you. Perhaps we could meet up in the morning and share a taxi to the gallery? My appointment with Beth is at ten.'

Max saw the taxi draw up before Beth did. Rushing out of the gallery, he had opened the door and engulfed Abi in a hug before she'd had the chance to even say hello.

Pulling back a fraction, but keeping hold of Abi, Max looked down at her, his eyes scanning her frame as if he was inspecting her for bruises or blemishes that might have been inflicted by Simon. 'Are you alright? He didn't hurt you, did he? What did he want?' Not giving Abi the chance to reply, Max pulled her against him and kept talking, 'Are you sure you're alright? I'd have come to the hotel last night if you'd let me know you were back.'

'For heaven's sake, Max,' Beth came out of the shop, 'Give the woman a chance to speak. Oh, hello?'

Beth's breath snagged in her throat as she noticed that someone else was climbing out of the taxi. He was carrying a large black portfolio and had a grin so suggestive that long-suppressed physical desires lit up all over Beth's body. It could only be the potter. Damn, he's hot!

Aware that Beth and Max were looking at her questioningly, about why she was sharing a taxi with the potter, Abi said, 'Oh, sorry! Yes, this is Jacob Denny, the potter you were expecting, Beth. I'm so pleased you called some of the folk on the list. Believe it or not we sat next to each other on the train yesterday, and as his taxi was passing the Cairn this morning we thought we'd share one, so that he found the gallery easily. Small world, huh?'

Beth beamed, hoping that the heat that was infusing her cheeks wasn't actually visible. 'Mr Denny, welcome.'

'Jacob.' He stuck out his hand in greeting as Abi made the introductions.

'This is Beth, who you're on your way to meet, and this is Max, great friend and decorator of this parish!'

Max gave Jacob his usual hearty welcome, 'Pleased to meet you. Which part of this grand county do you hail from?'

Jacob laughed. 'Well, Hayle actually, but my folks live just north of here in Pendeen these days.'

Desperate to have a private word with Abi before she spoke to Jacob, Beth said, 'Max, I don't suppose you could take Jacob inside and make him a cuppa? Jacob, perhaps you'd like to have a couple of minutes alone to get a feel of the space on offer, and then I will be with you.'

The moment the men had disappeared inside Abi pounced. 'Oh my God, you fancy him, don't you!'

'Damn, is it that obvious?' Beth coloured a deeper red.

'Totally.'

'Oh, hell. Do you think he'll guess? I don't want to put him off, I think a potter would be a brilliant guest for our first month, especially as his website showed that he produces lots of miniature pieces that could sell well before Christmas.'

'As long as you don't actually start drooling, you'll be fine!'

'I'm not that bad!'

'Don't panic, I'm joking.' Abi gave her friend a hug. 'I can't tell you how wonderful it is to be back. I have so much to tell you, but in the meantime you'd better go and see to the potting Adonis!'

'You most certainly do have a lot to tell me! I saw that cuddle with Max. That was a cuddle that lingered!'

Ignoring her friend's suggestion, Abi said, 'I'm so glad you've been pressing on with preparations for the gallery studio. What are you going to call it? It really should have a name.'

'I've been trying to think of one, but no luck so far.' Beth smiled, 'I'm just glad you're back. I had a horrible thought that Simon would emotionally blackmail you into staying up there.'

Abi grimaced. 'He was way more underhand than that. I'll tell you later. Now, go and see Jacob.'

Beth looked worried again, 'Aren't you coming in with me?'

'I've met him, hun, and anyway, I want to talk to Max and go and check on Stan.'

As Beth disappeared, Abi took her mobile from her pocket. She'd been putting off looking at it, knowing that there would be missed calls and messages from Simon. She hadn't wanted to deal with them until she was back where she felt she belonged.

There were three missed calls and two texts. The first text was angry. The next was contrite. So I guess one was from the café while he waited for me – and perhaps he popped his head into the estate agent's when I didn't show? The thought made her start to smile despite her annoyance. Listening to the messages could wait. It would do Simon good to sweat for a bit after what he'd done.

Beth felt proud of the space in which she and Jacob now stood. To stop herself worrying about the possibility of Abi not returning, Beth had thrown herself into the final stages of decorating and setting up her gallery. An electrician had been booked to come that afternoon to improve the lighting system, and a new set of easels and moveable picture-hanging systems sat waiting to be installed, propped against the pristine white paintwork of the two walls that weren't largely glass.

The blinds that would be required to perfect the amount of light had been ordered, and a heap of furniture brochures sat on her grandad's old workbench waiting to be read.

Beth hardly dared breathe as she awaited Jacob's verdict. Eventually, she had to break the silence. 'So, what do you think? Could you see yourself over there,' she pointed to the far side of the gallery space, 'displaying your work, with Abi working over here?'

Jacob nodded slowly. 'I think I could. You'd need a few plinths to display things on, but yes, yes, I think so.' He cast a professional eye over the space. 'Will you have spotlights?'

'The electrician's coming this afternoon. He is going to put in an adjustable system of independently controlled ceiling lights.'

'Perfect.' Jacob's smile widened. 'If you're prepared to invest in that, then I know you're serious. The right lighting can make the difference between a successful gallery and an unsuccessful one.'

Not wanting to look at Jacob in case she flushed and gave herself away, part of her wishing that he wasn't a nice person as well as gorgeous, Beth said, 'I hope you're right. I don't actually know what the right sort of lighting is, but I'll do my best.'

'I could stay. I mean, I can push off if you like, but I'm not due back at my studio until tomorrow, so . . .'

'Would you?' Beth looked up, caught his green eyes, and felt her insides do a tiny backflip. 'I'd appreciate any help you can give.'

'No problem.' Jacob pulled his portfolio forward, and resting it on the bench, opened it up, 'Maybe you'd better have a closer look at some of my work, before you decide if you want me to rent the space for a month?'

Embarrassed at him having to suggest that before she'd asked, Beth stepped closer. 'I'd love to.'

Trying to ignore the static between them that Beth was sure she was probably imaging due to severe wishful thinking on her part, she studied the photographs. Every single one seemed to reach out to her. Beth had to restrain herself from stroking them. She couldn't begin to imagine how she'd feel when she saw the actual pottery.

'These are gorgeous. I would love it if you're still willing to take the first month. I'm starting each month on the tenth day, which means the initial slot will run from the tenth of September to October ninth. For a week or so before that, you could have a few little pieces here rent-free. I'm planning to display some pictures from the local school for a family afternoon before the official kick-off.'

Jacob, his eyes shining, said, 'What time is the lighting man coming?'

'Two o'clock.'

'How about I take you out for lunch, and you can tell me about all your plans before he comes? Then I suspect I'll be saying "yes please" to the space.'

Chapter Twenty-five

'I almost phoned you last night, and again this morning, and quite a few more times actually, but I didn't want to interfere.'

Max didn't look at Abi as they walked around the corner and up the hill towards Stan's house. After the enthusiasm of the hug she'd received as she got out of the cab, Abi felt a little awkward, and oddly distanced from Max, even though they were walking just inches apart.

'I almost phoned you as well, but I didn't want to look at my phone. I knew there'd be messages from Simon, so I turned it off. Sorry, Max. I needed to sort things out in my head a bit, and I needed to do that on my own. Does that make sense?'

Max sighed. 'It does.' Digging his hands into his pockets, Max added, 'You'll have to forgive me, Abi, I am a helper by nature. I love to help my friends. It's tricky to stand back and see someone I care about being treated badly and do nothing, even when doing nothing is the right thing to do.'

Abi resisted the desire to throw herself into Max's arms. She had a feeling she wouldn't want to ever let go if she did that, and she needed to keep a clear head for now. 'Do you know, I think you might be the kindest person I have ever met.'

'I've never been sure if that sort of comment is a compliment or not? Doesn't it make me sound a bit of a doormat – or worse, controlling?'

This time Abi laughed. 'Max, believe me, I have been a door-mat for years, and you most certainly aren't one. And as for being controlling – Luke was a control freak par excellence. You couldn't be less like him if you tried.'

The freckles on Max's face were noticeably highlighted by the abrupt colouring to his face, 'And is that a good thing? That I'm nothing like Luke, I mean? We were about to talk before Simon stole you away, and well, you are accustomed to a standard of living I could never offer you, even though I think I . . .' The decorator's voice faded away, as if he was afraid to utter the end of this sentence.

'Max.' Abi stopped walking, and moved to stand in front of him. 'We will talk properly soon, I promise.' Allowing the instincts of her body to break the rules her brain had so recently imposed, Abi took his hand then carried on walking as she talked. 'For now I'll say that the fact that you are nothing like Luke, or indeed Simon, is the best thing about you, even better than the fact you are kind, cute, generous, good-looking and, quite possibly, the loveliest man I have ever met.'

Then, so as not to attribute too much importance to the trickle of physical attraction that was dancing up and down her spine, and break the relieved silence that was coming from Max, Abi added mischievously, 'Apart from Stan, of course, he's the nicest man of all! So, how was your cream tea? I was gutted to miss that.'

Stan beamed at Abi, giving her a hug which felt paper-thin compared to the one she'd received from Max, but was no less welcoming. 'Welcome home!'

Sadie buffeted her way through all their legs to rest her saggy head against Max's knee. 'I'm so glad to see you. I was worried I'd played a part in your kidnap for a while there!'

'I'm sorry you were frightened, Stan,' Abi gave him another brief hug, feeling better now she had seen he was alright for herself, 'Apart from being a total git, Simon is a superb game player, which is why he's so good at his job. It wouldn't have occurred to him worry about other people.'

Following Sadie, who was determined to take Max out into

the sunshine, Abi sat at the patio table, her eyes falling on the crumbling garden wall. Each time she visited the house she saw more signs that the whole property was badly in need of doing up. It wasn't tender loving care it lacked, it was basic maintenance.

'So then,' Stan rested his walking stick against the table, and placed his hand over Abi's, 'what's been happening? I want to hear all about it.'

As she told Stan the whole story, Abi could see Max clenching his fists, and she was glad Sadie was there for him to stroke out his angry frustration on her behalf.

Stan was stunned as Abi explained what Simon had done, 'And the estate agent let that Simon take the house off the market? Just like that, without asking you first?'

'He assumed Simon was my husband, and as you saw for yourself, he can be very plausible. He could also prove he was Mr Carter on paper. He had one of Luke's bank statements. It had the right name and address and everything on it. There was no way for the estate agent to know it was the wrong Mr Carter, and I must admit, it was partly my fault.'

Max was looking thunderous, an expression which appeared terribly foreign across his good-natured face. 'How on earth can it have been your fault in any way?'

'Before I left for Cornwall the first time I was nervous about putting the house on the market. I was concerned the estate agent would sense my inexperience and try and undervalue the house, so I asked Simon to be there as well. Even though I asked him to explain to the agent that he wasn't my husband, he didn't. I let him take over. It was easier that way. But I shouldn't have done that.' She grimaced at the memory of her former weaker self. She had changed so much in such a short time, and she was convinced that it was largely because she wasn't in Luke's domain anymore.

Stan spoke before Max had the chance to berate Simon further. 'Well, I think your need for help was quite understandable in the circumstances. So is your horrid brother-in-law out of the equation for good? Is the house sold?'

Abi shrugged. 'I've been avoiding Simon's calls, so I guess I'll have to talk to him at least once more, but the house is as good as sold. I've had the agents change the locks on the house, and I'm going to employ one of those house clearance firms as soon as I have either found a place here, or the buyers, the Adams family, decide they're ready to move in. I can put stuff in storage if I have to. I do wish I knew what Simon had planned when he tried to get me to rent my house out, but I guess whatever it was, he can't do it now.'

There was a silence of about ten seconds as the two men regarded each other with smiles on their faces. 'What am I missing?' Abi looked from one to the other, 'Did I say something?'

Stan nodded to Max, as if indicating that he should take over the mantle of conversation, 'We didn't want to say anything to you until we were sure you were coming back, but we've been pretty busy in your absence.'

Picking up a pile of flyers that Abi had assumed were just junk from the local newspaper, Stan waved them towards her. 'Max has been helping me pick a place in the new sheltered housing complex in St Buryan. As I was trying to tell you before you were stolen away, Abi, I'm selling up, and I'd like to offer you the chance to buy this place first, before it goes on the market. If you want it, of course. There is no obligation whatsoever.'

Abi's chest constricted. 'But I can't take your home, Stan. It'd make me look like the worst kind of vulture. Your daughter would hate me for one thing! I admit I always loved this place from the outside as a child, but my intention was only ever to take a look around! I never wanted to evict you! It was simply a nice fantasy about my dream house. That's all.'

Stan smiled. 'Which is probably why Simon stealing you away like that was a blessing in disguise, even if it was scary. We didn't know if you were coming back or not, so any decision I made about where to spend my remaining time on this good earth was made in the knowledge that I might have to sell the house to complete strangers. You aren't pressuring me, Abi. You've just come along at exactly the right time in my life. I'm so very grateful. As to Sally hating you, of course she won't.'

'I . . . I don't know what to say . . .' Tears of happiness pricked at the corner of Abi's eyes. 'Umm, Stan, do you think I could have another look round? A proper one. On my own?'

'Of course, my girl. I'd forgotten Simon interrupted your chance to explore last time. Away you go! Take all the time you need.'

Abi kissed his bald forehead as she got up, and Stan began to chuckle.

'What is it? I'm not going to find another old relative lurking in one of the rooms am I?'

'No. I just can't believe you've sold your Surrey house to the Addams Family, that's all!' Stan chuckled, 'I used to love that show.'

Abi's heartbeat thudded in her ears as she wandered through the house on her own. Although she'd been there before, this time it felt very different. Now she wasn't just dreaming of Abbey's House becoming her home, it was a very real possibility.

Deciding to put her misgivings about Sally's feelings on the matter to one side for now, Abi walked upstairs, running her finger up the banister as she took each hessian-carpeted stair at a time. The stairwell was narrow, but thanks to the butter-coloured paintwork and light wallpaper it wasn't dark. She could already picture some Margaret Clarkson watercolours hanging on the walls.

The upper landing was no more than a square of bare floor-boards, which led to three doors: one straight ahead, one to the left, and one to the right. Working systematically, Abi opened the door to her left, and found herself in a bathroom. Compact, with a corner bath wedged along one wall, a sink under the wide-silled window, and a toilet next to a freestanding wooden towel rack, it was neat and clean, but well worn, and already Abi found herself imagining it with a new white bathroom suite – one in keeping with the period features, of course.

Unlocking the little window, Abi could see a glimpse of the coast. Leaving the bathroom quickly, she dashed into the next room, and without taking in the fact that it was a bedroom, she threw open the window. As she stared outside, the hairs on the back of Abi's neck stood up. To the right the roofs of the houses in Sennen, leading out to the harbour and the sea and cliffs beyond, framed her view. Abi knew that it no longer mattered what the rest of the house was like. She had to live here. To be able to sit here, on the wide window seat she currently knelt on, in her own bedroom, and see that vista every morning was enough. It was worth every single penny she'd have once the Adamses had bought her old home.

Forcing herself to consider the rest of the room, Abi looked at the bedroom. It was obviously the one Stan used, as it had signs of his inhabitancy all over it. Trying not to feel like she was intruding, she took in its double bed placed in the middle of the far wall, the small oak wardrobe, chest of drawers and dressing table and chair, she felt the smile of hope she hadn't been allowing herself to show spread across her face.

Moving into the third room, expecting it to be another bedroom of about the same size, Abi took a sharp intake of breath stopped in her tracks as she pushed the door.

Not only was the room twice the size as the previous one, Abi could see clearly that this was where the house had been knocked from two separate houses into one. A line of bare bricks had been left between the white-painted plaster walls to mark the old divide.

An unmade double bed was dwarfed by the space. Again Abi made a beeline for the window, and stared through the glass. A feeling of contentment filled her from her toes up. The view from this larger window, unbelievably, was even better than from the other bedroom. She'd been wrong – Stan's room was great, but this room was her room. This was where she was going to live. There was even enough space for her to draw if she set up a desk and easel by the window. There would certainly be enough light during the summer months.

Abi had just decided that this huge room must have filled the entire upstairs of the second terrace, when a closer look at a full-length curtain on the wall to her right revealed a hidden door. Feeling as if she was a character in a fairy tale, Abi pushed open the door. A neat cream ensuite washroom, complete with shower, stared back at her.

With one last look through the window at the sea, Abi headed back downstairs.

She had already seen, and fallen in love with, the kitchen and its larder, and she knew the living room that led on through to the garden was cosy and comfortable, and just needed a spring clean, new carpet, and blinds instead of its thick light-obscuring curtains. That left two more doors to peep behind for the first time.

With excitement buzzing through her veins, Abi stood outside the first one. It looked like a shed door, and when she pushed it open she found herself in a huge walk-in cupboard, full of coats, shoes, and long-forgotten piles of wellington boots. Her heart ached for Stan as her gaze fell on two pairs of tiny children's wellington boots. They'd probably belonged to the grandchildren he missed so much.

The last door led into the dining room. It, like the large bedroom above it, was huge, and with its one small radiator, and large picture windows Abi judged must be as cold as ice in the winter months.

No expert on antiques, Abi was sure that the large polished mahogany table in the centre of the room, with its matching set of ten chairs, must be Chippendale or something similar. The more she looked at the sideboards and shelves, all stuffed with books, vases, jugs, china, and endless ornaments, the more Abi comprehended how long it was going to take for Stan to pack all his stuff.

Pulling out a dining chair, Abi sat in the quiet, letting the peace of the room engulf and comfort her. It felt right being there. Sighing with a quite contented pleasure, Abi allowed herself ten minutes of indulgent daydreaming about how she'd keep the character of the cottage just as Stan had it, but would also put her own mark on it, before she got to her feet.

It was time to go back to the boys.

'Well then, my girl, do you want to buy the old place?'

Abi couldn't find her voice. It was all too good to be true. She nodded, beaming broadly.

'Great stuff!' Stan clapped his hands together, 'Max and I have been chatting while you explored. We're going to clear the house as best we can between his jobs, and if I don't like the decor in my new place, then you're going to add me to your client list, aren't you, Max?'

'No, I'm not.' Max laughed, 'I'm going to decorate it for you as a friend, free of charge, between paid jobs. Least I can do for you being so kind to Abi.'

'I do have one favour to ask though, Abi.' Stan grinned at Abi's suddenly serious expression as she listened, 'I know you're awfully busy with Jack's granddaughter, but as you'll have seen, this place is packed to the rafters with stuff I'm never going to need again. Do you think you could bear to help me pack up, sort, and sell off my possessions?'

'Of course I can! But are you sure you want to get rid of much? Everything is quality stuff.'

'The flat I'm viewing tomorrow is tiny by comparison, there won't be room.'

'But won't you miss it all?'

'Some of it, yes. But I won't miss being in a house I can't afford to heat properly, and worrying about dusting it all!'

'Then yes, of course I will help you, Stan. It'll be a privilege.'

Chapter Twenty-six

Max had gone to fetch some paint colour charts from the van, and Stan was beginning to look tired. With her mind stacked full of everything that she had to do now she was back in Cornwall, Abi found herself in need of thinking space as much as Stan was in need of a nap.

'Shall I take Sadie out for a bit of a walk, Stan?'

'Would you? That would be really helpful. The old girl doesn't get a proper stretch of her legs too much these days.'

Unhooking the lead from the cupboard she'd discovered a few moments ago, Abi found the presence of the retriever comforting as she walked out of the cottage that was to become her own. Despite her elation, Abi could feel tension knot within her as she mentally listed all the things she had to do. There were business cards to make for Beth, other artists to track down for after Jacob's month, assuming Beth took him on (which Abi was sure she would, considering how hot she found him), and there was only so much longer she could put off calling Simon, all her possessions in Surrey needed sorting, she had to find a local solicitor for the legal side of the move, and then there was Max . . .

'Penny for them?'

Abi hadn't noticed Max catch up with her as she sauntered, very much at Sadie's elderly pace, along the road. 'I think the amount of stuff vying for attention in my brain right now might cost nearer a pound!'

Ruffling Sadie's ears, Max smiled. 'I'll bet! So, how are you going to celebrate?'

'Celebrate?'

'You have your dream house! You're going to own Abbey's House!'

The grin on Abi's face widened. 'I am, aren't I? Assuming nothing goes wrong.'

'It won't. I'm not saying it won't take a while to sort, but it will happen.' Max gestured to his van, 'Why don't I take you up to Land's End? There's a nice easy mile-long walk, which Sadie shouldn't find too much for her elderly canine legs. We can watch the sea for a while.'

'I'd love that! You sure you have time?'

'It's Saturday, I'm not working.'

'But?'

'I know I'm in my overalls,' Max tugged them off over his boots, revealing summer trousers and a short-sleeved checked shirt which made him look more handsome than ever in Abi's eyes. 'I thought Stan might want some painting or gardening done or something, so I came equipped.'

Climbing into the van with Sadie, Abi whispered into the retriever's ear, 'He's a good man, that Max Pendale.'

The breeze from the sea was incredibly welcome against the beat of the August sunshine as Max and Abi watched Sadie frolic in the long grass like a puppy.

'So, do you want to talk about that massive to-do list clogging up your head, or shall I engage you in mindless chatter while you admire the view?'

'The mindless chatter option.' Abi stared across the hundred yards of grass that kept them and the dog a safe distance from the sheer drop of the cliffs, and over the sea.

'Do you know the Legend of the Whooper?'

'That's not some local double entendre, is it?'

Max stared down at the top of her head as Abi kept her eyes on a pair of gulls dancing in the air above the cliffs before them. 'The Whooper of Sennen Cove is a creature that is believed to send a whooping thick mist into the harbour whenever there's an oncoming storm so that the fishermen can't go out, and therefore prevents them from getting lost in fog, or their boats wrecked on the waves.'

Encouraged by the laughing smile in his companion's eyes, Max continued, 'And can you see over there?'

'Just! I'm shorter than you, remember.' Abi stood on her tiptoes in the direction Max was pointing.

'Well, shortarse, that is Gwenver Beach. It's really popular with the local surfers. In the past, rather like Sennen Cove itself, it was a base for smugglers to hide out and store their ill-gotten gains.'

Abi stared out in front of her in fascination, her mind full of images of pirates smuggling barrels of rum, and bizarre mythical beasts plucking fishermen from the jaws of certain death in howling storms, as Max continued his heritage lesson.

'Standing here makes it clear why this region of Cornwall is known as Penwith. Penwith is the Cornish word for extremity. You'd need to travel a long way before you could find a cliffscape more extreme in its rugged beauty than this one.' Pausing to put Sadie back on her lead so they could start walking in a straight line, Max added, 'Another time, if you'd like, I could take you for a walk along the Mayon and Trevescan cliffs. Mayon has a cliff castle on it.'

'Wow, really?'

'Yep. Mayon or maen is the Cornish word for stone. We won't take Sadie with us when we do that though, as it's a sheer drop from the top of the cliff. Well worth a look, on a good day you can see basking sharks in the sea from there.'

'It's a date.'

'Is it? A date I mean, not just two friends having a walk?'

Replying by way of a nod, Abi asked, so quietly that Max only just heard her over the hum of the cliff breeze, 'Is Abbey's House really going to be mine, Max?'

'If you can afford it, and you genuinely want it, then yes.'

They walked in companionable silence for a while, until they reached a bench and Abi sat down, partly to give Sadie's legs a rest, but partly because, with Max by her side, and the sea stretching out so reassuringly before her, she knew she was strong enough to listen to the messages Simon had left on her mobile.

Asking Max if he minded her polluting the peace and quiet with her phone, Abi felt even better when he tucked her under his shoulder. She was protected by Max's solid torso from whatever vileness Simon could pour into her ear, and there was a gorgeous-smelling shoulder to cry on if necessary.

Her mouth dry, Abi pressed the button that would relay her messages. As she'd anticipated, the first of the three messages Simon had sent her was full of recriminations for standing him up at the coffee shop, and from the sound of it, had probably been made while he was still sitting there expecting her to turn up.

'You OK?' Max hadn't liked how pale Abi had gone as she listened.

'Apparently I'm an "ungrateful social climber" and, and I quote, "quite possibly an adulterous harlot who obviously never loved her husband and can't be trusted."'

'Well that's rich, coming from the man who propositioned his recently dead brother's wife and then committed a con trick against an estate agent.'

Although the accusations of adultery had hit home, hearing Max's response took the sting out of Simon's words a little, as Abi moved onto message number two. 'This one was sent a couple of hours later.'

Listening hard so she could hear above the sound of the sea, wriggling deeper into the comfort of Max's arm, Abi heard a more defensive Simon speaking. 'I have had a call from Nigel Davison. You will not believe what that idiot told me. God knows what sort of communication breakdown they had, but I never pretended to be Luke. As if I'd do that to my own brother! I understand now why you weren't at the café. Obviously I intend

176

to sue for defamation. I hope you are being sensible and holding out for the full price if you still insist on selling? Living there yourself would be much more sensible, of course.'

Thinking hard as she replayed the message for Max to hear, she found she wasn't at all surprised that Simon was denying all knowledge. 'He won't really sue them, will he?'

Max held her hand tighter. 'No chance. He'd lose face.'

Abi smiled, grateful for his common sense, 'Of course. That would not be a possibility worth consideration for Simon. He's just trying to win my sympathy, isn't he? Luke always said Simon never could take responsibility for his actions.'

'I did notice he never actually said sorry.'

Playing the third message, Abi laughed out loud 'Here, listen to this.' She put the speakerphone on and turned up the volume. 'This one is about four hours later. Mr Davidson was obviously keen for no more damage to be done to his reputation!'

'Abi, where the hell are you? I'm at Luke's house, and the bloody keys don't work. What have you done? This is outrageous! I'm thinking of contesting the will. There is no way my brother would have wanted you to exclude his family like this.'

Max shook his head in disbelief. 'The man is raving! He's unhinged.'

Rather than feel panicked, as she suspected she would have done if she'd listened to the message when alone, Abi found that Simon's bluster and emotional blackmail didn't work on her anymore. Not with Max keeping her tucked under his arm the whole time. Even so, she couldn't stop herself from asking, 'You don't think he will contest the will, do you? I mean, it's a bit late, everything was sorted ages ago.'

'He's being all piss and wind. Ignore him!'

'Good advice! Although I can't help wondering why he's so keen for me to live there still. It makes no sense. One minute he wants me to move in with him and rent the property, then the next he wants me living in it.'

'Well I suspect, and I may be wrong . . .'

'But you doubt it?'

'But I doubt it. That if you were still there he could work on you coming around to his way of thinking. Then, in time you might give in, move in with him, and he could use the vast monthly rent he'd make from your house to fund whatever he had planned in . . . Oxford, was it?'

'That's the place he mentioned, but I guess we'll never know for sure.'

Sadie rose to her paws, obviously feeling rested enough to toddle slowly back the way they'd come. Reluctantly leaving the comfort of Max's shoulder, Abi got up as well. 'I think we're being told something.'

'Looks like it.' Max patted Sadie's flank affectionately, 'Ready to go home, old girl?'

Sadie wagged her tail enthusiastically. 'I think we should take that as a yes.'

Feeling a huge sense of relief that she had faced up to Simon's messages, Abi knew she'd still have to phone him, or he'd just keep calling – or worse still, turn up again. Although if he had any sense he wouldn't set foot in Cornwall again. The reception he'd get from her friends would not be a welcoming one.

Following Sadie back down to the beach, Abi knew there was one more thing she couldn't put off saying. 'Max?'

'It's OK, I know, and I understand.'

'You do?'

'Yes. You're wary about us going too fast. Simon may talk a load of rubbish, but he hit a nerve with that adulteress dig, didn't he?'

'Sorry, Max, but yes, he did. I'd hate anyone to think that of me. And it is so soon after Luke. I wasn't exactly happy with him, but I did love him, you know, when he was being him and not all high society social climber-ish.'

'I know, and it's alright. As I said, I understand. I should warn you, however, that every now and then I might just have to hold your hand or cuddle you, and it is unlikely that I'll be able to go too much longer without kissing you again. I may be kind, but my patience is not infinite when it comes to beautiful women.'

Abi giggled. 'Is that so?'

Max faked solemnity, 'I felt it fair I should warn you.'

'Then I think it is fair that I should warn you,' Abi attempted to copy his grave expression, 'that I will be requiring a great deal of hand-holding, hugs, and, indeed, several of those kisses you are so good at but are reluctant to give out. It's just, as my dad used to rather euphemistically call it, "the second course" that I can't offer you yet. I want to, but I can't. Not yet. I'm not quite ready. Would you settle for taking me to the local pub quiz instead?'

Max laughed. 'A poor replacement compared to a "second course", but I'd love to. Now come here. I'm going to prove to you that I am not in the least bit reluctant about anything.'

By the time they'd finished kissing, Sadie was looking extremely bored.

Chapter Twenty-seven

Sitting in the garden of the First and Last pub in Sennen, Beth took advantage of the fact that Jacob had gone to fetch them drinks and a menu. She flipped open his portfolio and examined his work without her gaze feeling the irresistible need to stray towards his face every few seconds.

Beth knew she was behaving like a lovestruck teenager, but she couldn't seem to help herself. And she had a sneaky suspicion, or possibly a chronic case of wishful thinking, that the feeling was mutual. Jacob had certainly met her gaze enough times accidentally-on-purpose to pique her interest.

He's probably like this with anyone female, she told herself as she studied his photos again. It's been so long since I fancied anyone that wasn't in a movie that I've forgotten how to read the signs.

The images of his work looked even better in the natural light of the sun than they had in the gallery. Still not quite able to believe that Jacob was actually there, with her, in Cornwall, about to agree to exhibit his work in her almost finished gallery, and that he was even more gorgeous than she'd hoped, Beth felt a touch of guilt.

She hadn't told Abi that she'd emailed Jacob on the strength of his website photo alone. It had only been when he'd confirmed he was interested in seeing the gallery that Beth had, with her fingers firmly crossed, checked to make sure his pottery was as professional-looking as his website.

Now, having spent some time with Jacob, Beth could finally swallow her guilt at her lack of professionalism. Her instincts had been spot on, even if they had been initially led by lustful fantasies about his body and not by the calibre of his work.

'What do you think?'

Beth hadn't heard Jacob walk up behind her across the grass, and gave a little shriek of alarm. 'Sorry, I was so engrossed. These are incredible. I'd love to see them in real life.'

'Thank you.' Rather than sitting down on the bench on the opposite side of the table, Jacob sat next to Beth so he could guide her through his portfolio.

Wondering how the hell she was supposed to concentrate when Jacob was so close to her, Beth clutched hold of her glass of lager and forced herself to get a grip. *This is ridiculous, woman. You're a professional, and just because your lust chip has been activated, that is no reason to let it take over! Concentrate!*

'What sort of size pieces are you interested in?'

Keeping her eyes fixed on the photographs before her, Beth said, 'A variety. I thought a few small pots that could be sold for what most people would consider birthday or Christmas present-type prices, and then some more exclusive unique pieces which we wouldn't necessarily sell, but would act as good marketing items for both you and me.'

Pleased with her speech, Beth took refuge in a long draught of her drink, and watched Jacob's fingers smooth the page that was open before them. She couldn't help noticing that although his hands had obviously been scrubbed clean, there were tiny traces of grey clay beneath his fingernails that betrayed his craft. Beth found herself wondering if they ever went away entirely.

'Sounds good.' Jacob turned to the very back of the portfolio and showed Beth a collection of pictures she hadn't seen before.

'Wow!' Her eyes widened. She longed to touch these pots, to run her fingers along their rims and down their sides. 'Pots' didn't do these creations justice. They were of epic proportions, and she found herself wondering if Ali Baba and the Forty Thieves would pop out of them at any moment. 'We have to have some of these at the gallery! However did you fit them in a kiln to fire them?'

Jacob laughed, 'It was a nightmare. After I'd made the first one I vowed I'd never do another. But once it was fired and varnished, it just screamed out for a partner, and then another and, well . . . I've sold a few now, so I will be doing more.'

'How much do you charge for them?'

Jacob repeated the figure three times before Beth got hold of the idea that she was looking at a pot worth three thousand pounds. 'Seriously?'

'I can only fire one of them at a time, you see. When I make smaller items I can stack the kiln space right up, and so the production time and costs are lower. Then once it's fired, which takes a very long time on something so large, with such thick walls, then it has to be finished off. It's the time it takes that I'm charging for.'

'And your skill. I mean, look, I could just wrap my arms around them.' And you. Beth squashed down the unhelpful thought and added, 'Are you interested in exhibiting with us for a while, then? You don't sound as though you need to.'

'Definitely. My studio attracts the odd passing tourist, and I have pieces for sale in a few London galleries, not to mention a couple of my mugs and "Welcome to Cornwall" egg cups and stuff in some tourist shops, but I need to expand my profile. Let's face it: pottery like this is a luxury. These days people have more important things to buy! If I'm going to survive, then I have to ensure that the people who do have the money for such treats know I exist in the first place. Galleries are the best way to do that.'

Beth played with the edge of the plastic-coated menu that lay on the table next to her, 'And you're sure you want to be our first artist? I mean, word hasn't got round yet. It could be that no one turns up.'

'As long as I don't have to be there all of the time, that I get full rein with presentation, and I get to book in ahead to be the artist in residence next July, then you are on!'

'You drive a hard bargain, Mr Denny!'

Jacob turned his emerald eyes on Beth, 'That's not the only thing I drive hard, Miss Philips.'

Beth's stomach did a back flip. With a lump in her throat, not meeting her companion's eyes, she took refuge in her desire for food. 'Are you hungry?'

Jacob winked, dissolving her embarrassment. 'You have no idea! I'd like some food too. Toasted sandwich?'

'How about "A Load of Old Cobblers"?'

Beth dug Jacob in the ribs as they waited in the gallery for the electrician to come and sort out her new lighting rig. 'That is the worst name for a gallery ever!'

'Trust me, I've seen far worse.'

They were sat in the middle of the floor. Beth was showing Jacob the pictures from her schoolchildren. 'I would like the name to pay some sort of homage to Grandad, though.'

'He meant a lot to you?'

'Everything. He was the best man ever. Everyone thought I was mad to give up on having the chance of a husband and family to be his carer, but there was never any question as far as I was concerned.'

'Well it's hardly too late for you to get married or have kids, is it?'

'No, but then I didn't know how long he was going to live for at the time, did I?'

'True enough.' Jacob picked up a picture of a little girl building a sandcastle and smiled as he asked, 'Don't answer this if it is too personal, but was there someone who would have been your husband by now if you hadn't looked after your grandad?'

'Oh, that is personal.'

'I said it was.'

Beth shrugged. 'There could have been. I was never sure, which I guess tells me all I needed to know. We'd dated for about a year, but he was settled in a teaching job in Bristol and didn't want to move down here, and neither of us wanted a long-distance relationship, so that was that.'

'I see. And no one since?'

'Not for the last three years, and then nothing that lasted for long. Mostly tourists that were here one minute and gone the next. How about you?' Beth found herself asking a question she wasn't sure she wanted the answer to in case it was accompanied by a great deal of disappointment. 'Is there a Mrs Denny lurking in Pendeen or Hayle or Westbury?'

'Westbury is where my gran lives. She's a canny soul who I totally adore. She's not mobile anymore. I take a trip up to her every few weeks to make sure she's alright. My parents are in Pendeen, and in Hayle you'll find no one resident in my dinky little flat beyond myself and a tomcat called Oscar, who very much thinks he owns the place.'

Trying not to look pleased, Beth decided to test the water a little further, 'And any gorgeous girlfriends waiting on the end of the phone for you to let them know what this new gallery is like?'

Jacob laughed, 'Not one. There is someone I've met who I quite like, though.'

I should have known. Beth got up to look out of the window, under the guise of seeing if the lighting man was outside struggling to park, so that Jacob didn't see disappointment in her eyes. 'That's nice. I hope she'll appreciate your work if you get together.'

Jacob collected up the children's pictures and put them on the work bench. Then joining Beth at the window, Jacob put his arm around her waist.

'I met the girl I like extremely recently. There's something about her. I can't decide if it's her enthusiasm for my work, the love she obviously had – still has – for her grandfather, the bravery at starting her own business venture when she really doesn't have time, the fact she wants the first display in her gallery to belong to primary school children, or the fact she is extremely pretty, that won me over first. I was thinking of asking her out on a date tonight. What do you think? Do you think she'll say yes?'

Chapter Twenty-eight

Abi was exhausted. The last three days had been spent in a flurry of activity, which had begun with ordering business cards for the newly named Art and Sole Studio Gallery, and had gone on to include designing posters for the grand opening, booking caterers for the evening, making up invitations on her laptop, phoning up a huge number of artists (most of whom had said no outright to taking a space anytime in the next eighteen months as they were already booked up), acquiring cardboard boxes for Stan, finding a clearance firm for her house in Surrey, and choosing a solicitor.

Jacob, who had become a frequent feature in the studio, and Beth were working so well together on laying out the artists' side of the gallery that Abi had started to feel a bit in the way. She knew was being irrational, and should be grateful that another willing pair of hands was assisting in a race against the clock to be ready in time for the designated children's launch party on September the second, since it gave her a chance to devote herself to all the tasks she'd taken on for Beth and give some time to Stan and her purchase of Abbey's House.

Abi had been so busy that Max had gone on his own with Stan to the Chalk Towers sheltered accommodation complex in St Buryan, to view the two vacant flats in the hope that he'd like one of them. In the end it had been a case of him loving them both, but having checked that the lifts were easy to work, Stan had picked the one on the third floor of the converted Victorian mansion, so that he could see the sea from his bedroom.

Glancing at her watch, a stab of nervous excitement crept up Abi's spine. There would be an estate agent assessing the value of Abbey's House right now. Abi had offered to be there if Stan wanted, but had been relieved when he'd said no, as she felt a bit awkward about it, as she'd be the one who'd benefit from a lower price. Abi didn't want anyone to be able to say she'd influenced the valuation.

What with everything that was happening, Abi hadn't really had time to think about the fact that her childhood fantasy was coming true. Part of her didn't want to risk thinking about it, just in case it all went wrong. What if the valuation was too high after all? What if the sheltered accommodation people turned down Stan's offer on the flat?

The only thing keeping her whirl of uncertainties and anxieties in check was how much she was looking forward to going to the pub quiz with Max in two nights' time. Part of her mind kept reverting back to memories of their walk along the cliff path, and how much promise she'd seen in his eyes. He hadn't said as much, but Abi was sure Max would never let her down. She knew it was simplistic, naive even, to feel that way; but something in her knew it was true. She just hoped she could promise Max the same.

One thorn in her side however vied for her attention, and Abi knew it was standing in the way of her being truly content and happy in her newly adopted home.

That thorn was called Simon.

He could be getting up to anything in Surrey. She couldn't put off phoning him for much longer. Since his original onslaught of messages, she hadn't heard a thing from him, and that was somehow more unnerving than the barrage of insults she'd been expecting. Although Max had told her it was impossible to contest a will that had already been settled, Abi was convinced Simon would have something unpleasant up his sleeve to spite her. He wasn't a man who tolerated not getting his way.

On a more positive note, she had heard from Nigel Davison,

who'd told Abi that because the Adams family intended to rent out their current home, there was no sale to wait for, and they could move on with the handover as soon as Abi had engaged a solicitor.

Deciding that she was in danger of overthinking things too much if she stayed sat on her own in her hotel room for much longer, Abi gathered her newly presented set of keys to the Art and Sole Studio Gallery. Resisting the urge to phone Max, just to hear the comforting sound of his voice while he tackled a cottage in Mousehole, Abi decided today was the day to set up the studio section of Art and Sole as she wanted it.

She was glad that Beth and Jacob, who'd both gone to Jacob's workshop to choose which of his range of ceramics should be put on display as a taster, would be out of the way. It wasn't that she didn't like Jacob. Not only was he a friendly guy, he was a total godsend when it came to how much help he was willing to give them – advice about which artists to approach, and which pieces were too similar to those sold in the Roundhouse – and he was making Beth blissfully happy, but today Abi wasn't in the mood to see them so into each other.

Even as she thought it, Abi told herself off. Beth deserved to be happy. After years of putting everyone else first, from her pupils, to her friends, and her grandfather, Beth was due someone to make a fuss of her for a change. You're jealous, that's what it is.

Abi knew she wasn't jealous that Beth had someone. After all, she had someone of her own. Max was at the forefront of her mind more and more, and she missed him when he wasn't there. It had been sobering to realise that whenever Luke had been at work, even in the early days of their relationship, Abi hadn't given him much of a thought when he was out of sight.

As Abi had lay in bed at three in the morning, failing to sleep under her summer eiderdown, she'd decided that it had been because they worked in the same building, and could literally bump into each other at any time. But now, as Abi strolled slowly towards her car, she knew she'd been kidding herself. The love she'd had for Luke had been genuine, but it hadn't been like how she loved Max. And the cosy, happy-ever-after feeling she had when she was with Max frightened Abi as much as it thrilled her.

She wished she could be more like Beth. The bloom of happiness that radiated from her friend when Abi had found Beth had not spent the night alone following Jacob's visit to her new business venture, was almost tangible. But Abi wasn't the sort of person who could accept happiness so quickly – not any more. Even though she logically knew that Max never would treat her like Luke had, she had to convince herself she wasn't going to be bullied by someone she loved all over again. That meant that she couldn't just jump into bed with someone, even if it did, as Beth had told her, 'feel so right'.

Grinning up at Jacob from where she was sitting, Beth stretched her legs over the clay-smeared studio floor with a seductive smile, before pulling her clothes back into place.

Jacob, who was sat next to her, grinned back. 'There is very little that looks quite so sexy as a dishevelled schoolteacher.'

Beth looked around her, hunting down her stray items of clothing amongst the gorgeously intoxicating scent of clay that infused the racks of finished and semi-finished products waiting for discarding or firing that surrounded them.

'You are a very bad boy, Mr Denny. Now get dressed or we'll never get manage to pick what we need for the gallery.'

'Yes, miss!'

'Stop with the teasing, pottery man, or I'll be picking all the wrong things for the gallery. I told Abi I'd be back by one o'clock to help her to find some people to show their stuff in October and November.'

Throwing Beth's T-shirt at her from where it had landed in a dusty heap of half-thrown pots that had never made the grade and were waiting to be pummelled back down into throw-ready clay, Jacob scrambled into his own shirt. Brushing clay specks and porcelain dust from his jeans, he led the way into a giant walk-in cupboard.

'Wow!' Beth knew she'd just entered a ceramic lover's heaven. With shelves from floor to ceiling, there was so much to select from that she simply didn't know where to look first.

'Shall we start with the easily sellable stuff, and then work our way up to the pieces that are of a better quality, but have price tags to match?'

'Sounds good to me.' Beth was breathless, and not because of their unscheduled romp. If she hadn't already fallen in love with Jacob, then everything about the place would have won her over there and then. She was extremely glad Jacob was there to guide her, or there was a real danger that she'd pack up the lot, and make it all a permanent fixture in the gallery.

Half an hour later Jacob had collected together two dozen blue glazed rustic-style mugs with Celtic cross patterns, six matching jugs of various sizes, and three large vases which were varnished with mixed swirls of brown, and had been burnished so well that whichever direction Beth examined them from, they looked a slightly different colour. They seemed almost magical, as if they changed colour before her eyes.

'OK, so that's the small ware sorted. I have more of all of those items in stock, so if by any miracle we sell out I can nip back and top up supplies.'

Carefully wrapping every item in a copious amount of bubble wrap, Beth made a mental note to add buying in supplies of paper bags and packaging for those people who bought items from the gallery, as she gestured to the three urns she had already labelled as Ali Baba pots. 'We have to have those. I know they are worth a fortune, and they won't sell, but if they don't scream out loud how skilled you are with your hands, than I don't know what does.'

Jacob laughed, 'Is that so? Apart from you just now, you mean?'

Beth threw a bale of bubble wrap at him. 'Stop hunting for compliments, Mr Denny, and get wrapping up that pot!'

Chapter Twenty-nine

Her arms full with a cardboard box of groceries, Abi used her elbow to knock on the front door of Abbey's House. Stan had offered her a key, but it didn't feel right to take it. Not yet anyway. She wanted to own the house properly before that happened.

'Oh, you are a treasure,' Stan opened the door as wide as it would go and stepped back so Abi could edge past with his food shopping.

Following his friend into the kitchen, Stan leaned against the wall as he watched Abi moving around, putting his shopping away. 'That'll save Mrs Teppit a job. You're a good girl.'

'It's no problem at all. I'm quite enjoying getting to know my way round all the local shops. Funny how a person's perspective of a shop is so different when they stop being a tourist and start to be an actual resident.'

'You'll be a local before you know it!'

Abi laughed. 'I have been assured by Barbara at the hotel that becoming a local takes a decade at least!'

'Twenty years minimum, but you'll walk it!'

Placing the empty cardboard box onto the table, Abi pointed towards the kettle. 'Can I get you some tea, do anything else for you, before I set off again?'

Stan looked at the cardboard box by way of an answer. 'Do you need that?'

'I thought I'd leave it here for you to pack a few bits into, if you want it. Otherwise, not really.'

'Can you sit down a minute?'

Stan sounded so serious that Abi pulled out one of kitchen chairs straight away. 'What is it? If you've changed your mind about the sale, I'll completely understand.' Her insides clenched tightly, but her determination to show no emotion in case that was exactly what Stan was about to say stayed firm.

'Oh, nothing like that. Quite the opposite in fact.' Stan looked down at Sadie, his ever-present companion and ruffled the top of her head in her favourite manner. 'This old girl and I have been together for the last ten years, you know.'

Abi said nothing, but she could feel a lump forming in her throat. If Stan was about to tell her that Sadie was ill she wasn't sure she could handle it, and wished more than ever that Max was there rather than slapping emulsion on a wall somewhere.

'Well, the thing is, although I know moving to St Buryan is the right thing to do, and I haven't changed my mind about leaving here, well . . . I wondered if you'd consider letting Sadie stay here with you? I know it's a lot to ask, but I've just found out that the flats don't allow pets.'

'Oh, Stan!' Abi was horrified on Stan's behalf, 'I'm so sorry. Are you sure you still want to go? You and Sadie are a pair. You belong together!'

Stan was silent as he looked down at his companion, and Abi could see he was composing himself before going on. 'I'm sure. We've thought long and hard about it, haven't we, old girl?'

He was speaking more to Sadie than Abi now, which gave Abi time to suitably arrange her composure. 'We know that you and Max will love her, and I'm sort of hoping I'll be able to visit and you'll bring her to see me sometimes.'

Nodding fervently, Abi didn't know what to say as she looked into Sadie's big brown eyes. 'Stan, you'll always be welcome, and of course Sadie can stay. I'd be glad of her company, to be honest.' More gently she added, 'But you do know that Max won't be living here, don't you?'

A smile broke through the sober expression on Stan's face,

'Not at first perhaps, my girl, but he will. He's a keeper, that one, so make sure you grab him quick before someone else does.' Stan stared down at his faithful canine friend for a few unspoken seconds, before rallying again. 'So, how about proving to me what a good girl you really are and putting the kettle on before you go? I could do with a cuppa after all that un-British-like emotion.'

Familiar now with Stan's kitchen, Abi did just that, wishing she hadn't driven there so she could have something a bit stronger. 'Actually, Stan, I was meaning to tell you something. I wasn't going to yet, because it rather assumed a lot, but . . .'

'Assumed what?'

'That Abbey's House could be mine, although I know we've agreed between ourselves – and with the valuation coming in lower than the sale of my place in Surrey, that I can afford it, but . . .'

Stan finished her sentence for her, 'You don't want to take anything for granted until the deal is signed and sealed.'

'Sorry, yes. It isn't that I don't trust you; it's just that I've had this dream for so long, and I never thought it would happen. I am scared to jinx it.'

'That I understand. So,' Stan cupped his frail hands around his mug of tea, 'what were you going to tell me, on the assumption that life plays fair and the sale goes through – which it will, by the way. Even if I peg it you can buy it.'

'What?' Abi frowned, 'What do you mean?'

'When the solicitor bloke came to sort the private sale stuff, I asked him to change my will. It now says that if I croak it before the sale is complete, you still get to buy Abbey's House, but that the money will go to Sally in Australia instead of to me.'

Tears escaped this time, as Abi leaded forward over her drink, hiding her eyes beneath the hang of her fringe, 'Oh, Stan, I . . .'

The old man raised his hand, 'No, let's take all the thank yous as read. We all have to go sometime, and if we can do good on the way then all the better. I phoned Sally at the crack of dawn, and she was fine with it, so it's settled. Now then my girl, what were you going to tell me?'

'I have decided to keep the spare bedroom as your room. The only visitors I'll ever have will be my brother and his family, and that would be once in a blue moon, so I don't actually need a spare room. Especially as the main bedroom here is big enough to sleep a family of five!'

'But, Abi . . .'

'No Stan. I'm firm on this. You let me into your home as a total stranger, just because my parents joked about me living here when I was a child. That took kindness, and you have been nothing but kind ever since. Keeping a room here for you so you know that you are always welcome is the least I can do. After all, you'll want to come and holiday in Sennen with Sadie, won't you?'

Stan was very quiet for a while, and Abi sensed he was a little overcome and would probably appreciate her suggesting something practical to do. Putting her plans to go back to the studio on hold, trusting that Beth and Jacob would do very well without her, she picked the cardboard box back up. 'So then, Mr Abbey, you said something the other day about sorting out a few of your bits and bobs in the dining room. Shall we take our tea through and get cracking before we drown in sentiment?'

A beam broke out on Stan's face like the sun coming out from behind a cloud. 'An excellent plan.' He pushed himself up with the aid of the table and his stick, and pointed to a tray by the sink. 'Why not pop the tea and that packet of biscuits you just bought on the tray, and carry them through. I don't see why we shouldn't nibble while we work.'

An hour later Abi was beginning to understand what a mammoth job she'd undertaken. 'I can't believe how much stuff you've got!'

'It sort of accumulated over the years. My Mary was a bit of a hoarder. She had a good eye, mind. She was a dab hand at spotting bargains at car boot sales and jumble sales. Sometimes she'd sell things on and make a few pounds here and there. After she died I couldn't face coming in here for a long time, but slowly I got braver, yet I haven't ever done anything about all her stuff. I'm afraid to tell you that what you can actually see is just the tip of the iceberg. The cupboards are full to the brim, and I wouldn't look in the attic until you've had at least one bracing snifter of whiskey.'

Already the dining table was covered in dozens of Victorian oil lamps, a host of kitsch china Cornish pixies, more Spode than Abi had ever seen in one place in her whole life, and a whole box of things that could well be worth something, if only she could work out what they were.

As the dining room table was the sole part of the room that ever commanded Mrs Teppit's attention, the ornaments all came complete with a thick covering of dust, and Stan and Abi were taking it in turns to sneeze as each new item was given a hearty blow to see what treasure lurked beneath. 'I wish I knew about antiques.' Abi turned what she considered to be quite an ugly china frog over in her hands, 'I have no idea if this is worth a king's ransom or should be given to the vicar for the next jumble sale.'

'Nor me.' Stan was squinting as his reading glasses failed to pick up the tiny inscription on the back of a china plate. 'I loved my Mary with all my heart, but I never did get her obsession with odds and sods.' He sighed quietly. 'I wonder if Max knows anyone who does house clearance?'

Abi brightened up a bit. Sorting through all this lot with Max could be fun. 'I'm sure he does. He seems to know someone for every occasion. I'll ask him after work. He might even know an antique dealer who could cast an eye over this lot, I'm sure a few of these pieces are valuable, and I know the Spode is worth something, although I've no idea how much.'

Neither Stan nor Abi noticed the hours zip by as they chatted happily through their sorting. Having adopted a three-pile system (definitely junk, not sure if it's junk, think it's worth something), they started to work faster, and it was only when the doorbell rang that they were pulled out of Stan's reminiscences.

Beth and Jacob stood on the doorstep. 'Hi, Abi. We were getting worried; you haven't been answering your phone. Is everything OK?'

Abi checked her watch. 'Oh goodness, I had no idea that was the time already. Why not come in and say hello to Stan?'

Leading her friends into the dining room, Abi called ahead of them, 'Stan! We've been at this for four hours! It's Beth and Jacob. He's the potter I was telling you about. I was supposed to be helping them in the studio. I totally forgot I was so engrossed. Jacob, this is Mr Stan Abbey. Stan, this is Mr Jacob Denny.'

Stan held his hand out to Jacob, who shook it firmly as he and Beth surveyed the scene they found with a mixture of awe, horror, and fascination.

'Blimey!' Beth picked up a bronze ashtray from the junk pile, 'where did you get all this, Stan?'

'My wife collected pretty much everything. Abi and I have been having a sort-out. I'm sorry if I held her up.'

'Not at all, I was just checking up on her. Anything we can do?'

Stan shrugged. 'Not unless you have a talent for antique-spotting.'

Jacob was moving around the dining table, his eyes roaming over its contents with a barely suppressed exhilaration, 'Do you know what this is, Mr Abbey?'

'Please, call me Stan. And no, me'andsome, beyond the fact that it is a funny-shaped blue and white pot, I know nothing.'

Abi smiled, 'I can go one further. I would hazard a guess that it is a funny-shaped blue and white vase of oriental origin. After that, I also draw a blank.'

Jacob didn't say anything, but put the blue and white bottle shaped vase back down with considerably more reverence than Abi had placed it on the table in the first place, before picking up a pair of pewter candlesticks. The excitement in his expression was being to bubble over into his voice, as Jacob started muttering words like 'Sotheby's' and 'Bonham's' in such a way that made Beth, Abi, and Stan look at each other, but not dare to speak, as the potter danced around the table, moving more and more items towards him.

After a while Stan could stand it no longer. 'Young man, am I to guess by your manic movements that I have a few things here worth a second glance?'

Jacob cleared his throat carefully. 'Mr Abbey, Stan, I could be wrong of course, but I don't think I am . . . well, not totally wrong, my dates might be out a decade or two of course, but . . .'

Beth, seeing that Jacob was about to go off at a tangent, said, 'Jacob, will you please sit down. It's like trying to make sense out of a jumping jack!'

'Sorry, yes, of course.' Jacob pulled out a chair and sat down. 'Before I followed my heart and became a potter I studied antiquities, with a mind to becoming an auctioneer. I'm no expert, of course, but my eye isn't too bad, and if I were you, Stan, I'd get an expert in here fast.'

Stan laughed, 'I appreciate your enthusiasm, me'andsome, but these are just bits Mary picked up, I'm sure they can't be worth all that much.'

Jacob stroked the side of the vase, 'I tell you what, Stan, if you like, I'll get a friend over here to value some things for you; but not this vase.'

'Why not the vase?' Abi had picked up on Jacob's undercurrent.

'Because this is getting wrapped in bubble-wrap and nestled in a sturdy box as soon as I've nipped to my studio to get it for you.'

The other three people in the dining room looked at each other blankly. Jacob hardly dared risk speaking the words out loud in case he was wrong, but sure he wasn't, he said, 'If I'm right, if I am . . . then I don't think it's a good idea to keep a Ming vase lying about the a house without a pretty high-tech security system!'

Chapter Thirty

All thoughts of going back to Art and Sole to get Abi's opinion on how the children's pictures should be hung were forgotten. Every eye in the room fell on Jacob.

Beth regarded her grungy-looking new boyfriend with disbelief. 'You trained in antiques? Are you sure?'

Jacob laughed, 'Clothes don't always maketh the man, you know, and yes I did. I even had sensible hair and a suit.'

'A suit . . .' Beth sounded dreamy, before becoming conscious of everybody's eyes landing on her. She quickly said, 'Stan, this is your show. Do you want Jacob to help find a buyer for a few of these knick-knacks?'

Stan reached over and weighed the pewter candlesticks in his hands. 'My Mary loved these. I always thought they were a bit ugly myself.'

'Ugly?' Jacob was horrified, 'Stan, they're seventeenth-century! Maybe even sixteenth-century.'

'I never did like the way they had an extra bulbous bit of pewter around the main stick, it always looked to me as if they had a beer belly.'

Abi giggled as she looked at the candlesticks. She could see what Stan meant, Jacob however was deadly serious. 'Those bits are called ball-knops.'

Beth raised her eyebrows. 'For real?'

'For real. These are worth in the region of seven thousand for the pair.'

'Seven grand!' Abi and Beth shouted at the same time, before turning to Jacob. 'Are you sure?' Beth asked.

'As sure as I can be. The fact they are a pair is the main thing, and if you look carefully,' Jacob turned one of the sticks around, 'you can see that on the sconce there is a series of marks that look like scratches, that's the maker's signature.'

Stan pointed to the vase. 'And that? What would that be worth?'

Jacob thought for a while. 'I'll be honest, I'm less certain. Auctions are so fickle, it all depends who turns up to them. However, if this is Ming, and it'll need to be verified, then anything from seven to ten thousand.'

'Oh my God!' Stan's hand flew to his mouth. 'Abi, I think I need that glass of whiskey.'

'Me too!' They'd been working for hours and Stan must be as hungry as she was. Abi regarded him. 'Are you serious about a whiskey, or shall I go out and get us all a fish supper?'

Stan laughed, 'I haven't had so much fish and chips in years. I'd love that. Everyone is welcome.' He beamed at all of the people standing before him, 'I can't remember the last time I had so much lively company.'

Abi looked at her new friend affectionately. 'It'll be good practice for all those riotous parties you'll be having in St Buryan! Right, I'm starving! I'll call Max and see if he wants to join us.'

Stan nodded. 'Quite right. I always used to be famished after a day at work in the mine, so I'm sure Max is after a day decorating a bathroom. You'll need to tell him about Sadie as well.'

'Sadie?' Beth looked quizzically at Abi.

'I'll tell you on the way to the chippy, if you'll give me a hand. Are you coming, Jacob, or are you staying in Stan's Aladdin's cave?'

'I'll stay, if that's OK, Stan? I'll take some photos of these on my phone and send them to a friend at Peter's Auction House.' Jacob suddenly sat back down as if he was less certain of himself. 'I'm being a bit bull in a china shop, aren't I? Do you want to think about all this, Stan, you might not even want to sell them? I mean, you don't even know me.'

'You carry on and take those pictures, young man. Making enquiries won't hurt, even if I decide not to sell. Just don't promise your auctioneer friend anything until I've had time to think about what Mary would want me to do.'

The following morning Abi, Beth and Jacob sat with Jacob's antique dealer friend Peter in his office as he held the pair of candlesticks. He'd already examined them to within an inch of their lives as far as Beth could see, and she was finding it difficult not to ask him to hurry up and tell them if Jacob's guess about their value had been correct.

Abi glanced at Beth, understanding her need to know, but not wanting to risk rushing Peter in case he got things wrong. She couldn't bear the idea of Stan being disappointed. Part of her wished Jacob had kept his thoughts to himself about how valuable they might be, just in case their hopes had been raised incorrectly.

After what felt like an eternity, Peter placed the candlesticks on his desk and stretched his arms over his head, 'Well, Jacob, you were right. These are a pair of English pewter ball-knop candlesticks, and if I was to be pushed date-wise, I'd say we were talking roughly 1680.

'Oh my goodness!' Abi's eyes widened. 'You were right, Jacob.'

'No need to sound so surprised.'

'I'm sorry, it's just I didn't dare get too hopeful, for Stan's sake.'

'I know. I wish he'd come along.' Jacob hadn't felt comfortable taking such valuable items away from the owner, but Stan had insisted the excitement was too much for him, and that if Jacob had been right about the candlesticks and the vase, then he'd make an appointment for Peter to come and have a hunt through the rest of his stuff.

Peter picked one of the pewter pieces up again, turning it in

199

his hands, 'If I was putting these into an auction catalogue, which I must admit I'm rather hoping is something I will see happen, I'd describe them as "a pair of sixteen-centimetre, seventeenth-century English pewter ball-knop candlesticks, with writhen ball-knop and gadrooned bases." Sounds impressive, doesn't it!'

'It does.' Beth was about to ask how much they were worth, but Peter was ahead of her.

'And I'd put an approximate sale price of six thousand on them, with the expectation of higher if you attracted a collector.'

Trying not to look smug at how close his estimate had been, Jacob gestured towards the vase, which lay semi wrapped in its box where Peter had done no more than take the lid off and peek inside. 'And the vase? I admit to being less certain about that. I know I should be hot on anything ceramic, but the Ming period is so wide, and there are so many variables.'

'It lasted from 1368 until 1644. It was an extraordinary period of innovation in ceramic manufacture and development.'

Jacob nodded. 'The stuff those guys tried with kilns for the first time was awe-inspiring.'

Peter looked at the assembly of curious faces. 'Do you guys want me to dive right in, or would you like a cup of tea to calm the nerves a bit?'

Everyone spoke at once. 'Dive in!'

'You got it!' Peter smiled; the anticipation in the room was infectious. With the same sort of respect that Jacob reserved for a wedge of clay he was about to place on his wheel and turn into something amazing, Peter slowly unwrapped the vase, and held it like a newborn baby.

'Right, yes, this is Ming.'

A collective exhalation of air was expelled by his three guests as the antiques expert went on.

'I would say late Ming, early 1600s perhaps. Certainly from the time of the Wanli Emperor. That was when the Chinese stopped producing pottery that was only for themselves and started to export to Europe.'

Abi was fascinated, and couldn't stop herself from leaning forward in her chair as she admired the blue and white hues. 'I had no idea that pottery was mass-produced for export so early on.'

'From much earlier on a worldwide scale actually,' Jacob chipped in, 'but it was the early seventeenth century before that applied to Ming, right, Peter?'

'Absolutely. You can tell Jacob had a good teacher, can't you, girls?'

Beth nodded, 'Who did teach you, hun?'

Jacob looked sheepish, and tilted his head towards the auctioneer.

'A very good student you were as well. I still haven't forgiven you for going all hippie on me and falling in love with new clay rather than antique clay.'

Abi was getting impatient again, 'And so is this one of those exported pieces, then?'

'It is. I would say it was probably produced in one of the kilns at Jindezhen, which is where the main production centre for ceramic export was at the time.'

'Wow.' Abi sat back again, 'So, if Stan decided to put it up for auction, what are we talking price wise?'

Peter lay the vase back down in its protective bed, 'Now this time I am more hesitant. It's not worth as much as if it had been from the earlier Ming period, but still a considerable amount.'

'Considerable being?'

'You must understand I can only give you a rough estimate. Once you get to auction it all depends on the people there that day.'

'We understand.' Abi exchanged glances with her friends, who were all indicating their agreement.

'Right then,' Peter pushed a few buttons on his computer screen, 'if you guys want to go through to the salesroom and grab a coffee from the machine, I'll do a quick bit of checking, and then I'll make a quote.'

He smiled up at them, 'Don't worry, I won't keep you in suspense for long!'

Peter hadn't been able to resist Stan's invitation for him to come and explore the rest of Mary's boot sale bargains.

The moment she heard that the vase was Ming, Abi had called Max, who had dashed from his client's house in his lunch hour to see Stan. The old man was as consumed with excitement as his young friends, and had invited Peter to come over as soon as possible.

That evening, everyone was sat at Stan's dining room table once again. Peter was sorting through the pile of goods that Jacob had earmarked as interesting, as Stan asked for the third time, 'Are you absolutely sure it's Ming, Peter?'

Used to dealing with people who were either very disappointed or in a shock of disbelief about the steep valuations he gave, Peter patiently repeated himself, 'As sure as anyone can be. What you have here, Mr Abbey, is a blue and white double-gourd vase from the late sixteenth or early seventeenth century. I wouldn't like to say which.'

Stan stroked a gentle finger across the lotus pattern, which was separated by what Peter had described as ruyi bands. 'I always knew my Mary had good taste.'

'She most certainly did, Mr Abbey, and while I can't see anything else here that is of such value as the candlesticks and the vase, you have several items which should fetch anything from twenty pounds up to a few hundred. You could make a fair bit at auction with some of this. Although, I would advise, if you were to sell the candlesticks and the vase, that you consider contacting Sotheby's, Christie's, or Bonham's.'

'Honestly?' Abi nearly dropped the china lighthouse she was just consigning to the charity shop pile.

'For sure. That way you'd get maximum coverage, plus serious collectors and the world's major museums would be alerted.'

Stan couldn't quite believe what he was hearing. 'Peter, are you saying I should send my things to London to be sold?'

'If that is what you decide to do, sell them I mean, then yes. But I'm only advising you. The choice is one hundred per cent yours.'

'But if I sent them there, you wouldn't make any commission, would you, which seems unfair after all your hard work.'

Peter smiled at the old man whose hand hadn't left the fur of his golden retriever the whole time he'd been there. 'That's true, but I couldn't live with my conscience if I told you otherwise.'

Stan was quiet for a while, and no one else in the room moved. The air became heavy with the tension of waiting for their friend's decision, and both Abi and Max and Beth and Jacob held hands.

'Right then. I have three things to say.' Stan sat a little more upright in his seat, and looked down at Sadie as if to check she agreed with his decisions.' First of all: Jacob, Max, Beth, Abi – thank you. Since you all came into my life I have begun to live again. Before then I was slowly stagnating. Secondly, Peter, you are very kind, and I would like it, if you'd take on the work, to arrange to put the vase into whichever major auction house you think would take it. I am going to keep the candlesticks. I know I think they're ugly, but Mary loved them, and I loved her, so those I'm going to take with me to my new home. Then I'll leave them to my daughter when the time comes, and she can decide what to do with them.'

Abi's heart constricted, she hadn't known Stan long, and although his age was obvious, she found the fact of his mortality hadn't really registered properly until now. The idea of him not being around hit her hard, and instantly brought with it enough guilt about feeling sadder at the prospect of her friend's death than Luke's, made her drop Max's hand. Simon's words shot back through her with renewed venom. Harlot. Adulteress.

Aware that Max was looking at her questioningly, Abi was glad that Stan was still talking so she didn't have to explain the sudden withdrawal of her hand.

'And last of all, Abi?'

She snapped back to attention. 'Stan?'

'I've been thinking, it's totally up to you of course, but as this place will be yours very soon, I wondered if you'd like to move in now. Get yourself out of that hotel; save all that travelling back and forth to St Just. I mean, Jack's old cobbler's shop is only a short walk away. If you can put up with me and Sadie then you'd be very welcome.'

Chapter Thirty-one

Sadie sniffed the plant life at Abi's feet as she read the inscription on the storm-weathered bench. Its plaque stated it had been placed 'In Loving Memory of Edna, who loved this view from childhood'.

'And I've loved Abbey's House since childhood, Sadie, but does that give me the right to invade Stan's space before it's properly mine?'

Sadie's brown eyes shone as Abi answered the retriever's unspoken response. 'I know it's what Stan says he wants, but does he really, or is he simply being kind?'

Sitting on Edna's bench, Abi stared across the sea, zipping her leather jacket up as the breeze turned more gusty. As Sadie huddled against her legs, her patient air calmed Abi's confused thoughts. 'And what about Max, Sadie? He's so lovely, but I'm not sure I deserve him. What if I can't love him as much as he wants me to?'

It had been a long day in the studio. Although Abi and Beth had plenty to do, and the time had gone fast, Beth hadn't been able to prevent herself from asking, just before Abi got ready to leave for the evening, why she was being 'so tight with Max?'

Even Abi's successful acquisitions – a lady who quilted exquisite throws and pictures for the studio gallery in November and a local watercolourist for January – hadn't lightened the suggestion that Abi had hurt Beth's best friend.

Abi wasn't even sure herself why she hadn't answered Max's

phone calls the previous evening or all day. Watching the seagulls for a while, Abi couldn't shake the disappointed look that had crossed Max's face last night when, after their evening at Stan's with Peter, he'd asked if she'd like to go for a drink with him and she'd made some feeble excuse about wanting an early night to think about Stan's offer. Then, with Simon's accusations still ringing in her head, she'd told him she didn't want to go to tonight's pub quiz either.

Abi was sure Sadie was trying to tell her it wasn't feeble at all to need to think, but that she couldn't hide from her feelings forever or she'd lose Max to someone else – or worse, he'd start to think her as heartless as his ex-wife.

Crouching down, Abi wrapped Sadie in a cuddle. 'You're a wise old thing, aren't you? Tell me, do you want me to move in early?'

An enthusiastic wagging of the tail answered her question. 'OK then, I will.' Abi stayed where she was, the warmth of Sadie's fur giving her courage. 'And Max, is it time I stopped being a coward there?'

The wagging went into overdrive.

'Do you think he'll forgive me for being such a fool?'

Sadie's tail gave one more decisive wag.

Standing up, Abi gave Sadie a 'thank you' pat, and they strode off towards the Old Success Inn, in the hope that Max would have gone to the quiz anyway. She didn't want to say what needed saying over the phone.

Checking with a friendly man in the pub garden that she was allowed to take Sadie into the bar, Abi took a deep breath and, trying not to make a sound as the quizmaster finished his introductions to the evening's event, spotted Max on his own at the back, his head bent over a quiz sheet.

Not wanting to interrupt the heavy air of concentration that had descended over the room, Abi, hoping she hadn't blown her chances with him completely, whispered, 'Max? Can we join you?'

Max's face did not break into its usual friendly grin when he saw Abi, but he did look delighted to see Sadie, who he greeted with silent enthusiasm as the first question was read out. That was when Abi knew for sure what an idiot she was being. If she hadn't gone all withdrawn and distant for the past twenty-four hours she could have had a greeting like that.

Without saying anything, Max pulled out the chair next to him and handed Abi a spare pen.

Accepting his unspoken invitation, Abi sat down, hoping that she could at least impress him with her general knowledge, even if she couldn't impress him with her recent behaviour.

'An easy one to start with, ladies and gentlemen.' The host, a large jolly man, who with his white beard would have made a superb Father Christmas, had a twinkle in his eye which suggested to Abi that he meant exactly that. It was most certainly a warning of the horrors of cerebral acrobatics to come.

'Which Cornish landmark is most associated with the legend of King Arthur?'

Max had written Tintagel before Abi had even taken the lid off her pen, and she felt a hit of defeat. He hadn't even looked at her to see if she agreed with his answer. She knew it was easy, and that he didn't have to ask her opinion, but it still felt like a slight. You only have yourself to blame, Abi told herself as the quizmaster asked, 'The St Austell Brewery, from where we get many of our excellent alcoholic beverages, introduced which beer initially as a short term special, but it proved so popular that it became a permanent fixture on their brewing list, and has since become their best-selling pint?'

Abi didn't have the first clue, but Max was writing down the word Tribute with an air of satisfaction that hinted at the memory of many a satisfying pint consumed.

The questions continued, and Abi was beginning to feel a complete dunce as she didn't know the answers to any of them. Each one was based on the local area, the area in which she had chosen to live, and she knew nothing.

At last, after what seemed like hours, the quizmaster widened the scope of his questions. 'Which museum can be found on Great Russell Street in London?'

Max shrugged and looked at Abi.

Picking up her pen, she wrote down The British Museum with an air of relief that was so obvious Max couldn't prevent himself from dropping his hostile exterior.

The atmosphere began to thaw between them as the next question made them both laugh out loud. 'Over which centuries did the Ming Dynasty rule in China?'

After that they worked as a team, their hands occasionally touching as they both stroked Sadie's fur, and although they didn't catch each other's eyes, a level of truce was telepathically agreed upon until they had the chance to talk.

'Final question, ladies and gentlemen; and as usual, it is a bit of a stinker.' The host paused, in the annoying fashion of a television gameshow presenter about to announce the winner, until at last he asked, 'Which country spawned the original version of the children's fairy tale Cinderella?'

'Oh, God knows.' Max groaned. So far they'd had an answer for everything, even if they weren't completely convinced in one or two cases.

Abi pulled the paper towards her and wrote down the answer.

'For real?'

'Yep.'

'How did you know that?' Max looked impressed, and despite his better judgement, the feelings he'd been doing his best to suppress for the petite woman next to him came rushing back.

'I'm a children's book illustrator. I've tackled a few fairy tales in my time.'

The quiz host called out, 'OK, if you could put your names on the top of your quiz sheets, I'll be over to collect them up in a minute. Why not grab yourselves a drink while I tot up the marks?'

Max opened his mouth to speak, but Abi held up her hand so

she could go first, her words coming out in a mad rush in her hurry to get him to forgive her. 'I'm sorry. I've behaved so badly, and I really have no defence except that I felt so guilty. I couldn't seem to shift what Simon said about me cheating on Luke. And I do know that thinking that way is insane because we'd never even met when Luke was alive, and that he has been gone for months now, but Simon hit a nerve I guess, and then when Stan asked me to move in, and then he started talking about not being here forever and all I could think about was Luke dying and how I let him down, and how I might let you down, and . . .'

'Abi, it's OK, I . . .'

'No Max, it isn't OK. Sadie and I were talking about it just now.'

'Sadie and you?' He looked at Abi with an affection which clearly stated that she'd gone a bit mad.

'She's a very wise old girl, aren't you, sweetie?' She was met with a nod from Sadie. 'See!'

Taking a sip of the glass of wine that some secret code between Max and the barman had caused to appear at their table, Abi returned to her explanation. 'I've been afraid to like you. To more than like you. And I know we've already held hands and kissed, and we said we'd go slowly and everything, but I felt bad that I've not been more forthcoming. I see Beth and Jacob together . . . they're so happy, and their relationship has gone from nothing to full-on in seconds. I'm not sure Jacob's had a night at home since he first turned up. I really want to be able to give you that, but I'm not that sort of person, and . . .'

This time Max interrupted. 'And of course, neither of them have been hurt before. Not like we have. Lucinda chewed me up and spat me out. I didn't think I'd ever get over it, and I certainly didn't think I could ever contemplate being with someone else. And you've been widowed, and spent years trying to be what your husband wanted you to be, and not who you are. That sort of thing takes time to get past. So, although I'd be lying if I said

I wasn't more than a little keen to see if there are any interesting birthmarks, tattoos, or secret markings on that body of yours, I also need time to trust. It isn't just you.'

Max held Abi's gaze before adding, 'I also know I take things way too personally. I felt rejected when you dropped my hand over at Stan's, and I was cross with myself because I knew you'd have a good reason, but I still convinced myself you'd changed your mind about me. I even thought you might back out of the sale and leave Stan high and dry.'

Abi looked horrified. 'I would never do that in a million years!'

'I know.'

They both looked at Sadie, who was giving them a stare that quite clearly implied they were as bad as each other.

'So will you take Stan up on his offer to move in?'

Abi shrugged 'I'm not sure. What do you think?'

'You've offered to keep his room as his for as long as he wants it, even after he has moved out, and Stan is no fool, Abi. Trust me, he wouldn't have offered if he didn't mean it. I think it might be good for you. A transitional period for you both.'

There was the bang of a pint glass on the bar, and all the attention in the room returned to the quizmaster. 'As ever, folks, it was a close-run thing! But, ahead of everyone else by just two points, we have a winner. Before I reveal who that is, however, let's go through the answers.'

'We never used to have all this faffing about before Dave got addicted to watching *Who Wants to Be a Millionaire*?' Max muttered under his breath.

Abi giggled as they listened to Dave start to read out the list of answers. After about ten, she looked at Max. Unless her memory was playing tricks on her, they had got all of the answers correct so far.

Max put his hand over hers as they got to question twenty, and still Abi was sure they hadn't put a foot wrong.

'And the final answer, ladies and gentleman, which only one

team got correct, the answer to which country did the original Cinderella come from is . . . Egypt!'

The collective groans of 'No way!' from the other teams as Dave revealed the correct response, drowned out Max's cry of 'Oh, good girl!'

As he hugged her, Abi said, 'That's what Stan keeps telling me I am.'

'Not too good, I hope!' Max's eyes twinkled as a blush travelled over Abi's cheeks and relief flood her system.

She was spared having to reply by the sound of Dave announcing 'Tonight's winners, with a total of twenty-five points out of twenty-five, are Max and Abi.'

Graciously receiving their round of applause, Abi's face flushed when Dave came over to the table with their prize of a bottle of malt whiskey and said, 'Welcome to the Old Success, lass. I've no idea where you've sprung up from, but you obviously bring Max luck. The poor old soul has spent a lifetime coming second. Never seen him win before.'

As Dave returned to his other customers, Abi turned to Max. 'Is that right?'

'Sort of sums me up. Always the runner-up. Never quite good enough. Lucinda used to say that a lot. I can hear her now: "Oh for goodness' sake, Max, all you have to do is try that little bit harder." She wasn't one for being second-best.'

Abi had the feeling that Lucinda and Luke would have got on like a house on fire. 'Sounds familiar. Luke was always on at me for not being ambitious. He never understood that I was happy as I was.'

Max held Abi's hand. 'That's the difference between people who earn their living doing things to make other people happy, and people who earn their living to make money. All that ambition can't make folk content in the end, can it? I mean, if it did they'd be happy with what they have, rather than be in the constant pursuit of more, surely?'

Ignoring the fact that they were in a public place, Abi leaned

211

forward and kissed Max lightly on the lips, 'If you keep saying things like that, Mr Pendale, there is a strong chance that I'll never let you go.'

'That's good, because I have no intention of letting you let me go! So, shall we walk Sadie home to Abbey's House?'

'How about walking us both home to Abbey's House?'

'You're going to move in then?'

'If Stan still wants me to, then yes. Let's go and tell him together.'

Chapter Thirty-two

'Beth?' Abi was working from the laptop, which was sat on her desk, now a firmly established part of the studio gallery.

'Yes, hun?' Beth stopped singing along to the radio, and laid down the invitations she'd been stuffing into envelopes.

'Are you sure you want to have two launches? Don't misunderstand me, I think having a family launch to let the children see their work, and then an official launch is a wonderful idea, but can the budget stretch to it?'

'I know it's a bit of an extravagance, but I want to do this. And anyway, only the official launch is coming out of the business account, which is now in the black thanks to you securing exhibit deposits from three more artists. The family do is for me, so I'm paying for that myself.'

'You can't do that! I mean, I must go halves with you. It isn't fair that you have to pay for that on your own.'

Beth shook her head. 'I insist, but if it makes you feel better you can pay for the postage on this lot!' She waved the pile of addressed invite envelopes in the air. 'But the food, drink, balloons, and so on are on me.'

'But . . .'

Beth held up her hand, 'Listen, Abi, you'll be working on your illustrations while the kids crowd round you and put you off big time. Believe me, it's payment enough to have you to deal with the incessant questions from Brandon and his fellow handfuls.'

Abi laughed. 'If you say so!'

Running her eyes down the list of emails before her, Abi gulped. She had been putting off mentioning to Beth that she needed to get back to her work as soon as possible. Now there could be no more delaying the moment. 'Talking of my illustrations, Beth, I think I've pushed my publisher as far as they'll go. I need to start producing some work again.'

'Oh, hell! I'm so sorry. I had no idea you had people waiting for work.' Beth looked horror-struck at the possibility that she'd been interrupting Abi's schedule.

'Not at all, you haven't. They owed me time. I didn't take any time off after Luke died. I just ploughed on, hoping the world would go away; hiding in my work. That was fine at first, but you can't keep going like that for long. So when I finally snapped and ran down here, Genie Press gave me the bereavement leave they'd offered me earlier. Plus of course, my hours are flexible, and I can work whenever I like.'

'But now the leave time is over and the work is piling up?'

'That's about it. Although, don't worry, no one is cracking the whip or anything. I'm very lucky. There are three of us doing the pictures for the publisher, and they take on three books at a time. We each take it in turns to pick the book we want to illustrate next.'

'Hey, that's really cool! So you have a one in three chance of illustrating your favourite of the three each time.'

'Exactly. And as it's so much easier to draw pictures for a book you like, then it's a really good way to work. For now I simply have to confirm to the guys at Genie that I'm back in the game.'

'You will say yes, won't you?'

'Of course, I just hoped I'd have another couple of weeks so that we could get this place properly up and running.'

Beth smiled at her friend. 'Your job is wrapped up in this place, hun; we need you to have work to do, so people can pop in and go gooey over your illustrations.'

'Bless you. Talking of which, the author of *The Pickle Twins* and Genie have agreed that we can print a few of the stills from the book to put up on the walls – if you want them, of course.'

Clapping, Beth was thrilled. 'Do you think you could have them here in time for the launch day?'

'I already have them! I drew them after all.' Abi tapped her laptop affectionately. 'Once I've painted or drawn them on paper, they get digitally zapped onto my baby here. I just needed permission from the author.'

'I don't suppose you have the actual original sketches as well as the computerised versions?'

Abi smiled. 'They weren't exactly on my running-away list.' She was thoughtful for a while, 'You're thinking of having a pictures-in-development show going on?'

'It would be good for the kids to see the work that goes into their favourite books.' Beth got up and pointed to the space on the wall behind Abi. 'This was the only space I wasn't sure how to fill. A few examples of your works in progress would be perfect.'

Abi suddenly felt nauseous. 'It would mean a trip to Surrey to fetch them. I'm not sure we have time before the family launch.' Abi didn't add that the last thing she wanted to do was risk going back to the house in case she bumped into Simon. Even though he couldn't get into the house now, and the chances of seeing him were remote, the idea was still unsettling.

Beth returned to where she'd been working at her grandfather's old bench. 'Don't you have to go back and pack up your things some time, though? I mean, the sale is all but tied up, isn't it? Surely the buyers will want to move in soon?'

Abi had deliberately not mentioned that very fact to Beth. There had been so much to do, but now, after a week of full-on activity at the gallery, as well as countless trips back and forth to the printers in Redruth to get posters and flyers sorted, the workload was cooling down. The business cards had arrived, and thanks to Jacob's contacts and Abi's persuasive emails and telephone calls, they now had eight months of the following year booked up with an enthusiastic and eclectic collection of artists.

Trying to divert Beth's attention away from Surrey, Abi asked, 'Which should I pick then? It's my turn to choose a story first. A space story involving squidgy aliens, a pretty pink fairy princess tale, or a farm run by teddy bears story?'

Beth frowned. 'You wouldn't be dodging my question now, would you, Mrs Carter?'

'Yes I would. So, which shall I do?'

'Not sure I fancy seeing any more pink princess stories in my lifetime. My parents always bought them for me. They never seemed to catch on to the fact I was a tomboy and that anything pink and fluffy was at the absolute bottom of my wish list.'

'I have to admit, they're my least favourite type of story to illustrate. Although they're handy if I'm tired or pushed for time. Pretty princess stories are so formulaic that I can churn out similar-but-different pictures over and over again.'

Beth grinned. 'A little cynical perhaps?'

'Oh yes!'

Reading the descriptions of each story over Abi's shoulder, Beth said, 'I'd go with the space one I think. Got to love a squidgy alien!'

'Deal! I'll tell them that's the one I want, then I can start getting some initial designs for the main characters down on paper.' Abi hammered off an email, and headed to the kettle. 'Cuppa before I trot the invites down to the postbox?'

'Please.' Beth steered the conversation back to where Abi didn't want it. 'When are you going to go and pack up in Surrey? I know you said you were going to get a house clearance place to take all the furniture away, apart from your sofa, and a removal firm to pack up everything and ship it down here, but that isn't really what you want, is it?'

Beth studied Abi carefully as she made them both a cup of tea. 'Is it, Abi? Do you honestly think you won't regret it if you don't say goodbye to the place? There must be some things, like your artwork, that you would hate to lose. And don't you want to pack up the rest of your own clothes? I'd hate the idea of some big burly removal man scooping up all my underwear and dumping it in a packing case.'

Abi listened as Beth voiced all the thoughts she'd already had many times since the solicitor had informed her that completion for the Surrey house sale was in twelve days' time. The same day, in fact, as the family launch of the Art and Sole Studio Gallery

Pushing the point, Beth added, 'I could manage if you went. Jacob has almost finished the commission he's working on, and could help me out with the finishing touches to this place. And surely it would be better for you to go now, before you're immersed in the world of squidgy space aliens?'

Abi's eyes fell on the crate that was holding the newly framed children's artworks, all ready to be hung before the opening. 'I know you're right, but I wanted to be here when you put up the first display.'

'You will be. I wouldn't dream of starting without you. Anyway, I have to get on with sorting out next term's lessons for my new class. I've usually done all that by now!'

Abi swallowed, not wanting to voice the real reason she didn't want to go. Instead she said, 'I'm not sure I should leave Stan right now. He's only just got used to me being there. It seems cruel to leave him after three days. Not to mention letting down Sadie, who has quickly got used to going for proper walks again.'

'These are all sounding like convenient excuses to me, young lady!'

'I know.'

Putting her arm round her friend, Beth asked softly, 'So what is it? You don't think Simon will be there, do you?'

'Logically no. I don't see how he could be. He has no access to the house. I'll have to get some keys from the estate agent myself if I go.' She sighed heavily. 'It's silly, but I've moved on so much. Going back there . . . it's so full of the old me. I didn't like that me very much. I could never quite forgive myself for being such a doormat, and yet I couldn't fight the sensation off. Some days

217

I'd wake up determined to be assertive, but Luke would say something, or give me a certain look, and all my fight would evaporate. The house felt crammed full of those feelings of defeat and failure.'

'But you do want your things? Your special things, I mean, not the furniture, which I can understand you leaving behind, especially as Stan is selling nearly all his stuff with the house and you won't need much.'

'I guess I'd like a few bits and pieces.'

'And it would be great to have your pictures here. You must have loads of art supplies you'll need eventually. You don't want to entrust those to delivery men, do you?'

Abi was suspicious. 'You seem to have thought about this rather a lot.'

'Might have done.' Beth looked partly caught out and partly mischievous. 'It occurred to me that you might be nervous about going back, and you might not want to go alone.'

'What have you done?!'

'Nothing. Honestly.'

'Beth!' Abi didn't believe a word of it.

'OK, I may have suggested to Max that his van would hold much more than your car when it came to bringing stuff back here, and I might have taken a call for you from the estate agents yesterday saying the family are ready to exchange, and told them that you'll be there tomorrow to clear out the first load of your stuff.'

Abi stammered, 'W-what? Tomorrow? But there is so much to do here. And what about Max? He might not want to drive nearly three hundred miles to fetch a load of boxes, and then all the way home again in one go. And he'll have clients waiting for him and . . .'

Beth looked smug. 'Max is willing, a separate hotel room has been booked for each of you for the night, the van is full of empty boxes for you to fill up, and I'm taking Sadie out tomorrow night while Jacob takes Peter back to Stan's to sort out a few antiques for one of the local sales.'

Abi's mouth opened and closed as if she was a floundering goldfish, which was pretty much how she felt as Beth gave her a hug.

'Now be a good girl, turn off your computer, and go back to Abbey's House. Pack your toothbrush and get an early night. Max will be collecting you at six o'clock tomorrow morning.'

Chapter Thirty-three

When Max knocked cheerfully on the front door of Abbey's House at ten to six, it was opened by a fully dressed Stan.

'Morning, me'andsome, all ready for your trip, are you?'

'I didn't expect you to be up, mate. Abi didn't wake you, did she?'

'Trust me, the older you get, the earlier you rise. Abi's in here.' Stan shuffled through to the kitchen and indicated a dressed but somewhat weary-looking Abi who was wincing her way through a mug of extremely strong coffee.

'Are you OK, lass?' Max frowned at the spectacle of Abi practically mainlining caffeine. 'You aren't sick, are you?'

'Only with nerves! I really can't face this.'

Max looked at Stan, who merely shrugged. Pulling out the chair opposite, Max reached across the table and held Abi's hand. 'But you went before, and you were brilliant standing up to that stupid estate agent like that. I was so proud of you!'

'Were you? Thank you,' Abi sighed. 'Look, Max, this is so kind of you, and I know I have to go up there. Beth is right, I need my things. I'm already missing some of my art supplies, and I'd hate to lose all my original drawings and stuff.'

'But?' Max spoke as though coaxing a young child.

'But I never did have the guts to call Simon again. Some of the stuff in the house is Luke's, and I'm sure he'd rather it went to Simon and his parents than have it sold off.'

Max thought carefully before saying, 'There must be some

things of Luke's you want yourself as well? A few objects that remind you of the good times? Photos and stuff maybe?'

Abi took her hand from Max and began to roll her wedding ring around her finger. 'This. This is what I want to keep.' She paused, not sure whether to continue, but as Stan had backed out of the room on the pretext of seeing what Sadie was up to, she felt she had to go on. 'When Luke gave me this we were happy. Sometimes it seems absurd now. But we were. He enjoyed being the one who went against convention then – in a businessman-type way at least. He seemed proud to have a wife who didn't fit the mould.'

'Until he got promoted.'

'Yes. I was never sure exactly what it was about the promotion that changed him so dramatically and so fast, but for Luke it was suddenly no longer funny to have a wife who wanted to earn her own living, didn't like cooking for business reps, and who wanted children. All things which most certainly would not have fitted in with the lifestyle he saw for himself. I know it sounds antiquated, and the height of non PC-ness, but that's how it was.' Abi yawned. 'I'm sorry, I know I've told you all this before. I didn't sleep too well. I might not be the best company on the drive, and it's such a long way.'

Max stood up. 'I think you should take a pillow and get your head down. If we leave now you'll be able to grab a good three hours' kip before I need a coffee and a bit of breakfast.'

Abi got up and put her arms around his comforting bulk. 'You are wonderful.'

Picking up her overnight bag for the hotel, Abi also knew that her nerves had as much to do with being in a hotel with Max later as they did about going to her old home. Even though they were booked into separate rooms, Abi was sure she'd feel much better when the next two days were behind them and they were safely back in Cornwall.

Abi hugged Stan, asking if he was sure he'd be alright, making the old man laugh out loud. 'Girl, me and Sadie have been fending for ourselves for years. Be gone!'

Settling herself in the front of the van with her head on the pillow, Abi had her eyes closed before they left the street.

Seated in the van, higher than she was used to, Abi couldn't believe how safe she felt. Luke had always driven to show off to as many people as possible. Max's driving, like everything else about him, was careful and steady. The knot of apprehension in Abi's stomach began to unravel in the presence of the kindly Cornishman.

'You asleep yet?' Max pulled his vehicle through the narrow village street.

'Sort of.'

'Good girl.' He concentrated as the van somehow breathed in enough to let a lorry pass on the other side of the narrow road before they pulled out onto the A30. 'Abi, can I ask you a personal question?'

'Yes.'

'Do you still want children?'

'Yes.'

'Good. So do I. Now go to sleep.'

Abi's heart tightened with a flickering warmth of happiness she hadn't expected to feel until she was back behind her studio desk drawing pictures of squidgy aliens.

Beth stared at the calendar on her phone. How could it possibly be the twenty-fifth of August already? She was used to the school summer holidays passing with lightning speed, but this year the time had simply dissolved. And although she hadn't had much actual holiday time, Beth found she had a far bigger sense of achievement at the end of August than she usually did.

Standing in the middle of the gallery studio, Beth reflected on how much had happened since Max had rescued Abi in the pub restaurant on her first evening in Cornwall. Not only did Beth now have a definite future for her grandad's old shop, but she had a new friend, a business partner, and a gorgeous boyfriend. None of that would have happened if Abi hadn't come looking for her house.

Briefly wondering how Abi and Max were getting on, and hoping that Max wouldn't be freaked out when he saw what luxury Abi had been used to living in, Beth turned her attention back to the task in hand. 'Right then,' she told the gallery, 'time to go and bulk-buy orange squash and plastic cups, order cupcakes and chocolate cake for the family launch, not to mention some champagne, orange juice, and posh nibbly bits for the official launch.' Picking up the business's brand new chequebook and bank card, Beth set off to spend money.

Jacob was in his element as Peter picked out a few middle-value antiques from Mary Abbey's supply of car boot sale bargains, to sell individually or in group lots at Peter's Truro auction house.

'You know,' Peter turned a pretty set of miniature mining lanterns in his hands, 'some of these won't make that much in an auction house, but might do well in a tourist shop. Has Beth considered selling a few bits in the gallery? If she had a month when she couldn't find an artist willing to pay the fee, then there are enough bits and pieces here to sell for Stan. They could split the profits?'

'That's an excellent idea. Thanks, mate.' Jacob wrapped a china figure of a tin miner in a layer of packing paper. 'I'll ask Stan when he wakes up.'

'That's a hell of a snore he's got on him.' Peter smiled at the echo of the old man's snores, which were coming through the open doorway from where Stan was having his afternoon doze.

Peter laid down the last item for the sale as his mobile buzzed into life. A few minutes later he hung up. 'Well then, it's all systems go.'

'What is?' Jacob pulled a spare cardboard box from beneath the table and began to load it with the things for the sale room.

'The Ming vase. It's got into the next sale in London.'

'No way! That is fantastic. Thanks, mate. So, when is the next sale?'

'Well, we got it in as a late lot, so quite soon. I hope that's alright, but Christie's aren't people you turn down if they offer a sale slot.'

'Christie's! As in major London auction house Christie's who get buyers from all over the world?'

'The very same.'

'How the hell did you pull that off?'

'Charm, mate, all charm.'

Looking far from convinced, Jacob stood up and hooked his phone from his pocket. 'I'll see if Stan is awake so I can tell him, then I'll call Beth. This is brilliant. They'll be over the moon. 'When is the date exactly?'

'Second of September.'

'You lived here?'

'Yes.' Abi got out of the van, and peered about her furtively, half expecting Simon to jump out at her from behind the bushes.

Stretching his legs, Max walked to the back of the van and pulled out two empty boxes. 'Ready to do this?'

Abi, who was clutching the set of keys they'd collected on the way, nodded with little conviction.

'Come on, lass, once we get your things, we can leave everything else for the clearance people and the removal firm. Three hours maximum and then we'll be off back down the motorway in search of our Travelodge and an evening meal.

It felt very strange putting a new key into her front door, but as Abi stepped inside, the familiar feel of the place swept over here. Although Max was right behind her, Abi was aware that the ghost of Luke didn't feel as if it was going to pop into her mind and start ordering her about as it had used to.

Remaining practical, Max said, 'So then, I know you want the sofa from the kitchen. Anything else from in there, or shall we hit the living room first?'

'We need to go in my bedroom, the bathroom, and my studio. Nowhere else.'

'Sure?'

'Positive. Come on, let's get this over with.' Abi strode to her studio with a speed born of the desire to escape as fast as possible. 'Do you see the chest of drawers there?'

'I do indeed.' Max looked at the basket-weave chest, which he could tell at a glance had cost a fortune.

'Can you put everything inside in a box while I go and rescue the clothes I want from the bedroom?'

'Sure, or I could pick up the whole chest and secure it in the back of the van? That's a decent piece of furniture. It would look great in the studio behind your desk back home.'

Loving how he referred to her space in Cornwall as 'home', Abi agreed, 'It would. Thanks, Max! It'll be much quicker to move in one go as well. The only other things I want from in here otherwise is that pile of unused canvases, those three portfolios, and the easels. Can you manage all that if I sort my suitcases?'

'I certainly can, ma'am.'

'You're a star.'

'I will expect a reward later.'

A flicker of uncertainty shot through Abi. Did he mean sex? She knew she wanted to, but not yet. Not today, not when she was heavy with fatigue and as jumpy as hell after a visit to her old home.

Max smiled. 'Don't look so worried! I just meant an extra portion of chips with dinner. I'll get this lot sorted.'

Feeling a little foolish, but knowing it was her own fault, Abi went into the bedroom she'd shared with Luke and pulled a set of designer luggage from the walk-in wardrobe. It was more like a small room than a wardrobe, and it was almost empty. She'd given all Luke's suits and jumpers to charity weeks ago, and as she'd never been into clothes, her side of the space was far from full.

Unhooking her few remaining dresses, Abi bundled them into the first case with more haste than care, before dumping in a few pairs of shoes and her one pair of decent knee-high boots. Next came the jumpers and T-shirts, followed by her underwear, which was scooped up in a giant armful and dropped at the top of the case, before she squeezed it shut and went to see how Max was getting on.

Abi's phone rang as she bumped the case on wheels down the stairs.

'Hi, Beth. We're just packing up this end, how's it going at home?

Abi picked up on Beth's excited but panicked voice as she relayed the news. 'What? Christie's! That is incredible! Stan must be chuffed to bits. When's the auction?'

When Beth answered, Abi's happy expression disappeared as fast as it had arrived. 'Please tell me you're kidding? We'll never all make it in time . . . OK . . . right, well, I'll tell Max and . . .' Abi reached the front door and was about to wheel the case to the van when she stopped dead. The colour drained from her face. 'Simon.'

'What?' Beth groaned 'What's he doing there?'

'I'll have to go.'

Abi hung up and ran towards the van. She got there just in time to see Max give Simon a black eye.

Chapter Thirty-four

'Simon! What the bloody hell are you doing here?'

'Oh, that's rich! What are you and the overstuffed gorilla doing here?' Simon was cradling his eye, 'who I'm about to have arrested for assault, by the way.'

Abi ripped the mobile out of Simon's free hand. 'Really? And how will your company feel when they hear that you have been arrested for trespass and acting in a manner likely to cause an affray?'

'You weren't even here. You have no idea what happened. That oaf took a swing at me from nowhere.'

Max was fuming. 'I was in the van. I didn't hear him coming. Suddenly I was being hauled backwards and shouted at. He was accusing me of burglary. I acted on instinct. It was self-defence.'

Abi crossed her arms and stared at her brother-in-law, her blood was pumping through her veins so fast it felt as if she was running on pure anger and adrenalin. 'What sort of burglar raids a house like this, in broad daylight, then only takes a chest of drawers and some old art supplies? Which he secures in the back of his van extra-carefully before dashing off? And, come to think of it, what's so weird about a house that is for sale having goods taken away in a van anyway?'

'It isn't a removal van!' Simon was looking wrong-footed.

'No, it isn't. But it is a van you've seen before, when you gate-crashed my life in Cornwall. Which is a good point, isn't it?

I could add kidnap to the charge sheet. I have plenty of witnesses to that incident.'

With a careful eye on Max, Simon put a hand on Abi's elbow and tried to steer her away so he could talk to her in private, 'Look, Abi, I was worried about you.'

Shaking him off angrily, Abi stood her ground. 'No, you weren't. And anything you have to say you can say here, in front of Max. He's been more of a friend to me in the last few weeks than you have been in all the years I've known you. Max has helped me, supported me, and looked after me. He does not make me feel stupid or inadequate, and he has managed to work out that quality of life and making people happy is more worthwhile than making money to buy and show off things you don't need.'

Max came up behind Abi and put his arm protectively on her shoulder. 'If you'd stopped to think, Mr Carter, you'd have worked out that we are here to collect Abi's things. Perhaps you could tell us why you're here?'

'I don't see why I have to answer to you!'

'You don't. But you do have to tell Abi.'

'I've been keeping an eye on the place. You obviously don't care what happens to my brother's things, so I thought I'd try and find out who the new owners were and make sure they didn't sell off Luke's belongings.'

Abi groaned her annoyance as she regarded her brother-in-law's anger screwed up face. 'You're insane, or paranoid, or both. But on the other hand, perhaps your appearance is timely. I was going to call you when we were finished. You can have the remainder of your brother's things. I have all I want.'

'Yeah, right. Like I'm going to believe that!'

With a restraining hand on Max's arm, Abi said, 'Simon, this is the very last time I am going to ask you this, because I have no intention of ever seeing you again after today: what do you want? What is all this insanity about?'

'You! You, of course.'

His always-in-control mask slipped a little, and just for a second Abi wondered if she was looking at the real Simon. With a faint hint of defeat in his voice, he carried on talking.

'Luke never appreciated you. He never saw what you could become.'

Abi's eyes narrowed. 'What I could become?'

'Yes! You could look incredible if you let yourself. The perfect businessman's wife. I could have made you that woman.'

Abi opened her mouth. No coherent words would form on her tongue as Simon reached forward and took her hands. 'It's not too late, Abigail! We could use the money from renting this house out to secure a place I've made enquiries about for us in Oxford. You'd love it. So close to all the right connections for my business – and with you in place as a permanent hostess and –'

'Stop!' Abi's shout echoed around the driveway, cutting across Simon, which wiped the beseeching expression off his face to be replaced by its usual arrogant countenance. 'You've secured a place for us in Oxford? For us?'

Abi was incredulous, as she and Max exchanged glances that clearly stated they thought Simon had lost his mind. 'What century are you living in? You have no idea who I am, do you?' Even after all Simon had done, Abi couldn't stop herself feeling pity for him. 'Is this your idea of a relationship, Simon? Really? How awful for you.' She shook her head, 'All these years you've looked at me, building up a picture of what you want to see in your mind, but you've never noticed the real me at all. You've never really seen me.'

Simon's angry embarrassment put the arrogant businessman within him well and truly back in charge. 'You've made a big mistake trying to keep all of my brother's things from me, Abigail.'

'Haven't you been listening to me? I said I have taken all I want from my memories of Luke. The rest is yours.'

'And why would I believe you?'

Max's temper was beginning to crack again, 'If you'd like to follow me, Mr Carter, you'll see that Abi is, as ever, telling the truth.'

229

Stalking after them, Simon walked into his brother's old home and followed the line of Abi's pointing hand. A neatly stacked pile of Luke's music collection, the modern art Abi didn't like, and various other bits and pieces from his life, along with the keys to his Porsche 4x4, sat waiting with a note on them asking the removal firm to deliver them to Simon's work address.

'Satisfied?' Abi looked her brother-in-law in the eye. 'Do you know, for a second back there I felt sorry for you. I thought, just for a moment, that you were telling me the truth. A blinkered, unrealistic truth, but the truth nonetheless. How dare you pretend to care for me, when all you want are my assets and me for a dressing-up doll with a fake smile to please your clients! Luke would be ashamed of you. I hope whatever memories and money you can glean from his possessions will make you happy.'

Simon's greedy expression contorted into a mixture of humiliation and disgust that made Abi wonder about his true feelings for her once more, 'You've kept nothing. You didn't love him at all.'

Abi put an arm on Max's side to restrain him from punching Simon again. Speaking with extreme care, she addressed Simon as if he was a bomb that was about to explode. 'I loved Luke. I think he loved me too, in the beginning, but I couldn't be the trophy wife he needed and he grew to resent me. Dislike me, even. I tried hard to be who he wanted me to be, but I couldn't do it. In the end I made him unhappy, and I'd do the same for you. I have my wedding ring, which I will always love, and the sofa we used to sit on together in the early days before he became obsessed with keeping up with the Joneses, and pushing himself harder and harder just so we could show off material things we didn't need. If he hadn't been like that he might still be here now.'

Simon picked up the car keys. 'Is it in the garage?'

Max shook his head. 'For a moment there I thought you might have learned from your brother's mistake. A mistake which cost him his life, as well as the most beautiful, kindest woman in the world. Seems I was wrong.'

★

Dropping the house keys back at the estate agent's, Abi signed all the outstanding documents required to complete the sale and gave instructions to Nigel Davison about the disposal of the remaining furniture. They quickly arranged for a truck to come to fetch her sofa, the dresser, and a few other items that, once Simon had disappeared and the fear of him popping up again was gone, Abi had chosen to take back to Cornwall after all. Now, as they began the two-hour drive to the Travelodge where they were spending the night, Abi put her hand on Max's leg.

'The most beautiful woman in the world, huh?'

Max's face flushed. 'Maybe.'

Abi smiled into the fading light of the day. She felt exhausted, but finally free from the chains of guilt that she had allowed herself to be wrapped in for so long. 'I think you really have earned that extra portion of chips.'

'Christie's!'

Abi laughed as the chip Max had just speared on his fork fell off in mutual shock with its would-be consumer. 'Yes. Isn't it wonderful? Stan is chuffed to bits apparently.'

'I can't believe how fast Peter got that sorted. Is it a specialist oriental ceramics auction?'

'No, it's a general auction. Peter did tell Stan that he'd get more if he waited for the next specialist auction in six months' time, but Stan said he could be dead by then, so they should crack on.'

'Sounds like Stan! Ever the realist.' Max chewed slowly. 'I bet he'll be determined to go up to London to the auction himself. I can hear him now: "One more adventure to add to the score sheet, me'andsome!"'

Abi giggled, 'I bet you're right, and Stan should be there. Shame I won't be there too.'

'Why ever not?'

'That's the problem with going for the first available auction. It's on the second of September. No way can I leave Beth to cope with the family launch of the gallery on her own, especially as she is hoping that I'll entertain the children with some of my pictures.'

'Oh hell, I hadn't thought of that!'

Hiding her disappointment that she wouldn't be there with Stan while he saw his treasure make thousands, Abi took a sip of wine. 'Will you be able to go with him, Max? Beth said that Jacob had offered, and I know they get on well, but you've known Stan a bit longer.'

'I wouldn't miss it for the world.'

They'd stopped eating almost an hour ago. Abi couldn't face another drink, yet she didn't want to be the first to mention bedtime. The rooms they'd been allocated were next door to each other, and she felt odd at the thought of them, having been so close all day, lying in beds so near to each other and yet so far apart. Abi knew she couldn't suggest abandoning one of the rooms so they could share after all the fuss she'd made about taking things slowly. How could she do a complete about turn and tell Max that all she wanted was to be held in his arms all night?

'Are you alright? You must be shattered, I know I am.' Max pushed his empty tea cup away, 'I'm going to have to turn in or I'll be falling asleep at the wheel tomorrow, and I'd quite like to make an early start if that's OK?'

'Of course, yes.' Abi got up too quickly, and knocked the remains of her glass of water over. 'Oh hell, oh I'm so sorry.'

Dabbing at the puddle of water as it spread over the table, Max said, 'Not to worry, you're tired. It's been a long, emotional day. Come on.'

Abi's heart began to beat quicker with hope as he took her hand. 'Bedtime, young lady.' As they walked up the stairs, Max hooked his arm around her waist.

'Here we are then.' Max stopped outside her door. Leaning down, he gently lifted Abi up off her feet so that they were face to face, and kissed her with so much tenderness Abi thought she might cry.

Putting her down again, Max patted her on the shoulder. 'Don't worry, I don't break my promises, as much as I'd like to ravish you and then cuddle you to sleep, I respect your need to wait.'

Only a second later, Abi was on her own in the corridor, wishing she'd had the guts to tell Max that his suggestion of ravishment had sounded very nice, thank you.

Chapter Thirty-five

'My life has turned into a never-ending list of things to do!'

Beth sank onto the sofa in her living room, next to Jacob who was scanning his laptop for last-minute hotel deals in the area of London near Christie's.

'You'll get through it, love, don't worry.'

Beth flipped through her notepad, looking at all the tasks still to cross off before she could even think about the gallery opening properly. 'We're almost ready for the family afternoon, and it shouldn't take too much to swap things around for the official launch, but are we ready to start selling for real? I mean, I haven't even had a go at using the till yet. What if I can't work it? How embarrassing would that be! And the man hasn't brought the credit card machine, and the phone line needs changing for that as well, and I'm gutted I can't come up to London with you guys for the auction.'

'Me too.' Jacob smouldered at her over the top of his computer. 'I was looking forward to corrupting you in new and interesting places.'

'You are unstoppable!'

'True.' Jacob stopped what he was doing for a moment. 'It is a shame though. Stan would have loved you and Abi to be there as well, but he understands that you need to be at the gallery. To be honest I think we're as sorry that we won't be at the family opening as you are at missing the auction.'

'You will look after Stan, won't you?'

'Of course. We'll be fine. Max is going to drive us up, as there's room for three in the front of his van, and it's nice and upright, so Stan will be comfortable. Then we'll have three rooms together – if I can find them – and with Max on one side of him and me on the other Stan will be just fine.'

Beth snuggled down onto Jacob's shoulder and stared at the computer screen with him. 'Thanks, hun.' Yawning, she closed her eyes. 'At least Art and Sole is beginning to look like a gallery.'

'So the schoolkids' pictures are up now then?'

'Yes, Abi and I hung them this afternoon. Took ages, but I must admit they look great. It's going to be tough keeping the blinds down over the shop windows in this hot weather, but I don't want people to see them before the big day.'

'Ahh, got one! Well, three.' Jacob pressed the 'Book Rooms' button before anyone beat him to it, and opened his wallet for his credit card to confirm the booking. 'Now all we have to do is find Max a suit. Do you think he has clothes other than boiler suits?'

'Oooh, bitchy! That's my best friend you are talking about!' Beth laughed. 'He does indeed. He looks all handsome when he's dressed up.'

'Does Abi think so?'

'I'm sure she does. She hasn't spoken about Max much since she got back from Surrey. In fact, she's been pretty quiet all round now I think about it, but we've been so busy, what with her illus-trating job starting again and the gallery and everything. I haven't had the chance to talk to her properly. Maybe we'll have a girls' night out after the launch to celebrate that, and to toast your suc-cess in London. What time does the auction start?'

'Not until six, so at least we won't have to spend more than one night up there. Keep your fingers firmly crossed for some Ming lovers to turn up.'

Beth smiled, 'Of course I will.' Then suddenly she sat up straight, 'Oh God, I've just thought.'

'What?'

'What if the gallery sign doesn't turn up on time? I was supposed to call the signwriter today to confirm a time for the erection, and I forgot all about it.'

Jacob put down the computer and pulled her onto his lap instead, 'It will be fine. You can call him about his erection in the morning, and deal with this one now . . .'

'Abi, Abi? Are you alright? I can hear voices.'

Abi opened her bedroom door, 'I'm sorry, Stan, I should have told you. Come and say hello to Oliver.'

Stan looked about him, and saw no one. 'Oliver?'

'Over here, look.' Abi steered Stan across the room and pointed to her laptop, 'Ollie, this is Stan. Stan, this is my brother.'

Ollie held up a hand in greeting. 'Hello, Stan. Abi has told me so much about you. Thank you so much for taking such good care of her down there.'

Stan gave Abi a confused look, before saying, 'Well I'm pleased to meet you too, young man. Although I should say that it's more a case of Abi looking after me, but . . . where are you?'

'I'm in Yorkshire. This is Skype. Great, isn't it?'

'Ahhhh.' Stan nodded, comprehension gradually spreading across his face. 'Sally, that's my daughter in Australia, she told me about it, but I didn't know where to start, so I never sorted it out.'

Abi pulled up a chair next to Stan, 'I could set it up for you, if you'd like me to. If Sally has a laptop or a tablet or something?'

'Oh, she has all the gadgets; it's just me who hasn't a clue!'

Ollie laughed from the other side of the country, 'Not just you, Stan. Took me ages to get to grips with it. My children set it up for me.' A noise in the background made Ollie turn around. 'Talking of which, Tina is out tonight and it sounds as if the kids need me, so I'll love you and leave you, Abi. Great to see you, Stan. Take care, sis.'

Stan was eager, 'Could we really? You know, see Sally while we speak to her?'

'Of course.' Abi was decidedly uneasy at the prospect of meeting

Sally, albeit via the magic of technology. What if Stan's daughter wasn't as comfortable as Stan had claimed about a stranger, not only buying her family home, but moving in before the sale was even complete?

'How do we do it then?' Stan leaned towards the computer as if it was some sort of awe-inspiring magical machine. Which Abi supposed it sort of was, it was just one that almost everyone who used it took it for granted.

'First we'll need Sally's Skype address, so you'll have to call her normally next time you can and get that from her. Once we have that I'll set it up, and you'll be able to see Sally when you chat.'

'And my grandchildren?'

Abi smiled at the eagerness of her friend, and gave him a hug. 'Yes, and your grandchildren.'

'I bet they've grown. Every time Sally sends a photograph of Pippa and Craig they look like they've grown another inch.' Stan swallowed, composing himself, and said, 'I'll call as soon as it's morning over there.'

'You'll be able to tell them all about the auction as well.'

'I can't believe it's so soon. And the gallery launch. I'm sorry you can't be at both.'

'Don't you worry about that. No one can be in two places at once.'

Getting up, Stan looked about him properly for the first time. All the boxes that Abi and Max had brought back from Surrey were still stacked along the side of the room. The only item that had been disturbed was one of the suitcases, which was open, and had obviously been rifled through, but not emptied.

'Why haven't you unpacked yet?' Stan's shrewd eyes scanned his friend. 'You know you can put your things anywhere you like. Especially now that you and Max have made such a good start on packing up my things, ready for my move.'

Abi felt a little awkward. She wasn't sure how to explain it to Stan without offending him, something which she wouldn't want to do for all the money in the world. 'I just haven't felt ready. To be honest, Stan, I'm not sure my things from the me that was then, fit the me that is now. Not yet, anyway. Does that make sense?'

'None at all, my girl, but I totally respect you for that.' Stan stood up and walked slowly towards the door. 'I'll leave you in peace.'

'Stan?'

'Yes, Abi?'

'Thank you.'

The old man gave her shoulder a quick squeeze. 'And you, my girl. And you.'

Once Stan had the idea of being able to see Sally and the children as well as talk to them, there was no stopping his determination to make it happen as soon as possible.

'Stan . . .' Abi knew she couldn't leave voicing her doubts about Sally's reaction to her any longer as her friend sat excitedly in front of her laptop.

'Yes, my girl?'

'What have you told Sally about me exactly?'

'Everything! How you knocked on the door, about your family holidays in the past, about Max, and walking Sadie, and bringing me fish and chips, and everything.'

'What did she say about it?'

'How do you mean?'

'Stan, if I was Sally I'd probably be worried. I could be anyone in her eyes, couldn't I? A con artist after your home, a thief, a gold digger even. It happens.'

Stan looked a little uncomfortable. 'Well, I did have to reassure Sally a bit. But don't worry, Sally's lovely. She'll adore you just like I do.'

Abi smiled, but felt far from reassured as she prepared the laptop for the call. 'I'll start it dialling, and then I'll leave you to it. You don't need to press anything. You should have this first call in peace.'

'You won't go far, will you? Stan looked worried, 'Just in case this thing beeps at me or something.'

'I'll be in the next room; I'll leave the door ajar. Shout if you need me.'

Trying to read a book so that she didn't eavesdrop on Stan's conversation, Abi found concentration impossible. She knew she'd been foolish to not seek a conversation with Stan's daughter before now. She desperately wanted Sally to like her, but she knew that her trust would have to be earned.

It was with a sense of relief that Abi heard laughter coming from the next room. A few seconds later, Stan called her through. Abi had thought he might, and the nervous perspiration that had been building up on her palms prickled slightly as she got up and went to join her friend.

Beaming with pride, Stan gestured to the smiling faces on the computer screen before him. 'Abi, may I introduce you to my wonderful grandchildren, Pippa and Craig.'

Smiling at the two young teenagers, Abi waved and said hello. 'I'm very pleased to meet you.'

Stan, looking as though all his Christmases had come at once, said, 'Is your mum still there, troops? I'd like her to meet Abi as well.'

'Sure, Gramps.' Pippa and Craig disappeared in a flurry of blown kisses and waves, as Sally slid in front of the screen, and sat down. Unlike the children, Sally wasn't smiling. On the plus side, Abi thought, she wasn't scowling either.

'You're getting the hang of this Skype business already, Dad.'

'I am, Abi's shown me how it all works. We had lots of little practice runs before we called properly.'

Turning her attention to an increasingly uncomfortable Abi, Sally nodded. 'Thank you. It's fabulous to be able to see my dad.'

'Not at all. It's the least I can do. Your dad has been so very kind, and so have you.'

Sally frowned. 'I have?'

'Yes.' Abi, hoping she sounded sincere rather than patronising, said, 'You don't know me from Adam, and yet I've sort of taken over at this end. I really didn't mean to. I suppose I'm trying to reassure you that I'm not a gold digger or anything, which now I've said that, makes me sound even more like one, doesn't it? Oh dear, sorry,' Abi felt increasingly flustered, 'that didn't come out right.'

Stan waved away what Abi was trying to say. 'Don't be silly, Abi, I know you aren't a gold digger, and Sally and I have talked it all through before.'

'You are very kind, Stan, but even so, if I was Sally, I'd want more reassurance than that.' Abi addressed Sally directly, 'Is there anything I can do to prove I'm genuine?'

Sally smiled, some of the reserve in her eyes softening. 'Well, it is nice to know someone is looking after Dad, but I confess I'd feel better if I knew you a little more.'

'I'd like that. Stan talks about you and the children so much, it seems odd that we've never physically met.'

Nodding, Sally glanced at her watch. 'Do you have time for a longer chat now?'

'Sure.'

'Dad, I'll call you again tomorrow. Time for Abi and I to get to know each other a bit better. I have to grill her!'

Stan looked worried, but Abi smiled. 'Sally's joking, we're just going to fill in the gaps between what you've already told each of us.'

'So, do you think you've convinced Sally you aren't after Stan's money?' Beth asked Abi as they watched two men, balancing on ladders, curve, smooth, and hammer the shop sign across the front of the studio gallery.

'As much as I can. We got on pretty well in the end. I can't blame her for being edgy at first. I would have been in her place.' Abi smiled at the memory of Stan's happy face when she'd reported back on how well she and Sally had got on, and that they'd already scheduled another Skype chat for later in the week.

240

As the last nail was driven home Abi and Beth raised their mugs of coffee in salute to their new enterprise.

'I can't believe it!' Beth felt a rush of grateful love for her new friend, 'It's actually happening. Here's to The Art and Sole Studio Gallery!'

Abi beamed. 'I can't wait to get working in there properly. I can't tell you how lovely it will be to have the occasional interruption!'

'Really? I was worried the visitors would put you off.'

'Not at all. I work better with people around. Plus, it can get awfully lonely working on your own. And, let's face it, we could go days without a customer, but at least I'll have the company of the artists that are visiting on and off. Will Jacob be sitting in all the time, or will he just be popping by sometimes? He can hardly bring his work with him like the painters and quilters, can he?'

'A bit of both. He's planning to be in his work studio all morning, and then bring in admin and stuff to do here in the afternoons. Sound good?'

'Perfect.' Abi looked up at the Victorian-style script of the Art and Sole sign. This was her office, her daytime home. 'I can't believe how lucky I am to have such a great place to work.'

Going back inside so that Beth could write a cheque for the sign men, Abi headed into the storeroom, taking extra care not to knock over any of the pots that Jacob had stacked up ready for his month in residence, when her mobile burst into life.

'Oh, hi, Max, how's today's wallpapering going?'

'Let's just say I prefer putting up plain paper to patterned! Lining up the little flowers on this stuff is enough to try the patience of a saint.'

Thinking that Max did have the patience of a saint Abi couldn't imagine how tricky it must be to have got him moaning when he added, 'Anyway, the woman I'm putting up this headache-inducing design for is the features editor for *Cornish Life* magazine. I've been telling her all about Art and Sole, and she is interested in doing an article about you guys, why you've started another gallery, what is different about it and so on. What do you think? You up for it? Would be a brilliant bit of publicity.'

'I'd love it! Any free publicity is good. I've done several adverts for the local papers, but they've all cost a fortune. But shouldn't you be asking Beth this and not me? She's the boss after all.'

'True, but this was an excellent excuse to call you in the middle of the day!'

Warmth flowed through Abi as she said, 'You don't need an excuse. I love it when you phone.'

'Do you?'

'Yes.' Abi felt the need to say so much, to tell Max exactly how she was beginning to feel about him, but deciding it was cruel to tell him over the phone when he was unable to leave his annoying wallpaper, she simply said, 'Fancy a walk and a drink tonight? I have a yen to learn a bit more about this area so that I can answer more of the pub quiz questions next time, and you're the one to tell me.'

Chapter Thirty-six

Abi's alarm clock rudely summoned her to life at five o'clock. There was an hour before Max and Jacob would be knocking on the door ready to take Stan up to London, and two hours before Beth would be expecting her at the gallery to go through the preparations for the family launch that afternoon.

The sounds of movement from the next room told Abi that Stan was up and getting ready. Pulling on some old clothes that would do until she had the chance to shower, Abi went downstairs to the kitchen to make them both a hot drink and some toast.

As Abi moved around the kitchen she wondered what if would be like to be here on her own, with just herself to make toast for and only one mug to fill with tea or coffee. She was surprised to find that the idea didn't appeal to her at all. The dream had been to live here alone, but somewhere along the line the dream had changed, and she hadn't even noticed.

Although Abi had contemplated asking Stan to stay permanently, the way he talked about moving up to the flats was so enthusiastic that she wasn't sure he'd want to stay. Anyway, she knew it wasn't Stan she wanted here with her – not really.

It was with a sense of shock, as Abi wondered how it would be having Max move in with her, that she realised she'd never seen his home. Was he ashamed of it? Or maybe of her? Don't be silly, it's not that he hasn't shown you, he just hasn't got round to taking you there. It's not as if he's desperate to get me on my own so

243

he can do interesting things to me is it! Sighing into the kettle vapour, Abi once again cursed her hasty declaration that her body was out of bounds. How could she possibly tell him that she'd changed her mind? That now Simon was off the scene she felt free to be who she wanted to be?

Her musings were interrupted by the sight of a smartly suited and broadly smiling Stan. 'What do you think? Will I cut the mustard up there with those City types?'

'You look very dapper indeed!' Abi smiled. 'Are you packed for your night in a swanky hotel with the boys?'

'I most certainly am.' He gave Abi a wink which she was sure would have been a pretty powerful weapon when he was a younger man. 'We'll show those city gals a thing or two!'

'Stan!'

The old man laughed as he sat down to the pile of toast Abi placed in front of him. 'I was up there for a time during the war. You should have seen me! You'd never have recognised me, girl. Bit of a catch I was back then.'

'I don't doubt it!' Abi sat with him, sipping her tea, 'You all ready then? Nervous?'

'I am a bit. I've always wanted to go to a real auction though. I love all those *Bargain Hunt* type shows. You never know, we could make a fortune.'

'You never know.' Abi, who was worried Stan had set his heart on them fetching a sum for the vase that was unrealistic, said no more on the matter.

Between munches of toast Stan added, 'I know what I'm going to do with the money when we have it.'

'What's that then?'

'I'm going to buy a plane ticket for Sally and the kids to come and visit. They want to come, but simply can't afford it.'

Abi grinned. 'That's a fabulous idea. I hope you make enough.' Having met Sally via Skype several times now, Abi had found herself more and more endeared to the single parent who'd taken her children off for a fresh start all on her own, something which Abi was sure had taken far more guts than she would ever have. Privately deciding that if Stan didn't make enough for all three tickets she'd offer to make up the difference, Abi said, 'How long does the money from Christie's take to come through after a sale? I can't imagine they write you a nice fat cheque there and then. They'll have to take their commission and stuff off won't they?'

'I don't know, my girl. Jacob will do, I expect, and that Peter said he'll talk us through it all.'

'Peter's going?'

'He's meeting us up there. Apparently Peter has never sent stuff to Christie's before, so he didn't want to miss it. Not done his reputation any harm, according to young Jacob.'

A knock at the door told them that Jacob and Max had arrived.

'Morning, Stan.' Max took Abi's hand as he came through the door. She swore he looked more attractive each time she saw him, especially when he wasn't wearing his work clothes. 'So, are you all ready for family time at Art and Sole?'

'Almost,' Abi held his hand a little tighter, hoping Max would pick up on the fact she didn't want to let go again, 'only the little bits and pieces to sort out now.'

Jacob picked up Stan's bag. 'You will put my pots out where I told Beth, won't you? I'd hate them to get broken by overeager young fingers.'

Abi, who had heard this request three times in the last few days, said, 'We'll put them exactly where you said. I can promise nothing about little fingers except that we'll do our best to protect your things. You don't have to have them displayed today if you'd rather not. We could leave all your stuff until the official launch.'

'No, it's fine, Beth might sell a few. Ignore me; I get a bit precious about my work sometimes.'

As Abi had heard that before as well she just nodded and, with a double-check that Stan had everything he needed, and a quick whisper in Max's ear asking that they should stop at least once every two hours so Stan didn't get too tired, she escorted Stan to the van.

Max hesitated by the driver's door. 'Good luck, Abi. You will call and let us know how it goes, won't you? I can't believe I'm not going to be there to support you and Beth.'

'You are supporting us; you've done so much to help.' She hugged him close, and looked up at Max's smile, which was a foot above hers. 'It's a miracle that the top of your head doesn't get frostbite from being all the way up there!'

'Cheek! It isn't my fault you're all petite and dinky-like!'

Lifting her off her feet Max gave her a quick kiss. 'Call me later, yes?'

Breathless as she was lowered to the floor, Abi blushed at the thought that Stan and Jacob could be watching, 'You bet. You call too. I want to hear all about it. In fact, could you hold your phone up so Beth and I can hear the bidding?'

'Great idea.' Max bent down and kissed the top of her hair. 'Have a brilliant day. Give my love to Beth.'

'Will do.' Abi waved as Max carefully reversed out of his parking spot, and the van disappeared back off towards London, following a route Max was beginning to know quite well.

Silver and blue balloons hung in five bunches from hooks on the outside of the Art and Sole Studio Gallery, an area of floor had been cleared to accommodate the visitors, and Abi's prints and original sketches had been framed and hung on the walls. They were from her favourite of all the books she'd illustrated, *The Bumble Tumble Monkeys*, about some mischievous monkeys that loved to cause havoc in the jungle.

A pile of the books were also available to sell, thanks to the publishers' eager agreement to having another retail outlet, and her latest work in progress from *Squidgy the Alien* was propped on her easel. Having taken the precaution of removing all her paints from harm's way, Abi laid out her watercolour pencils and opened her laptop to show the page of writing that she was currently illustrating.

Beth came to see what Abi had been working on between all the other things she'd been doing lately. 'That's amazing.'

'Thanks.' Abi put down her last piece of set dressing, the grey rag she used to blend her colours on the page, and turned to examine the gallery side of the room. 'It's all looking fantastic. Can I help with Jacob's pots?'

Beth smiled. 'That would be great. For such an easy-going bloke he is so darn anal about his work. You'd think he'd want people to touch them, but he gets all stressy about it.'

'He gave me the "keep them away from the children" speech again this morning.'

Beth groaned and rolled her eyes, 'I love the man to bits, but honestly! Pottery is supposed to be touched and used. And how anyone will be able to resist touching his Ali Baba pots next week once they're on show for a month I don't know. You wait until you see them in the flesh, as it were. You'll get no work done. You'll be popping across the shop to run your hands over them every five minutes.'

Abi had fazed out of what Beth was saying after her first few words. 'You love Jacob? Already?'

'Sure. I think I was already in love with his photo before he got here. Then his voice on the phone added to the lust factor. When I met him I knew for sure.' Understanding why Abi was asking, Beth added, 'Our situation isn't the same as you and Max. You can't compare it, you know.'

'I know.'

Beth paused to start spreading out plastic cups on a tray, ready to be filled with orange squash, 'You've fallen for him, haven't you?'

'That obvious?'

'Actually, no, it isn't. And of course, Max wouldn't ever push you for anything because he is too darn nice for his own good sometimes.'

Abi shrugged, 'That's just it, you see. It's my fault. I asked him to go slow, and now I've changed my mind. How can I tell him that, when he is going out of his way to be gentle and slow?'

'Snail pace slow?'

'You got it. Although actually, he did give me a lovely kiss this morning.' Abi giggled. 'When he kisses me he has to lift me off my feet in order to see my eyes at the same time.'

Beth smiled, 'He's a man worth waiting for, Abi. Don't forget, he's been hurt as well.'

Brushing her hands together decisively, Abi picked up a huge tin of biscuits and sat them next to Beth's tray. 'Shall we sort this launch business first, then when Max gets back I'll seduce him or something.'

Laughing, Beth said, 'That's the spirit! Do you think we've got time for a cup of coffee before we go and change into our glad rags? That Felicity woman from *Cornwall Life* will be here in an hour.'

'Loads of time. I was just planning to stick my clean jeans on and a nicer top. No point in dressing up for this one, especially as I'll probably get covered in paint. I'll do the glamour frock for the official launch.' Suddenly remembering this was really Beth's show and not hers, Abi added, 'If that's OK?'

'Sounds just the ticket to me! Come on, let's go upstairs and draw breath.'

Felicity arrived late, in a flurry of apologies about her car not starting, and then not being able to park. She was followed by a rather shy-looking young man equipped with a camera and posh-looking Dictaphone.

Dressed up to the nines, balancing with enviable ease on killer heels, and without a wrinkle on her exquisitely made-up face, Felicity gushed her way about the gallery as Beth explained the background, her grandfather's wish that she should take on the shop, and how Abi and her friends had helped her to decide on what to do with the space, Felicity oohed and aahed over the children's paintings. She was satisfyingly impressed by Abi's work, and instantly fell in love with Jacob's mugs and small pots which, ignoring his wishes entirely, Beth had put where she wanted, telling a rather concerned Abi that the place was insured and there was no point in trying to sell anything that no one could see properly.

Mark, the photographer, had just finished taking pictures of the two rather self-conscious women, both of whom were wondering if they should have dressed up more, when the sound of young voices alerted them to the arrival of their young guests and their parents.

Beth had expected Felicity to leave, but she was so charmed by the idea of a family launch rather than the usual 'little bits of things on sticks', that she asked to stay, and before long Mark was snapping away at the children standing by their framed pictures, beamingly proud parents by their sides.

Abi hardly had time to breath. The children were fascinated by her drawings, and by the time she had explained the process of how her sketches went from ideas to outlines to paintings and then got transferred onto the computer screen, her voice was hoarse and she was ready for some of the orange squash that Beth was passing around.

'You ready to read everyone a story then?'

'What?' Abi was horrified. 'Seriously?'

The choruses of approval from the children gave Abi no way to back out, and with a semi-murderous glare at Beth, she picked up the top copy of *The Bumble Tumble Monkeys*. Sitting on the floor, she immediately found herself surrounded by cross-legged children and several keen parents.

With a flash of encouragement from Beth, who was selling three of Jacob's pots to Felicity, Abi began to read.

'The Bumble Tumble Monkeys scrambled through the trees.

"There goes double trouble," said a voice beneath the leaves . . .'

Chapter Thirty-seven

Walking into the imposing entrance to Christie's, the three men took a lot list from the smiling receptionist, and followed her direction to the auction room. Peter was already waiting for them by the entrance to the salesroom. 'You made it, how wonderful!' He shook their hands. 'All set, Mr Abbey?'

'I certainly am, me'andsome. This is quite an adventure. When does it get going?'

There were a few people already sat down, bidding paddles in their hands, but most people were milling around while they waited.

'We have about a quarter of an hour until kick off.' Peter pointed to the side of the room where three booths waited for their occupants. 'That's where anyone expecting overseas or private phone bids will sit.'

'Are we expecting anyone like that tonight?' Jacob was scanning the growing crowd as if trying to work out which people had money, which were just sightseeing, and which were hoping for a bargain.

'I hope so, but I'm not sure.' Peter pointed to a row of seats set off to one side of the main crowd. 'I hope you don't mind, but I reserved those seats for you. That way you can see everything that is going on, but you won't get confused with the bidders.'

Stan chuckled. 'That's good, I was getting worried about scratching my head or something and making a million-pound bid by mistake!'

*

The lots moved quickly. The auctioneer was both charismatic and beguiling. It was like watching a magician at work. Max was sure that some of the bidders were only raising their stakes to please the auctioneer and keep the game going for longer.

Stan leaned over and whispered, 'How far are we down the list? I've lost track. It's all such a whirl.'

Max, who'd been having similar problems, traced his finger down the lots printed on the paper. 'That was the fifteenth one, I think, so we're up in five items' time.'

The atmosphere was electric. Everyone seemed poised to act, and as the men caught each other's eyes at the same time, the nervous tension in the room increased.

Beth kicked off her shoes and flopped onto the sofa. 'That was exhausting!'

'It certainly was. Although it may be some time before I forgive you dropping me in it with a story-telling session! Why didn't you warn me, then I would have had a practice?'

'Because if I'd told you what I planned you'd have said no.'

'This is true.' Abi poured two large glasses of wine, and pushed one towards Beth. 'I know we said we'd go out for a meal tonight, but I'm so glad we opted for the takeaway option instead. I'm shattered!' Dividing a generous portion of chicken chow mein onto two plates, Abi stabbed a fork into the top of each haphazard pile of food.

'Plus, of course, if Max does manage to turn his phone on so we can listen to the bidding in progress, then we'll hear it much better in here than in the pub.' Beth checked her watch. 'Surely their turn must be soon?'

'Is it us now?'

Stan had stopped looking excited, and was getting anxious. Max patted his arm affectionately. 'The one after this. Are you ready?'

'As I'll ever be! I think it might be time to call the girls.'

★

Abi's mobile buzzed with the arrival of a text. She frowned. 'Max wants me to get my laptop.'

Beth frowned, 'Whatever for?'

'He doesn't say. I hope it's got enough charge in it, I left the cable downstairs. Can you turn it on while I text him back to tell him we're getting it?'

'Is it working?' Stan stage whispered as Max nodded.

As the picture on Skype came to life, Max and Jacob leaned forward and waved into the video phone screen, with their fingers firmly over their lips to indicate that Abi and Beth should keep quiet.

The girls waved back happily. They were going to be able to see as well as hear the auction in progress after all.

Abi felt the buzz of her mobile again. It was Max.

This was Stan's idea. He's gone a bit Skype mad since you introduced him to it! We are up next. Better keep quiet x

Abi flashed the message in front of Beth's eyes. In mutual unspoken need, both women picked up their wine glasses. As the brown-coated handler lifted up Mary's Ming vase, the girls grasped each other's hands for support as the auctioneer announced Lot Twenty.

'Ladies and gentleman, Christie's is delighted to be able to offer you a particularly exquisite item this evening. As you'll see from your brochures, this nineteen and a half-inch high Ming Dynasty vase comes from the late sixteenth century. A blue and white double-gourd bottle vase, it has a square lower gourd. Decorated all over with a dense lotus scroll, the pattern is divided by ruyi bands. As this item comes from an inland collector there is no import tax to pay, though tax is of course payable should the buyer wish to export this item. If you are all ready, I'd like to start the bidding at £5000 for this beautiful object.'

Abi and Beth exchanged glances of disbelief as the bidding ricocheted into action. There was no hanging about; no dropping of the price to get things going like there always was when these things happened on the television.

Abi wished she could see Stan's face. She hoped he was alright and that the tension wasn't too much for him. He might be forever up for adventures, but he was still eighty-eight years old, and she didn't want him to raise enough money for his family to come and see him, only to be gone before they got here. Heart attacks, she knew all too well, came from nowhere.

The auctioneer was still taking bids. It was clear that there was something about Stan's vase that appealed to collectors, for the price was still rising by a hundred pounds a bid, and was already at £6900 without any sign of slowing.

Stan's hand was shaking a little against his stick. Sally and the children could come home for a while now. He had enough money. He had to bite his lip to stop himself from calling out that was plenty, thanks, you can stop now . . .

'Did I just imagine that?' Abi turned the microphone off at her end, so that she could speak to Beth. 'Did Stan's vase really go for £12,200?'

Beth nodded; speechless.

'I hope Stan's OK?'

'I bet he's thrilled. Oh, look!'

Max had turned his phone around, and the girls could see three broadly beaming faces staring at them. Each man gave them the thumbs up, before the screen abruptly went blank.

'Oh my goodness! If it was stressful this end, what on earth must it have been like their end?'

'I imagine all three of them will have slightly higher blood pressure than they went in with.' Abi picked up her phone, convinced it would ring; which it did in perfect unison with Beth's.

Abi walked into the kitchen so she and Beth could take their respective calls privately, 'Max, is Stan alright?'

'A bit flustered, but elated. We've come out of the salesroom

253

now. It was awfully humid in there, and Stan and I needed some fresh air.'

'I can't believe it went for all that money.'

'I'm not sure we can either. It even stunned Peter, and according to Jacob, that isn't easy to do. Jacob is going to stay for a while and sort all the paperwork, and I'm going to take Stan for some supper. I'll call you later. I want to hear all about the family launch.'

'No problem.'

'Catch you later, love.'

Max hung up, and Abi smiled. He'd called her 'love'. He usually called her 'lass'. That had to be a step in the right direction!

Beth hung up her own phone. 'Jacob sends his love. Sounds as if Stan is tired but happy.'

'That's what Max said. He's taking Stan off for a bit of dinner while Jacob sorts the paperwork out.'

Beth picked up on the happiness that shone in Abi's eyes. 'What else did he say to you?'

'He called me "love". Is it silly that it feels like a big step?'

'If it was anyone else it wouldn't mean a thing, but with Max it does. Hang in there. Like I said earlier, he's worth waiting for.' Beth lay back on the sofa. 'What a day! An auction and a launch. I didn't imagine the family launch bit going so well, did you? Suddenly it seems ages ago.'

'It was great! That Felicity must have thought so if she asked to come back again to report on the official launch as well. Sounds as though she's planning quite a big article, and if the amount of photographs Mark took is anything to go by, then it could fill the whole magazine!'

'He was a bit trigger-happy, wasn't he? Mind you, it might be a mixed blessing having Felicity back.'

Abi refilled the wine glasses, 'How do you mean?'

'Did you see the way she was ogling the photograph of Jacob that's up next to his details?'

'Really? No, I didn't.'

'And if she stroked those pots once, she stroked them a thousand times!'

Abi laughed, 'I do declare you are jealous, Miss Philips.'

'Damn right I am! Potentially, anyway. I was off men for years, by choice I grant you, but now I've found a lovely one I'm not losing him!'

Chapter Thirty-eight

'But, Abi, are you sure?'

'Of course. Look, Stan, this is the obvious solution, and the only way you'll have space to put them all up. I'll stay at Beth's place, and Sally and the children can have my room.'

It was three days since the sale, and already a nice big deposit had been made into Stan's bank account from Christie's. Now a bemused Stan was studying the computer screen Abi had on display before them on the kitchen table. 'And if you press that button right now, they'll all be booked on the flight from Sydney tomorrow? Just like that?'

'Just like that. Shall I?'

Stan nodded. 'Sally is so excited about it.'

'Then let's do this!'

Half an hour later, the tickets were purchased and had been emailed to Sally in Australia, and Abi stood in her room in Abbey's House. Glad that she had stuck to her decision about not unpacking her things until the place truly belonged to her, she stuffed as many of her clothes back into her suitcase as possible in readiness to move out the following day. It wouldn't take long to tidy up, or put up the two camp beds for the children. It would feel strange, though, leaving just as she'd started to settle in.

Telling herself off with a sharp reminder that even though Sally had stopped being suspicious of her motives concerning

Stan and his home, Sally had far more right to be in Abbey's House than she did, Abi headed downstairs to fetch Sadie. It would do them both good to have a walk. Although the summer sun had an autumnal tinge to it now, it was still pleasantly warm, and Abi knew she should make the most of it before the cutting winds that Max had warned her accompanied the coastline once summer was over, began in earnest.

Unhooking the lead from the cupboard, she wandered through to the kitchen to find Stan reading a letter.

'You OK, Stan?'

He waved the piece of paper in her direction, 'Take a look. It's all going through. The flat at Chalk Towers is mine as soon as I sign on the dotted line.'

A lump rose in Abi's throat as she saw the old man sat at his kitchen table. The kitchen table he'd shared with his wife, and his parents, and his grandparents before them. 'Stan, I've been thinking.'

'I know.' Stan pointed to the seat, inviting Abi to sit down. 'You're a good girl, and I have no doubt that you and that lovely man of yours have talked it all through. You have good hearts.'

'You guessed I was going to ask you to stay here with me, even when the house was mine?'

'I did.' Stan smiled bravely, 'Do you see that sink, Abi?'

Abi nodded without comprehension.

'Mary used to stand there. Every time I look at it I see her. When she went I moved north to stay with Sally, because, like you have recently discovered, it is very hard to stay in a place that reminds you so strongly of someone you've lost.'

Abi said nothing, understanding completely as Stan continued. 'When Sally moved away and I came back here I was full of mixed emotions. I wanted to be able to feel Mary's presence again, and I can. This house is full of her. But I was also afraid to experience all that loss again every day. It's a big house for one. It's a bit cut off from life when you don't walk too well. I'd be lying if I said I wasn't a bit lonely before you and Max knocked on my door.'

'But Stan, if you stayed you wouldn't be lonely. I'd be here with Sadie.'

He shook his head. 'I love you very much, Abi. You've been more like a daughter than a friend. In a few short weeks you've done more for me than anyone has in years, but I miss talking to people of my own age. That doesn't mean I don't want to talk to you and Max, but I want to be able to remember the old times with people who were there. Grumble about my aches and pains with people who have them too.'

Abi nodded again, 'You will always be welcome here. Always. I won't be demanding the keys back or changing the locks or anything.'

'A fact which makes me love you all the more, my girl. It's your turn now. Your turn to make this place your place, to love it, fill it with happiness and children and fun, and I have a feeling you'll do just that.'

Abi felt tears approaching as she held out her hand for Stan to squeeze.

'Now then, I'm sure Sadie would appreciate that walk I see you were about to go on. I think I need a little rest, then I'll call the bank. It's time to get this house move going once and for all.'

Hanging up the phone two days later, Abi looked at Beth as her friend washed up their breakfast dishes. 'Well, that's it then. I no longer own a house in Surrey.'

'How do you feel?'

'A bit weird, to be honest. Relieved though.'

'Shame it came through while you were staying here and not with Stan, he'll be so pleased for you.'

'He's so happy with his family right now, and we have so much to do, that I think I'll leave telling him to later. Maybe when Sally brings him to the gallery tomorrow night.'

'Talking of tomorrow night . . .' Beth picked up a pile of

RSVPs from their invitations, 'The postman has just brought another two positive replies for the opening.'

'But we're already full? I thought everyone we had invited had already replied.' Abi frowned. 'You didn't send out these extra two then?'

'No. I stuck to the list we discussed. All the local shopkeepers, all the artists we are to feature over the next six months, Felicity and Mark from the magazine, Barbara from the hotel, my old schoolfriend and long-suffering estate agent Maggie, plus the chap from the local paper, and Max and Stan of course. The only extra I was expecting was Sally.'

Abi took the two extra replies from Beth. 'Oh, well you know who this is from. It's the auctioneer; Peter.'

'Oh yes, of course,' Beth smiled, 'I remember Jacob saying he was interested, and I told him to take an invite out of the drawer to give him.'

'Well it looks as if Jacob took another invite as well.' Abi read the names off the stubs, 'Who is Sarah Clifton anyway?'

Beth went pale. 'Did you say Sarah Clifton?'

'Yes. Look.'

'I read that as Sarah Griffon. Terrible handwriting. You'd expect a television newsreader to have neat writing wouldn't you?'

'A what?'

'Sarah Clifton is the presenter on the local news, you must have seen her? She lives not far from here actually.'

'The one with the perfectly bobbed blonde hair? And she is coming to our launch? Oh my God!' Abi closed her eyes and counted to five before opening them again, 'You don't think she's coming here in her television role, do you?'

Beth sat down. 'She can't be. Jacob would have said, surely? Wouldn't he?'

'Not if he didn't want to worry us. And anyway, how come he knows a television presenter?'

Beth was already ringing him. 'Jacob, what have you done?

259

And before you answer I think I should warn you that I have Abi here, and my mobile is on speakerphone, so make your excuses good and clean!'

The girls could hear laughing. 'You got a reply from Sarah then?'

'Yes! What did you do?'

'Nothing. Well . . .'

'Jacob, I am in a position to seriously withhold services here, so tell me the truth right now.'

'Oh, double standards! I have to keep things clean, but you can threaten to withhold sexual services in front of Abi!'

Beth rolled her eyes in Abi's direction. 'You know full well that I meant that professionally. I could withdraw your pottery from my gallery! Now, talk.'

'All I did was pinch an extra invite from the drawer when I took one for Peter.'

'We've had a reply from a Sarah Clifton. That isn't the woman off the news, is it? Must be another Sarah Clifton, right?'

'She said yes?'

'Yes, Jacob, what is going on? We're already going to be packed out. We invited more people than we can actually fit into the place because we didn't think that everyone would come, but only three people have said no, so we're hardly going to be able to move around here to serve drinks, let alone swing a cat.'

'Was cat-swinging part of the plan then?'

'Jacob!' Beth pushed her notepad across the table to Abi, showing her the to-do list for the day. It was dauntingly long. 'If you don't start telling us what is going on I'll hit you where it really hurts, and lock your Ali Baba pots in the cupboard during the launch.'

'OK, OK. Yes, it is the Sarah Clifton who reads the BBC news for the south-west.'

'Seriously?' Abi chipped in. 'Why didn't you tell us you'd invited her, we could have been more prepared.'

Speaking before Jacob could reply, Beth doodled thoughtfully

260

on the corner of her notepad, 'OK then, so how do you even know Sarah Clifton? Am I going to have to stop her drooling all over you, as well as that Felicity?'

Jacob laughed. 'Trust me, Beth, women that leave so little to the imagination do nothing for me at all. I mean, blatant is so dull. Smacks of desperation.'

Abi laughed, 'Well, that's Felicity in her place then! So, how about Sarah?'

'Honestly, I don't know her. You'll have to ask Max. I pinched the invite for him.'

The girls looked at each other.

'Max?'

Chapter Thirty-nine

Abi had set up an easel by her desk, upon which was the third set of sketches of the little blue squashy-looking alien she'd been working on for her latest set of illustrations, and of whom she was becoming quite fond.

With its midnight blue sky, and the crater-covered planet surface in the foreground, the plan was, in between chatting and helping serve drinks, to finish colouring in the figure of Squidgy as he tried to catch a fish out of a water-filled crater.

In the spare room of Beth's flat Abi had already changed into the smart business suit that she hoped showed the right level of professionalism and practicality. Beth had wanted her to wear a cocktail dress, but as Abi pointed out, it wasn't terribly practical to wear something like that if she was supposed to be painting, and her only concession to posh clothing was going to be a pair of high heels which, she smiled to herself, should make reaching up to kiss Max a little bit easier.

Undoing one extra blouse button over her cleavage, and wishing that she had rather more to flaunt, Abi put her shoulders back and, with a critical look at her reflection, decided that it was pointless to add a fresh layer of lip gloss until the last minute, as she'd have licked it off several times by then.

She could hear Beth and Jacob giggling together as they got ready. Max had volunteered to escort Stan and his family to the launch, so she hadn't seen him yet. Abi studied her appearance again. Maybe she should have worn a dress after all? She was sure

Felicity would arrive in something drop-dead gorgeous to flirt with Jacob, but what about Sarah?

Beth had been gobsmacked when they discovered that Max had been the one who'd invited Sarah Clifton. Apparently he hadn't told them because he didn't want to raise their hopes, but the show really was coming to interview them about their opening. Abi had been delighted until she'd found out exactly how well Max knew Sarah. He'd sat her down at Beth's table the evening before, after Beth had winkled the truth about the invitation out of him, and explained himself fully.

'The week after I returned to live in Cornwall after my separation I met Sarah in the pub and we hit it off. I was so hurt and angry with Lucinda, and it turned out that Sarah had been similarly treated by her errant husband. As the Victorians used to say, "we took comfort in each other". It didn't last long, and the only real feeling involved was mutual relief that we could be found attractive by other people, and that there wasn't actually anything wrong with us. I was a bit ashamed of myself for using her like that to be honest. I never even told Beth.'

Beth had been gobsmacked when Abi had told her later about Max and the newsreader, her personal feelings in turmoil. Abi hadn't seen Max as a casual sex sort of guy – but as Beth had reminded her, everyone can be a casual sex person sometimes, especially when life has left you wrung out, dumped on, and feeling unattractive.

Max had remained friends with Sarah in a 'say hello when they bumped into each other' sort of way, and when Felicity had offered to do some publicity for the gallery in *Cornwall Life*, he'd thought about asking Sarah if the BBC might be interested.

'He's done us a massive favour,' Beth insisted, 'although I'm scared stiff. I've never been on the telly before.'

Now, as she ran a hairbrush through her hair, Abi forced herself to stop picturing Max and Sarah together and tried to focus on how she was going to make small talk.

'At least,' Abi told her reflection, 'I don't have to make any

263

bloody chococcino muffins!' Sighing, she pulled off her suit and put on a body-hugging peacock blue cocktail dress. 'Oh, sod it! How the hell else am I supposed to compete with a TV celebrity!'

'Jacob, close your mouth!' Beth dug her boyfriend in the ribs as he ran an appreciative gaze over Abi's outfit. 'You look incredible. I'm so glad you didn't go with the suit. You looked great in it, but chances to knock Max out don't come along all that often.'

'I'm not wearing this to impress Max. I don't want to let you down.'

'Bollocks.' Beth straightened her own charcoal grey, cleavage-enhancing dress, and slipped on her court shoes. 'So, are you ready to go and sell your soul to the goddess of mammon?'

Abi hovered nervously, 'You look gorgeous. If any of the dads from your school come in, they'll never be able to look at you in the same way again during parents' evening!'

Beth grimaced, 'Ugh, what a thought!'

Jacob, who looked like a gypsy James Bond in his tuxedo with loosened bow tie, held out both of his arms, 'Ladies, may I escort you all the way down to your empire?'

Taking a mutual deep breath, they answered, 'You may.'

Abi tried to stop her gaze from continually straying to the door. The gallery was already full of people, and Abi was glad she'd opted for the dress, as the place was packed with high heels and tight-fitting frocks.

The compliments for her work had been entirely effusive, and Jacob was positively drowning in compliments for his breathtaking ceramics, not to mention admiring glances and suggestive comments from many of the women.

Taking a breather behind the counter to refill her glass of champagne, Abi asked Beth out of the corner of her mouth, 'Don't you mind all those people hitting on Jacob?'

'Nah, it's quite flattering.'

'Flattering?'

'I get to take the hottest guy in the gallery home. They just get to buy a pot!'

Wishing she could think like that, Abi had just decided that she should stop looking out for Max, when she spotted Stan and Sally coming through the door. Immediately picking up two glasses of champagne, Abi made a beeline for them. 'I'm so glad you came. Now I feel like the launch is really happening!'

Stan gave Abi a half-hug so that he didn't spill his drink. 'You are always so kind!' He looked about, 'I must say, you girls have done Jack proud. He'd have loved this. His shop full of people all happy, all laughing, especially those girls.' He pointed to the potter's little fan club. 'That Jacob is an awful lot like Jack. Not surprising Beth likes him so much.'

Abi laughed, 'That makes sense. Where's Max, didn't he bring you?'

'He did, but he said he had to go and fetch someone called Sarah before he could come in.'

'Oh.' Abi's shoulder muscles tensed. 'He's bringing Sarah? I hadn't realised. If you'll excuse me, I'd better go and warn Beth that she's on her way.'

Sally put her hand out to Abi. 'It's OK, you know, he's just giving her a lift, he isn't "bringing her" in a date sense.'

Embarrassed that she'd given herself away, but grateful to Sally nonetheless, Abi whispered, 'Thank you,' before rushing off to warn Beth that the television cameras were coming.

'There will be some who'll say you're very brave to open another gallery in Sennen, when the village already has one of the most famous and established galleries in Cornwall in the shape of the Roundhouse. What makes your enterprise different?'

Having anticipated this question, Beth and Abi had rehearsed what Beth should say. As Abi listened to her friend talk calmly into the microphone about how Art and Sole was to be an enterprise to promote an ever-changing array of artists from the south-west as well as a chance to witness an illustrator in action, she was full of pride.

Sarah, who was as together and as pretty as Abi had expected her to be, was kind and friendly, and despite herself Abi could see exactly why Max had found her attractive. Once the interview was over, and she and Beth had been filmed walking into the gallery three times before the cameraman got the shot he wanted, Abi left Beth to the pleasantries, disappearing back into the gallery to make sure everyone was happy, only to find a gaggle of Jacob's groupies waiting at the till to buy some of his ceramics.

'You look gorgeous.'

Abi looked up from wrapping the last of Jacob's vases up in silver tissue paper, straight into Max's clear green eyes, and her stomach instantly did a backflip. She wasn't sure what it was about a man's evening dress that worked, and she didn't care. She was just glad it did. Her chest tightened as she felt her body react to his presence.

'You look pretty handsome yourself.' Keeping her voice light she asked, 'Where've you been? It's been mad here.'

'Part of the deal to get Sarah here was to mend her mother's toilet cistern. I've just this minute finished it.'

'What? Tonight? She made you do that tonight?'

'I dumped her. The only time I've ever done that in my life. It was horrid, it made me feel awful. I owed her, I guess. The timing was crap, but isn't it always?'

Abi felt her heart swell in the face of his honesty. 'Come on. Let's find you a glass of champagne.'

At last everyone had gone. Jacob, Beth, Abi, Stan, Sally, and Max stood in the centre of a rather depleted collection of Jacob's ceramics and a totally empty table where the pile of children's books had previously sat.

'We did it!' Beth yawned as she spoke. 'When do you think we'll be on the television?'

'Tomorrow night's programme, I should think.' Max started to collect up the empty glasses that had been abandoned on Beth's grandad's old bench, 'then this place will really be on the map. I bet you're busy next week.'

Abi let out a squeak. 'But next week I'll be on my own, you'll be back at school, Beth!'

'You'll be fine.' Beth looked at the empty tables and plinths that dotted the room. They'd even sold one of Jacob's Ali Baba pots to the ever-hopeful Felicity. 'And it won't even matter if you don't sell a thing. We made more money tonight than I projected us to make in the next month.'

'I beg to protest,' Jacob said with a smile, 'I'd like you to sell everything I have! But don't worry, Abi; I'll be here in the afternoons to chat to the stray tourists.'

A massive yawn from Stan reminded them how late it was, and how tired they all were. Sally immediately began to make 'time to go' movements, and with thanks and hugs, soon only the four friends remained.

Beth scooped the money from the till into a bag. 'Do you mind locking up, Abi? I want to get the takings safely sorted and put away upstairs before I crash out.'

'Not at all. I'll pile up the rest of the dirty dishes to clean tomorrow, and then I'll be up as well.'

As Jacob followed Beth upstairs with a suggestive smirk of things to come, Max put his hands out to Abi. 'You have no idea how much I want to follow Jacob's example and follow you up those stairs.'

'Well, you don't have to go . . .' Abi, who had hoped he'd do exactly what he suggested, saw that she was about to be disappointed.

'I happen to know that Beth's spare room bed is tiny, and the idea of making love to you with Beth and Jacob cheering us on from the next room is not what I have planned for our first time together.'

The hope that had begun to die rekindled again in Abi's veins. 'You have plans in that direction then?'

'Oh yes, Mrs Carter. I have plans.'

'And you're sure he's alright?'

'Stan is in his element.' Max grinned at the memory of the old man's face as he'd walked into the flat complex's main reception. 'I wish you could have seen him. Turns out he went to school with two of the other residents. The staff are going to have their hands full when those three are in the communal rooms at the same time!'

Abi had said nothing about how much she'd wanted to be there to see Stan safely settled, but there had been no room in Max's van for more than Stan and his stuff. Anyway, Sally and the children naturally wanted to help him unpack, and Abi hadn't wanted to butt into their family time, especially as it was so rare and precious. 'I can well imagine.'

With Max's reassuring presence close beside her, Abi scanned the garden, mentally deciding that most of it would have to be pulled out and replanted next spring.

'Now you can stop beating yourself up about evicting an old man from his home, which I know you've been doing, even though you did no such thing in the first place.'

Letting out a long slow exhalation of air, which Abi felt she'd been holding in for weeks, she spoke slowly. 'Once I've signed the paperwork I really will own Abbey's House, won't I?'

'You will. Lock, stock, and overgrown garden!' Putting his arms around her, Max followed her gaze across the long narrow garden. 'I'm sorry I have to dash off. I've got to get back to work.'

Abi smiled up at him. 'It's fine. I think I'd like to sort out my stuff on my own, after all, only I know where I want to put everything.'

'Fair enough,' Max kissed her forehead, 'I do have one condition, though.'

'Oh yes?'

'Make sure, and I realise I'm speaking with a lot of future hope here, that you have a king-sized bed put in your room. You may have noticed that short I'm not!' And with a brief glance of desire in Abi's direction, Max strode off down the path, and disappeared into the wilds of Penwith to paint someone's ceiling.

Chapter Forty

'Are you sure you don't want us to take Sadie?'

Max cuddled the retriever as he said, 'It's too dangerous for you up there, isn't it, old girl. We'll have a walk later, OK?'

With Sadie wagging her tail as if in agreed understanding, Max turned to Abi. 'I want to show you Mayon Cliff before the weather takes a major turn for the worse. It's best if we have a nice day for it. We'll get a much better view, and if we're lucky we'll see the basking sharks.'

Testing her toes in her new walking boots, Abi grabbed her fleece, 'Do you think I'll be alright in these? I've not broken them in as much as I'd like yet.'

'Only one way to find out. I'd wear some thicker socks than those if I were you though, keep them from rubbing you too much.'

'But that'll roast me! I hate having hot feet.'

'Well, if you end up in crippling agony I dare say I can carry you. You barely weigh as much as a feather anyway!'

Waving goodbye to Sadie, Abi locked the front door which now officially belonged to her. 'So, which way, Mr Pendale?'

'This way.' They walked past the old converted capstan house, followed the arrow painted on the coastal path sign that was half-hidden by the public toilet block, and began to climb some steps.

Abi started to puff, and Max laughed. 'Come on, city girl, you can't be out of breath already, there's another twenty steps to go!'

'I hadn't realised there would be so many people about now it's September.'

'It's because it's the last chance for a lot of people to do something with their children before they go back to school. Most of these folk will be off to the Land's End Experience.'

Abi laughed. 'By the way you spat that last sentence out I take it you aren't a fan of that particular tourist development?'

'This is one of the most outstanding places of natural beauty on the planet, why do we need a theme park to bring people to it? I'm all for family visitor centres and that, but here? Big mistake.'

'Not for all these people.' Abi gestured to the crocodile of families trailing up behind them.

'Don't be reasonable! Part of the scenery has been destroyed all for the sake of a *Doctor Who* exhibit and some other stuff.'

'Really? I rather like *Doctor Who*.'

'Well, so do I, but . . .' Max caught Abi's expression. 'You're teasing me, aren't you?'

'Yep!' She stepped up the last of the granite steps and took in a big lungful of air. 'This is Mayon Cliff, right?'

'This is it. There was an Iron Age hillfort here once, and now there's a little stone castle, and look, if you stare down there you'll see the harbour we've just passed, and that large flat rock you can see is called Cowloe Rock, the sea channel around it is called the Tribbens.'

'It's simply stunning.' Abi held onto Max's arm as the wind flapped at their faces, 'Do you know all the local placenames?'

'I sure do. Beth always says I sound like I swallowed a tourist guide, but really I just love the place. I was born and raised here. Once my marriage fell apart I couldn't wait to get back.'

As she watched the specks of people wandering about in the harbour below, Abi said, 'I can't imagine you living anywhere but here. You seem to fit.'

Tucking Abi under his arm, Max set them off in the direction of the old castellated area of Pedn-men-Du. 'Come on, if we keep going we'll leave all the holiday makers behind. Are you OK with a bit of a climb?'

'I am if the view stays this incredible.' Abi didn't know where to look first as she enjoyed the refreshing wind on her face.

Every few minutes Max stopped them to point out landmarks he didn't want Abi to miss; a strange shaped rock called the Irish Lady, another rock just offshore of the Castle Zawn headland called The Peal, and then the little cliff castle which Abi had to stop and marvel over as a little set of streams, that Max told her was called Carn Clog, trickled past their feet.

'Over there,' Max gestured to the line of people walking away from them, 'that's the way to the Land's End Experience. We, however, are going this way.'

Abi stood statue-still. She wanted to take in every inch of the landscape she was surrounded by.

'How are your feet?'

Wishing she'd taken Max's advice and worn thick socks, Abi fluttered her eyelashes at him. ' I am rather aware of my toes right now, and you might have been right about the socks.'

Max smiled, 'Just a few hundred metres, then we'll stop and rest those tootsies. OK?'

'What are we looking for?'

'You'll see.' Max ran his free hand through his hair as he checked over his shoulder to make sure they were alone. A few paces later, he said, 'Close your eyes.'

Abi wasn't sure she should, 'The ground is a bit unsteady. I might fall over.'

'I won't let that happen, trust me. It'll be worth it.'

Closing her eyes, Abi felt Max stand close to her left side and take her hand, then he passed his right hand all the way around her to hold her right hand. 'First one step, and then another, that's it. I won't let you trip or fall. Promise.'

Ten steps later, each one tentative over the sloping grassy ground, Abi could hear a roaring noise getting closer, making her hold onto Max tighter still.

'OK, you can stop.' Max turned Abi so she was stood with her back firmly against his chest, and wrapped his arms around her front, 'you can open your eyes.'

'Oh, wow . . .' Abi stared in awe at the view before them. It was one of the most spectacular sites she'd ever seen. 'Max, it's beautiful, what's it called?'

Pointing to a rock arch that was being battered by the waves thundering beneath them, Max raised his voice above the scream of the sea. 'That's the Armed Knight of Enys Dodnan, and if you follow the view you can see where the sea is churning and roaring around Pordenack Point.'

'It's magnificent. I can't believe we're the only people here.'

'You can see why I didn't want to risk Sadie coming here though, can't you. She could have been blown over the edge.'

Glad that Max was there to keep her on her feet as the wind whipped up around them, Abi pushed her hair from her eyes.

'We should sit down, it'll be more sheltered, and you can still see the view just fine.'

Glad to take the weight off her sore feet, Abi found herself sat between Max's outstretched legs, cradled in his arms, with his chin resting gently on top of her head. She'd never felt so safe, or so tiny, as she watched nature showing her its beauty and its power.

Even with Max's body heat against her, after ten minutes Abi began to feel cold. The fleece which had kept her so snug suddenly felt insubstantial, and she began to shiver.

Max brought his face down to her ear. 'Are you cold, shall we go?'

'A bit, but it's so amazing here, and peaceful – well, apart from the sea and the wind!' Twisting around, smiling up at Max, Abi leaned forward and kissed him. 'I love it! Thank you so much for bringing me here. It's exactly what I needed.'

Max's eyes met hers. 'I'm so glad you like it. This is one of my favourite spots in the county.'

Keeping her eyes fixed on his, Abi asked, 'Will you show me the other places you love sometime?'

'I'd love to.' Max wiped Abi's windblown hair from her face, before pulling her down so she was lying on top of him. 'But first, I think I'd better warm you up a bit.'

Abi didn't argue as his mouth met hers. The sound of the sea whipped away her cry of 'at last' as his large hands disappeared beneath her fleece on a gratifyingly accurate quest for her breasts that soon made every fibre of Abi's body buzz with happy desire . . .

'Come on then, I told Jacob and Beth to meet us on the beach for a late lunch.'

Letting Max pull her to her feet, Abi readjusted her clothing, 'You did? Why? I have so much unpacking to do now the bits from Surrey have arrived and Stan's happily playing ninja bridge with his friends at the flats.'

'Because you need a break, and because, if I remember rightly, apart from living in Abbey's House there were three other things you wanted to do in Cornwall, walk – which we are doing right now – have lots of picnics – Jacob should be manhandling a large and very full hamper into position as we speak – and you wanted to build sandcastles. Right?'

Abi was amazed. 'I can't believe you remembered that.'

'I remembered because it was obviously important to you.'

As they climbed carefully back down the steps to Sennen beach Abi could see Beth waving at her, a big smile on her face as she battled against the gusty late summer wind to lay a picnic rug over the sand.

'You arranged all this for me?'

'We arranged it,' Max bent down and kissed her upturned face, 'all of us.'

In the closing distance Abi could see Jacob and Beth setting out glasses, a bottle of champagne, and a huge cake.

As soon as they were in range, Beth ran forward and hugged Abi hard. 'Nice walk?'

'Very.' Abi blushed. 'Look at all this. Wow!'

Jacob waved the champagne bottle in her direction. 'What better way to mark the start of your official residency in Cornwall than a picnic of home-cooked pasties, cake, and champers?'

As the cork flew from the bottle with a suitably theatrical pop, Max pulled Abi onto his lap on the rug, and as Jacob filled their glasses he raised a toast. 'To Abi, the new owner of Abbey's House!'

'And to Art and Sole,' added Abi, 'Beth's new venture and my new job. If the feedback from the launches and our TV moment is anything to go by, we are going to have a very busy year indeed.'

Three evenings later Abi sat on her special sofa in the corner of the kitchen. Her kitchen.

She stroked the tatty blue fabric. If this sofa could talk . . . She had left Stan's kitchen table where it was in the middle of the room, but the arrival of her dresser had meant that the old side table Stan had kept his surplus groceries and bits and pieces on was now in the summerhouse, dotted with a myriad of flower pots.

The oven had been scrubbed to within an inch of its life and the Belfast sink gleamed in its freshly varnished wooden surround. The plates that had been in the larder had all been washed, and now had a new home being displayed on the dresser.

Abi hadn't been sure about inheriting so much of Stan's stuff with the house, but as he'd been adamant he didn't want it, and wouldn't have any need for it, she'd kept it. After all, she loved its eclectic nature, and the fact that none of it matched anything else appealed to her need to escape from the 'everything has to be coordinated' life she had left behind her.

Beth and Jacob had been surprised when Abi politely but firmly declined their offer of help to sort Abbey's House out. Max however had simply told her he understood. This task she had to do herself. It was her way of letting go of everything that had gone before and starting all over again. By herself. For herself. After that anything was possible. The new future that was out there for her could truly begin.

Tucking her feet up under herself, Abi let the ache of hard work in her muscles flow satisfyingly through her. Only Stan's room remained without the distinct mark of her personality on it, and even that had been tidied. His bedlinen was aired and ready for him whenever he wanted to visit, and the collection of Zane Grey novels he'd left behind was neatly stacked on his bed-side table.

A spare easel stood in the corner of Abi's bedroom, along with a stool and the cabinet of her art supplies that Max had insisted she bring from Surrey.

Max.

Holding her mug of hot chocolate tighter, Abi allowed remi-niscences of their walk across the Mayon Cliff infiltrate her mind.

Abi looked down at the sofa again. It was time her favourite piece of furniture had some brand new memories to add to its silent history.

Epilogue

Max found Abi weeding the dandelions that had taken root by the front door. Refusing her invitation to come inside, he passed her the large, heavy parcel he was carrying.

'It's from Stan.'

'Stan?'

'Your belated house-warming gift. Open it here. Trust me.'

'It's so heavy! Whatever is it?'

Max's eyes radiated pleasure as he supported the end of the parcel so she could unwrap her present.

'Oh, wow!' Abi couldn't take her eyes off the carved plaque of shaped wood that she was half holding, had half propped in Max's arms. Eventually her words came out as a whisper. 'Did you make this for Stan?'

'For Stan to give to you, yes.'

Max passed Abi the mallet he'd produced from behind his back like some sort of tool-carrying magician, and with a solemn look on his face that belied the glowing happiness in his eyes, he nodded encouragingly towards the front gate.

Abi pulled the old sign out of the ground with a satisfying heave. As she positioned the new one into the clay soil, Max wrapped his hands over hers, and they swung the mallet together, driving the new house sign home.

Abi's House.

If you loved *A Cornish Escape*,
why not read

A Cornish Wedding

Available from

ACCENT

Bookends

When one book ends, another begins...

Bookends is a vibrant new reading community to help you ensure you're never without a good book.

You'll find exclusive previews of the brilliant new books from your favourite authors as well as exciting debuts and past classics. Read our blog, check out our recommendations for your reading group, enter great competitions and much more!

Visit our website to see which great books we're recommending this month.

Join the Bookends community:
www.welcometobookends.co.uk

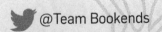 @Team Bookends   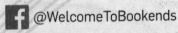 @WelcomeToBookends